Descending the stairs,
Candida saw the most handsome man
she had ever set eyes on in her life.

Hastily, Candida dipped a curtsey. As she arose, she heard him say in a deep warm voice, "May I bid you welcome to Stratton Hall."

Candida gazed into his smiling gray eyes, certain that he must hear the hammering of her heart. For in her wildest dreams, she had never expected her future husband to be so devastatingly attractive. Oh, she thought joyously, I have been worrying unduly!

"I trust," inquired the dark-haired man courteously, "that your journey to my home was not too fatiguing?"

"Oh, no Your Grace," stammered Candida. "Such lovely countryside . . . I was quite enchanted . . ."

His pleasant laugh interrupted her. "Oh, but forgive me! I have not introduced myself properly. I have not the honor to be the Duke of Stratton. I am Lord Berkeley. Bartholomew, the Duke, is my older brother."

Suddenly there was a crash, as if a table had been overturned. The door opened, and a stocky, red-haired man lurched into the room, his face florid with rage. Catching sight of Lord Berkeley and Candida, he bawled, "Ah ha! Wenching again then, brother! Well, she looks a pretty piece of petticoat!"

He stumbled and lost his balance. Clawing at the wall paintings for support, Candida's future husband collapsed in a drunken stupor at her feet.

Novels By Caroline Courtney

Duchess in Disguise
A Wager For Love
Love Unmasked
Guardian of The Heart
Dangerous Engagement
Love Triumphant
The Fortunes of Love
Love's Masquerade
Heart of Honor
The Romantic Rivals
Forbidden Love
Abandoned For Love
The Tempestuous Affair
Love of My Life
Destiny's Duchess

Published By
WARNER BOOKS

CAROLINE COURTNEY

Destiny's Duchess

A Warner Communications Company

WARNER BOOKS EDITION

Cover art by Walter Popp

Cover design by Gene Light

Warner Books, Inc., 75 Rockefeller Plaza, New York, N.Y. 10019

A Warner Communications Company

Printed in the United States of America

First Printing: August, 1981

10 9 8 7 6 5 4 3 2 1

Destiny's Duchess

Chapter One

"No!" Candida's blue eyes blazed. "The suggestion is preposterous! I shall never, ever agree!"

Sir Montague Gore smoothed down his immaculate wig and repressed a sigh as he regarded the angry young woman gracing his drawing room. Sir Montague was, at that moment, a deeply unhappy man. As a confirmed bachelor, the ways and wiles of womankind were a mystery to him. It was monstrous, complained the disgruntled society hostesses of Hampshire, that Sir Montague clearly preferred the company of his gun dogs to that of their unmarried daughters.

But eight months ago, Sir Montague's brother in marriage, Sir George Wellesley, had died, leaving him guardian to the nineteen-year-old Candida. It would be bad enough, mused Sir Montague sourly, being obliged to take responsibility for any young girl who had enjoyed the benefit of a mother's gentle guidance and advice. But Candida's mother had died in childbirth. Sir George—in Sir Montague's opinion, an over indulgent parent—had allowed his daughter to run wild.

As Sir Montague regarded the defiant tilt of her chin and the rebellious toss of her pale gold hair, he reflected that Sir George had done the entire male world a disservice in not impressing upon Candida that gentlemen should at all times be deferred to. They should be treated with the respect they deserved as the undoubted superior sex.

"You are very quiet, suddenly, Uncle! Can it be that at

heart you are ashamed of the cold-blooded plans you have hatched for my future?" Candida's high, clear tones rang through Sir Montague's reverie. He pulled himself together, and prepared to assert his authority over this impertinent filly.

But before he could speak, Candida had once more seized the initiative. "It is the most monstrous notion I ever heard!" she declared heatedly. "How dare you order me to marry a man I have never met, and about whom I know not the first thing of any importance!"

Sir Montague adjusted his eyeglasses and remonstrated severely, "Do not exaggerate the situation, Candida! Like all females, you are quite incapable of thinking logically. Of keeping to the facts."

So enraged was Candida at this remark that she turned her back on her uncle, and with a rustle of dark blue silk wandered across to the window. Not that the view was particularly inspiring. Sir Montague's estate was planned on formal lines. There were straight rows of trees and low yew hedges severely clipped into oblong shapes which to Candida's critical eye resembled green coffins. No flowers bloomed. Not so much as a single daisy was allowed to lift its head to the July sunshine. Sir Montague regarded flowers as frivolous and, therefore, strictly the preserve of the feminine sex.

"Candida!" protested Sir Montague. "Will you kindly afford me the courtesy of facing me when I am addressing you!"

His voice, thought Candida as she slowly turned to face her uncle, is so dry it sounds like gravel in a jar.

"It simply is not true that we know nothing about the Duke of Stratton," declared Sir Montague. "We are cognisant of the fact that he resides at Stratton Hall in the county of Sussex. His mother was Lady Margaret Hillier, daughter of the Marquis of Egmont. The family name of the Dukes of Stratton is Berkeley, and the family has lived in Sussex for over two hundred—"

He broke off, and said sharply, "Candida! I trust you are not yawning!"

Candida exclaimed rashly, "Indeed, Uncle, I am fair

ready to expire with boredom! For you have told me nothing of importance about the man you say I must marry. What of his character, his looks, his disposition? Is he kind? Is he handsome? Will he treat me with generosity and affection? Will he make a good father? Have we interests in common?"

Sir Montague pushed back his shoulders in his dark brown velvet frock coat and said stiffly, "He is a Duke, Candida! Why, most girls of your age and position in life would be delighted at the prospect of becoming Duchess of Stratton. Especially as the Duke is not a crusty, balding old man but a vigorous youngster of just thirty years!"

"Since the Duke of Stratton is clearly such a devastating creature that he has his pick of all the eligible females in the south of England, I wonder why he should write out of the blue demanding to marry me?" mused Candida, her eyes deceptively guileless. "After all, we have never met. I have no title. For all he knows, he could be taking on some pock-marked female with no teeth and a peg leg. Has he so much as requested to see my portrait?"

Sir Montague cleared his throat, and busied himself, drawing the Duke of Stratton's letter from the pocket of his gray silk waistcoat. He unrolled the parchment, and meticulously smoothed out the corners.

"The Duke," he remarked evasively, "is an extremely busy person. The Stratton estates extend well over two thousand acres. In addition—" Sir Montague peered through his eyeglasses at the letter—"I gather that the Duke has recently acquired the responsibility of a ward—a twelve-year-old girl who is so wilful in her ways that it is impossible to retain a governess for her."

From Sir Montague's tone it was evident that in the matter of rebellious young girls he was much in sympathy with the Duke of Stratton.

"So, he has expressed no desire to see my portrait," said Candida scornfully. "And of course, it would doubtless be asking too much of such an important person as the Duke of Stratton to pay me the simple courtesy of sending me *his* likeness!"

Sir Montague flung down the letter on the walnut bureau

which loomed against the pannelled drawing room wall. "Really, Candida, you have no one to blame but yourself for this turn of events. You have the impertinence to stand there before me complaining that your hand has been offered in marriage to a gentleman who is a stranger to you. But if you had only the good sense to take advantage of your London Season, you would by now have been happily settled with any one of the dozens of beaux who were dancing attendance on you in Mayfair."

Candida's mocking laugh echoed around the gloomy drawing room. "Oh yes, I confess, I was never short of dancing partners during my Season. But none of them, I fear, could ever be considered seriously as my partner in marriage. Such fawning, foppish creatures, those London men, with their wigs, their mauve satin evening coats and their manicured, polished nails. When I marry, Uncle Montague, I want it to be to a red blooded man, not a strutting peacock!"

Sir Montague winced as Candida's voice rose with indignation. "It saddens me, Candida," he pronounced sorrowfully, "that you have never had the benefit of a mother's guiding wisdom. Your dear Mama, I know, would have taught you that it is most unseemly for young ladies to raise their voices in the presence of their elders."

"I am quite convinced that if my Mama were alive today she would never countenance the notion of my marrying a man I would not recognize if I passed him in the street!" retorted Candida, quite unabashed by the severity of her uncle's tone.

"Indeed," replied Sir Montague calmly, "it was your mother's dearest wish that you should marry the Duke of Stratton."

"Come now, Uncle!" Candida protested. "My mother died barely an hour after I was born. And my father told me often how her delicate disposition had prevented her from journeying far. How then, could she even have made the acquaintance of the young boy who was to become Duke of Stratton—let alone formed the opinion that we two were destined for a happy marriage?"

Sir Montague replied gravely, "You are obviously unaware that my sister—your Mama—was the girlhood friend of the Lady Margaret, who married the old Duke of Stratton. Although your mother never set foot outside Hampshire, she corresponded regularly with Lady Margaret when she married. And on her deathbed, your mother's last whispered words were the expression of a fervent desire that you should marry Lady Margaret's eldest son."

Candida's pretty face was white with shock. She turned away, absently fiddling with the blue ribbons decorating the skirt of her dress. "But, but why was I never informed of this?" she stammered. "Why did my father never tell me . . . ?"

Sir Montague's cold blue eyes narrowed. Personally, he had considered it indulgently rash of Sir George to have allowed Candida the luxury of a London Season—and the pick of the capital's beaux.

"Dash it all, Montague!" Sir George had declared. "I am quite well aware that Majorie harbored this romantic notion that Candida should marry the eldest son of her dearest friend. But the young Duke of Stratton has devoted most of his twenties to prancing about Europe. I've never even set eyes on the fellow. I feel it would be best all around to allow Candida to enjoy her London Season. If she meets some dashing cavalier and falls in love with him, well so be it. I'll not forbid the marriage for my daughter's happiness is all that matters to me."

But Sir Montague had no intention of repeating this conversation to the fair-haired beauty sitting so dejectedly on his sofa. It would be fatal, he decided, to fill her lovely head with fanciful notions of love and eternal bliss. It was a burdensome business for a bachelor like himself being saddled with the guardianship of a high spirited girl. Far better to marry her off now (and to a Duke, no less!) and then he would be free to pursue undisturbed his quiet, country gentleman's life.

Accordingly, he crossed the room and awkwardly patted Candida on the shoulder. "No doubt your esteemed father, out of respect for your tender years, had no desire to trouble you with the sad events of your mother's last hours on this earth. I believe that it was his intention to guide you, quite naturally, into acquaintanceship and then marriage with the Duke of Stratton. Of course, what he could not foresee was the dreadful tragedy of the fire at Wellesley Park."

Candida's blue eyes clouded at the memory. She had returned from her morning ride to find Wellesley Park, her home, gutted by fire. Her father and her brother Charles had worked ceaselessly to ensure that all the servants were rushed from the blazing house. But then the two men had found themselves trapped and had died when the old timbered gallery had crashed in flames on top of them.

Sir Montague went on; "I assure you, it was ever in your father's mind that one day you should marry the Duke of Stratton. And with your father and brother so untimely called to rest, I feel it my duty to ensure that the wishes of your parents are fulfilled in the matter of your marriage."

Observing that Candida was still stunned with shock, Sir Montague crossed to the window, drawing strength from the orderly, classic lines of his estate. Yes, he mused, Candida must be married to the Duke of Stratton with the minimum of delay. If not, he could foresee that the calm of his life in Hampshire would be rudely shattered.

It was not just that Candida was a deucedly pretty girl. But the death of her father and brother had made her one of the wealthiest nineteen-year-olds in all England. With Candida's period of mourning now almost over, Sir Montague gloomily predicted that every fortune hunter in the land would soon be beating a path to his door. He shuddered at the notion of his peaceful house invaded by fops and young cavaliers, braying and shouting as they competed for Candida's favors.

Naturally, he had done his duty and taken Candida under his roof when her own home was destroyed by fire. Had she been a quiet docile girl who believed in being seen and not heard, then he would probably not have been so anxious to see her wed.

But Candida was a high spirited minx. She would, no

doubt, expect him to hold balls and routs to which her young blades would be invited. The drive would be choked with phaetons, the estate ravaged by hordes of young people trampling over his yew hedges.

Sir Montague shuddered. No, he resolved grimly. Candida would marry the Duke of Stratton and depart for Sussex. His mind was made up, and no slip of a girl would be permitted to change it for him!

Candida, still seated on the sofa, said slowly, "It seems strange to me, Uncle . . . if the Duke of Stratton were aware of the desire of his mother and mine that we should wed, why did he wait all this time to contact me?"

"I understand," Sir Montague said easily, "that the Duke has sojourned in Europe for ten years on his Grand Tour. He has been back in England for only a twelvemonth."

"His Grand Tour has lasted for ten years!" exclaimed Candida in horror. "Surely, Uncle, you would agree that this indicates an excessive degree of self-indulgence?"

Sir Montague did agree. Privately, he regarded it as monstrous for a man to fritter away ten years on the pursuit of pleasure on foreign soil. However, it would clearly not advance his case to admit this to Candida.

"On the contrary," declared Sir Montague persuasively, "I am convinced that you will find that the Duke's years in Europe have given him an excellent knowledge of the arts. He will have first-hand knowledge of all the paintings, the sculptures, the treasures of Europe. You were asking earlier if you had anything in common with your future husband. Well, there is your answer. You will have endless hours of pleasure discussing art, literature, and music."

Candida said stonily, "And when, may I ask, is our happy union to take place?"

"The Duke suggests that you wed in December," replied Sir Montague, "as by then a full year will have passed since your poor father's death. He very considerately wishes to give you time to recover from your grief before you undertake the responsibilities of marriage."

Observing the light of defiance once more beginning to

kindle in Candida's eyes, Sir Montague said softly, "Never forget, Candida, that your dear mother died in order to give you life. Surely you would not be so heartless as to refuse to fulfill her last request?"

As the tears streamed down Candida's face, Sir Montague knew he had won. He handed her his handkerchief, and courteously held open the drawing room doors as she rushed from the room. Then he rang for his Steward and ordered the brandy to be brought in. He was a man who normally believed in moderation in all things. But today he felt he deserved the large measure of brandy he poured from the decanter. He had completed a satisfactory afternoon's work. Tomorrow he would write to the Duke of Stratton confirming that Miss Candida Wellesley was honored to accept his proposal of marriage.

Miss Candida Wellesley stood in her bedchamber, lashing at the bedpost with her riding crop.

"I won't marry you, Duke of Stratton!" she shouted. "I won't, *I won't!* Take that! And that! I hate you. Although we've never met. I know you to be the most detestable man in the world!"

Exhausted, she threw down the crop and flung herself onto the cushioned window seat. "Oh Mama!" she sighed, "surely you never intended such a dreadful thing to befall me? You yourself married for love—my father often told me so. I am convinced you would not want me to wed a stranger. Even if he is a Duke."

Candida was sure that this was the real reason her Uncle Montague was so determined to see her at the altar with this loathsome stranger. The Gores and the Wellesleys were two of the wealthiest and most respected families in Hampshire. But no member of either had ever married blue blood. There was no doubt that Sir Montague relished the prospect of his increased social prestige when it became known that his niece was betrothed to the Duke of Stratton. He would be anticipating with pleasure the future scene over the after-dinner card table, as he was able casually to declare, "I was down in Sussex last week for the christening of my niece's son—

Queen Charlotte sent a quite exquisite silver christening mug . . ."

No, thought Candida fiercely. I will not give in to this plan. I cannot allow myself to be hurled into an arranged marriage. Uncle Montague cannot force me. I shall run away . . . I shall scream every inch of the way to the altar . . . I shall—

Oh, but what is the use of thinking like this? For all the time I am confronted with the fact that by refusing to marry the Duke I am denying my dear Mama her dying wish. And that I cannot do. For I should never be able to live easily with my conscience.

It would be all so much easier to bear if only I had some notion of the character, the looks, the temperament of this man who seems destined to be my husband. Oh, I have no doubt that before we are wed in December, a few social engagements will be arranged so that we may make one another's acquaintance. But inevitably, on this occasion he will be showing me his best face. It will be difficult to determine his true personality. If only there were some way in which I could be in his presence and observe him, without his realizing I was there. Then, if I discovered him to be a total ogre, I should have no compunction about high-tailing it to France, or Italy, or anywhere! For I am convinced my Mama would not have wanted me to marry the Duke if I truly found him detestable.

Candida remained on the window seat, her knees drawn up to her chin, her mind awhirl with plans. Dusk fell. But it was only when the moon rose over ths beech trees that Candida suddenly scrambled off the window seat and ran across to her writing table. In the candlelight, there was a blaze of determination in her sapphire blue eyes.

She unfurled a roll of parchment, shook her quill and began, in her elegant hand, *My dearest Clara* . . . .

The following morning, Candida entered the library and said quietly, "Forgive me for disturbing you, Uncle. May I ask if you have yet written to the Duke of Stratton accepting his offer of marriage?"

Sir Montague looked up from his leather chair and replied

testily, "Now Candida, I must warn you that those high winds last night gave me a very unsettled sleep and I am not in the best of tempers this morning. In particular, I am in no mood to listen to whatever arguments you have dreamed up to try and dissuade me from encouraging this marriage. The matter is closed. The issue decided. You will marry the Duke of Stratton in December. I shall be writing to him to that effect later today."

"Yes, Uncle," said Candida demurely. "I merely wanted you to know that, on reflection, I have decided it would be best to be guided by you in this matter."

Sir Montague favored her with a rare smile. "Capital, Candida! Excellent! You will make an admirable Duchess, my dear, and be a credit to us Gores and Wellesleys in Hampshire."

"I will do my best, Uncle." Candida restrained the urge to swat a fly which was crawling across her uncle's wig, and went on, "You mentioned yesterday that the Duke of Stratton was having difficulty finding a suitable governess for his young ward."

Sir Montague nodded and said irritably, "Frankly, I can't imagine why the fellow should imagine that a bachelor like myself would be able to help him. There must be scores of spinsters in Sussex who'd be grateful for the position. But," he sighed, "I gather the young girl is something of a handful and has scared all her governesses away."

Candida stood with her hands neatly clasped in front of her. "It is just that I know of a young woman in the village who might be suitable. A Miss Jane Wilton. Her previous charge was sadly smitten with the smallpox and died, so Miss Wilton is now urgently seeking a new post."

"Then I suppose I should call her here for an interview. My, how tedious!" complained Sir Montague.

Candida was well aware of her uncle's antipathy toward governesses. *They are always thin, scrawny creatures* he often declared sourly *and they regard one with a barely veiled expression of disapproval which brings back in all its horror the smell of schoolroom ink and the swish of the strap.*

Casually examining the intricate work on her uncle's brass inkwell, Candida said lightly, "Heavens, no doubt when I am Duchess of Stratton it will be my duty to interview governesses. How terrifying!"

She held her breath, praying that her uncle would take the bait. For if he did not, and insisted on inspecting Miss Jane Wilton himself, then all Candida's plans were surely dashed.

Sir Montague curled the end of his wig around his thin finger, and then thoughtfully declared that it might be a good notion for Candida herself to interview Miss Wilton. Candida fluttered her pretty hands and demurred. Sir Montague insisted. It would be good experience for Candida, useful training for her future responsibilities as Duchess of Stratton.

"There is more to being a Duchess than wearing a jewelled tiara and an ermine robe," Sir Montague advised Candida gravely. "I am sure you are aware that with the Stratton estate running to over two thousand acres, there will be scores of tenants and retainers whose wives and children will be your responsibility. If they are sick, you must visit them. If they are discontented you must ascertain the reason why. And, of course, at Christmas you will be hostess at the tenant's ball, ensuring that each child receives a gift . . ."

"Yes, Uncle . . . No, Uncle . . . Indeed, Uncle," murmured Candida obediently during this interminable lecture, digging her nails hard into the palms of her hands to stop herself from falling asleep with boredom.

But at last the sermon was ended. Candida declared that as she felt obliged to make a morning call on the baker's wife in the village, who had just been brought to bed of her first child, she would take the opportunity also to visit Miss Jane Wilton. It was agreed that Sir Montague would delay writing to the Duke of Stratton until Candida returned with confirmation that Miss Wilton had agreed to journey to Sussex.

Candida put on her bonnet, and devoted a pleasant few hours to meandering around the local village. The Baker's wife had been delivered of a bonny girl, named Honor. Her husband had fashioned his gingerbread mix into H shapes to "honor" the occasion, and the village children were crowding into the bakery, clamoring for the hot novel-shaped gingerbread.

After a suitable length of time had elapsed, Candida returned to Gore Lodge and advised her uncle that Miss Wilton would be glad to take up the post of governess to the Duke of Stratton's ward.

Sir Montague looked first well pleased, but then a frown creased his brow. "Did you in any manner intimate to Miss Wilton, Candida, that the young lady at Stratton Hall is of a decidedly difficult temperament?"

Candida nodded. "I thought it my duty to advise Miss Wilton of the full facts, Uncle. But she is a firm, sensible young woman. She was quite convinced that she would be mistress of the situation."

"Capital! Then I shall write to the Duke of Stratton directly!" Sir Montague indulged in a pleasurable sniff of snuff. "The Duke will no doubt be delighted to receive my letter. His offer of marriage has been accepted. And a governess has been found for his vexatious ward. All is right with the world, is it not, Candida?"

"Oh yes, Uncle!" Candida said, smiling sweetly.

Two weeks passed, during which time Sir Montague saw very little of his niece. Not that this concerned him unduly. He was a man who enjoyed his own company, and it suited him well that Candida was content to remain for much of the day in her own apartments in the topmost east wing of Gore House.

Conscious of his duty to make social conversation over the dinner table, he did once inquire of his niece how she was spending her days. Her reply, *Why, I have been sitting on my window seat, Uncle, and I have been sewing.* pleased Sir Montague greatly. Clearly, the rebellious, high-spirited Candida had seen the error of her ways. He had been right to be firm with her over the matter of her engagement to the Duke of Stratton. Sir Montague had always suspected that her father, Sir George, had treated his daughter with too soft a hand. The girl had taken advantage of him. But he, Sir Montague, had mastered the girl. *You will marry the Duke of*

Stratton! he had ordered. And after an initial token resistance, she had capitulated.

Not only that, but Candida was positively a changed character. Why, when she first came to reside under his roof, she had spent her days punting on the lake (such an unladylike activity in Sir Montague's view) . . . and out riding in all winds and weathers . . . or sitting up in the apple tree in the village, blowing blossoms down to tickle the bald head of the unfortunate curate.

But now that a suitable marriage had been arranged for her, Candida was a transformed person. She was quiet. She was demure, and sat in her chamber, engaged in that most feminine of occupations—sewing. Sir Montague felt a glow of satisfaction. All was right with the world indeed.

He was pleased when, returning from a bracing afternoon walk, he entered the drawing room and came upon his niece playing a particularly melodious piece upon the spinet.

"How happy you look, my dear," he said. "No doubt your thoughts were dwelling with pleasurable anticipation on Sussex and your new life there."

"That is exactly so, Uncle!" smiled Candida, her eyes cast down to mask the merriment she felt within her. "But I have also received a most welcome letter—from my Cousin Clara. She has invited me to go and visit her at her new home in Guildford."

Sir Montague approved of Clara. She was a comely, dark-haired girl who had married the Earl of Merrow and produced two children in the space of three years. That, thought Sir Montague, was exactly as it should be.

Candida went on: "If it would not inconvenience you, Uncle, I should very much like to leave for Guildford without delay. For to be sure, after I am married, I am convinced there will be very little opportunity for me to indulge in girlish chatter with my dear cousin."

Candida was perfectly aware that it would very well suit her uncle to have his niece safely installed in Guildford for a month or so. Sir Montague was itching to travel north for an enjoyable spot of grouse shooting.

Sir Montague nodded. "It seems an excellent plan, Candida. Of course you have my permission to visit Clara. As you so rightly point out, when you are Duchess of Stratton your life will be too full of marital responsibilities for you to journey far beyond Sussex." He held out his hand. "May I see Clara's letter?"

"Of course!" Candida smiled, taking the roll of parchment from her reticule. Sir Montague perused the closely written lines and remarked,

"How fortunate you are, Candida, to have a cousin who is so patently eager to see you!"

"Oh yes," murmured Candida, "I should feel quite lost without dear Clara!"

It was settled that Candida should depart from Gore Lodge in two days hence. Sir Montague courteously offered her his carriage for the journey. Candida, equally courteous, declined, insisting that her Uncle take the carriage for his journey to his beloved grouse moors.

"I shall be perfectly content with the stage, Uncle. And I shall, naturally be taking my maid Bessie with me, so I shall be well protected on the journey."

Bessie, a woman in her middle years with arms like great hams, was known to Sir Montague as a person who would stand no nonsense from anyone. Thoroughly at ease in his mind, he departed to his own apartments to give his valet orders about his journey north.

Candida hurried up to her dressing room where the faithful Bessie was repairing one of her mistress's petticoats.

"It is all arranged, Bessie," said Candida breathlessly. "You and I will travel by stage. But instead of coming all the way to Sussex with me, I shall leave you at Hazlemere, and you will be able to spend a month with your ailing sister."

Bessie's round face was troubled. "There's no stopping you, is there, Miss Candida? I must confess I don't like to think of your going all that way to Sussex on your own. And then for a lady like yourself to pose as a governess! What if Sir Montague ever finds out? He'd have not believed his eyes if he'd burst in here and discovered you with a needle in your hand, fashioning plain dresses for Miss Jane Wilton to wear!"

Candida laughed, "I had no choice, Bessie. For had I

ordered such dull dresses from my regular dressmaker in Alton, the intelligence would have been all around the village in no time!"

Unfortunately, Candida's first attempt at making a Jane Wilton dress had been a disaster—when she tried on the finished garment it was absurdly tight. Almost in tears, she had called in Bessie for advice, and the maid had pointed out that Candida had forgotten to allow a half-inch seam all around. But with Bessie's guidance, four plainly styled dresses had been made, in forest green, brown, dark blue, and dark red.

In a spirit of elation, Candida slipped on the dark red dress and paraded in front of the long glass.

"Sit up, now, Bessie, and pay attention," she rapped, with mock severity. "There! Do I not make a creditable picture of a governess?"

Bessie shook her head. "Your hair's not right, Miss Candida. All those unruly curls will never do!"

"Oh yes. Heavens, I had not thought of that!" Hastily, Candida rammed a severe black cap over her head, and pushed inside all the offending golden curls. "Is that better, Bessie?" she asked anxiously.

The maid laughed. "Mercy, Miss Candida! I've known you since you were born, and not a day has passed that you were not up to some prank or other. But this adventure is the most outrageous of all. Do you really think you will succeed in gulling the Duke of Stratton that you are a humble governess?"

Candida clasped her hands and declared fervently, "Oh, but I must succeed, Bessie! My whole future depends upon it!"

It was a perfect summer's day, with the occasional fleecy cloud scudding a shadow across the fields of ripening corn. Candida was in the best of spirits as she began her journey across the South Downs, the beautiful range of hills ridging the southern English landscape across from Hampshire to the majestic Seven Sisters cliffs in Sussex.

Candida had spent last night at a comfortable little inn

in the pleasant town of Hazlemere, having previously installed Bessie at her sister's cottage. Bessie, although obviously relieved to be with her sick sister, was prey to last minute doubts about the wisdom of allowing Candida to venture forth to Sussex on her own.

"Now you are not to worry, Bessie," said Candida firmly. "I promise, I shall keep all my wits about me. And if I do find myself in difficulty, I shall simply pack my bags and run away back here to you in Hazlemere."

And with this her faithful maid had to be content.

It was an uncomfortable carriage ride along the dry, rutted, dusty country roads; but nevertheless there was a smile on Candida's lovely face. So far, all her carefully laid plans had come perfectly to fruition.

Uncle Montague had been completely taken by the fictitious Miss Jane Wilton. How fortunate that he had not felt it his moral duty to interview her himself! Then Cousin Clara, dear loyal soul that she was, had responded instantly to Candida's letter imploring her to send an urgent invitation to Guildford.

Yet, of course, I dare not reveal to Clara in a letter the reason why this subterfuge was necessary, thought Candida. Poor Clara! She must be beside herself with curiosity. I must ensure that when my adventure at Stratton Hall is over, that I hasten to Guildford and tell Clara all. I am sure she will understand that posing as a governess is the only way in which I can respectably reside under the same roof as the Duke of Stratton. After a few weeks in his company, I should have had ample opportunity to judge his character. To decide, once and for all, whether he is the man I wish to marry.

The sun rose high in the sky, and the carriage rolled through the enchanting towns and villages of Horsham and Cuckfield. Candida was fascinated by the flint stone cottages and the beautiful Sussex gardens, vibrant with roses, honeysuckle and marigolds. Then she dozed, until at six P.M. the coach reached its final destination of Lewes.

In the bustling coachyard of the Bull Inn at Lewes, Candida suddenly found herself at a loss. She knew herself to be a good twelve miles from Stratton. Foolishly, she had given no thought as to how she was to cover that ground.

Then came a tap on her shoulder. "Miss Wilton?" inquired a burly man wearing impressive dark green livery. "I'm Morton, second coachman to the Duke of Stratton. I have orders to convey you to the Hall."

Candida sighed with relief. As Morton busied himself removing her box (borrowed from Bessie for the purpose) from the stagecoach to the smaller, utility coach which had been sent for her, Candida could not repress an inner surge of triumph. Since Morton, the driver, had recognized her instantly as a governess, it must be that her simple dark blue dress was utterly convincing.

As Morton handed her into the green carriage, Candida inquired, "How did you know that I would be on this particular stage, Mr. Morton?"

"I didn't, Miss. My orders were to meet every cross country stage for the next three days."

How very civil of the Duke, thought Candida, highly impressed. A wry smile touched Morton's cracked lips, and as if reading her thoughts he remarked, "A new and willing governess is regarded like gold dust up at the Hall. Little Lady Lucy, in particular, is most anxious to meet you!"

He chuckled loudly as he slammed the carriage door. Candida slid down the window and called, "Mr. Morton . . . I should be most grateful for any advice you could give me regarding my future charge."

The driver grinned. "You'll find out soon enough, Miss. But one thing I will warn you of: watch your head the first time you enter the schoolroom. The last governess came in for a drenching after Lady Lucy placed a bucket of water on top of the door."

And with these comforting words, he cracked his whip and Candida set forth on the last stage of her journey to Stratton. Candida's first sight of Stratton Hall was one she was destined never to forget. The impressive house, built eighty years before in the reign of Queen Anne, was set in a combe, guarded by rolling hills and a small beech wood. The sun was setting, flaming the mellow brick of the house to a slightly deeper hue than the corn waving in the roadside fields. To the side of the house was an ornamental lake, proudly presided over by two snow white swans, and beyond, Candida could ascertain an orangery and a vast sweep of lawn across which strutted a magnificent peacock.

Candida's heart contracted as she gazed on the house, with the sunlight glancing off the hundred windows. Oh, I love it, she thought passionately. How wonderful it would be to be mistress of Stratton Hall . . . to wander out in the mornings and feed the swans . . . to linger awhile in the sweetly scented orangery . . . to walk in the cool of those lovely beech trees. Yes, oh yes, I could be very happy here!

They began the long, slow descent from the chalk Downs, and through the sleepy, thatched-roofed village of Stratton. As the carriage passed under the massive wrought iron gates and rolled up the endless drive toward Stratton Hall, Candida found herself mesmerized by the house's large oak front door.

She willed it to open and reveal to her these people within, strangers to her now, but destined to play an all important role in her life. Young Lady Lucy for example. Candida had been so delighted at devising the role for herself of governess that she had not given a thought to how she was to manage her difficult charge. Was the girl really as wilful and rebellious as everyone claimed? What will happen, mused Candida frantically, if I find myself totally out of my depth with her? By all accounts she has already defeated any number of hapless governesses. I shall need all my wits about me if I am to come out on top in my encounter with little Lady Lucy!

And then, most important of all, there was the Duke of Stratton. Somewhere, within the mellow walls of Stratton Hall, was the man who would have her as his wife. What was he doing now, Candida wondered. Perhaps he has just partaken of a light supper, and is sitting in his library, enjoying a civilized glass of port.

Oh please, she prayed as the carriage halted before the front door, please let me like the Duke! Let him not be the ogre I fear him to be!

The front door swung open. The house Steward appeared, snapping his fingers at the scurrying footmen who hastened to open the carriage door, and remove Candida's box from the top.

Feeling suddenly nervous, Candida ascended the steps, and entered the splendid main hall, which was dominated by a wide marble and brass staircase. And then, descending the stairs, Candida saw the most handsome man she had ever set eyes on in her life.

He was tall and broad shouldered, and although dressed in the casual clothes of a country gentleman, it was obvious from his proud bearing that he was a nobleman. His rich, dark hair was defiantly unpowdered and unwigged. And as he drew closer, Candida saw that his eyes were of a deep gray, with the rugged lines of his face intriguingly enhanced by a long scar that ran along his left cheekbone.

Hastily, Candida dipped a curtsey. As she arose, she heard him say, in a deep warm voice,

"May I bid you welcome to my home, Miss Wilton. Welcome to Stratton Hall."

Candida gazed into his smiling gray eyes, certain that he must hear the hammering of her heart. For in her wildest dreams, she had never expected her future husband to be so devastatingly attractive. Oh, Uncle Montague, she thought joyously, I have been worrying unduly! Dear Mama was right after all. For I have met my future husband, and if this strange lightheadedness I feel is to be believed then I have fallen in love with him at first sight!

"I trust," inquired the dark haired man courteously, "that your journey was not too fatiguing, Miss Wilton?"

"Oh . . . oh no Your Grace," stammered Candida. "Such lovely countryside . . . I was quite enchanted . . ."

He laughed pleasantly. "Oh, but forgive me! I have been

most remiss in not introducing myself to you in the proper manner. I have not the honor to be the Duke of Stratton. I am Lord Berkeley. Bartholomew, the Duke, is my older brother."

The blood drained from Candida's lovely face. Disappointment tore at her heart and set her atremble from head to foot. Oh, but this was a cruel blow indeed! She had been so sure, so certain when she set eyes on this handsome man that he was indeed her intended. To him she could have given herself freely, willingly . . .

Candida was suddenly aware of a commotion issuing from one of the rooms leading from the hall.

"Where's that damned Steward?" shouted a male voice, clearly thick with wine. "I told him ten minutes ago to bring in more brandy. Stap me, I'll wait no longer, I'll fetch the deuced decanter myself!"

There was a crash, as if a table had been overturned, followed by innumerable glasses. The door opened, and a stocky, red-haired man lurched out of the room, his florid face livid with rage. Catching sight of Lord Berkeley and Candida he weaved toward them, bawling, "Ah ha! Wenching again then, brother! Well she looks a pretty piece of petticoat and no mistake!"

He stumbled and lost his balance. Clawing desperately at the wall-paintings for support, Candida's future husband collapsed in a drunken stupor at her feet.

Chapter Two

Candida stood immobile, frozen with horror and disgust at the revolting spectacle that confronted her. Yet, she was still strongly aware of Lord Berkeley's tall commanding presence at her side.

How would Lord Berkeley cope with this embarrassing situation? Would he apologize for his brother's inebriated condition? Or would he attempt to gloss over the matter with a careless laugh, a pretence that the Duke was prone to the occasional dizzy turn?

In the event, Lord Berkeley adopted neither of these options. Totally master of the occasion, he simply stepped over his brother's inert, sprawling body and taking Candida by the arm, guided her further down the hall where a woman in gray taffeta was waiting in the shadows.

"May I introduce Mrs. Brewer, our housekeeper—Mrs. Brewer, this is Miss Wilton, the Lady Lucy's new governess."

As the middle-aged woman kindly appraised the new governess at Stratton Hall, Candida was aware of a snap of Lord Berkeley's fingers. Immediately two footmen came running from a side room. They each took one of the Duke of Stratton's arms, and half-slid, half-lifted him from the hall into the room from whence he had come. Such was the smoothness and efficiency of the operation, that Candida opined that the Duke's drunkenness tonight was not a simple case of unusual over indulgence. It was horribly apparent that this was a regular—even daily—occurrence.

"Mrs. Brewer will escort you to your apartments, and assist you with anything you may need," smiled Lord Berkeley. "Lady Lucy is, of course, in bed. At least, I hope she's in bed?" He looked inquiringly at Mrs. Brewer.

The housekeeper nodded reassuringly. "Indeed yes, my lord. She's sleeping soundly. I always go in now, and check, since that time when she ran down to the village and rang the church bell at midnight."

Candida gasped, "Oh heavens! No doubt the entire village was aroused, and thoroughly alarmed?"

"Quite so," sighed Lord Berkeley. "The Watch, the excise men, the fire cart, the Rector, the local physician, and myself all converged in some confusion on the village square only to find, of course, that it was little Lady Lucy up to another of her pranks."

Aware that Lord Berkeley and Mrs. Brewer were closely observing her reaction to this adventure of Lady Lucy's, Candida was careful to allow no expression of shock or apprehension into her eyes. To show dismay now would be to admit defeat before her task had even begun!

Accordingly, Candida murmured serenely, "My, Lady Lucy certainly sounds like a high-spirited young lady. I am greatly looking forward to making her acquaintance. At what hour do her lessons normally commence in the morning?"

"Lucy is usually coaxed into the schoolroom by ten," replied Lord Berkeley with some feeling. "But I expect you would prefer to delay formal lessons for a day or so, Miss Wilton, to give you time to familiarize yourself with Stratton Hall."

Candida was immensely touched at his thoughtfulness. If I were truly a lowly spinster governess arriving at this grand house to take responsibility for a wayward charge, then yes, I should indeed be grateful for a time in which to get my bearings, she thought. But this is one aspect where I, Candida Wellesley, have the advantage. For unlike Jane Wilton, I am not at all overawed by Stratton Hall and its hundreds of rooms, servants, and subtle nuances of etiquette.

She smiled at Lord Berkeley and said firmly, "Thank you, my lord, but if it is convenient to all concerned, I should prefer to start lessons with Lady Lucy promptly at ten tomorrow morning."

Lord Berkeley's gray eyes glimmered with surprise, and admiration. "Very well, Miss Wilton. I will leave you, then, in the capable hands of Mrs. Brewer. But if there is anything which worries you, please do not hesitate to come to me. We want you to be happy here at Stratton Hall, Miss Wilton."

And with that he strode away down the hall, into the room in which the footmen had dragged his unconscious brother.

As the door slammed hard behind Lord Berkeley, Mrs. Brewer turned and led the way upstairs. She took Candida to a small, comfortably furnished apartment in the east wing. In addition to the bed, there was an oak writing table, and a well upholstered arm chair. Candida surmised that many an exhausted governess had collapsed with a sigh of relief into that chair at the end of a long hard day with the wilful Lady Lucy!

Candida's plain wooden box had already been placed in the small dressing room adjoining the bedchamber. Mrs. Brewer ran her finger along the marble topped washstand to satisfy herself that the maid had dusted properly. Then, she hovered by the dressing room door, and talked with Candida as she unpacked.

"No point in you coming into this post unawares, Miss Wilton," the housekeeper began bluntly. "It is best all around that you know a few of the facts right from the very start. Then there'll be no cause for misunderstandings."

Candida, naturally, was all ears. She was also aware of the close scrutiny the housekeeper was giving her underwear, her shoes, her personal effects as she unpacked. Fortunately, Candida had been thorough in her preparations. Having decided to adopt the *persona* of Miss Jane Wilton, Candida had ruthlessly discarded anything which did not totally suit her new role as governess. How she had longed to bring her new, lace-edged petticoat and those wonderfully fine silk stockings! Regretfully, she had lain such elegant finery aside.

Her petticoats were plain, and untouched by even a whisper of lace. Her hoops were small, at least a foot less in circumference than those worn by the most fashionable ladies of the day. Her stockings were well darned (thanks to Bessie, again!) and her only item of jewellery was the simple silver cross she wore around her neck.

Mrs. Brewer obviously saw nothing amiss. After five minutes of watching Candida unpack, her eyes glazed, and she wandered back to the washstand, peering into the flowered china jug in a vain search for dust.

"Of course, in many respects we all feel mighty sorry for Lady Lucy," Mrs. Brewer was saying. "It was tragic for the lass, losing both parents when she was only eleven. And to be fair to the Duke, it can't have been easy for him, either. He'd lived abroad for years, you see. So he returns home here to Sussex, and finds himself saddled with a red-haired tiger of a girl as his ward."

"It must have been difficult for the Duke to adjust to an English way of life after living in foreign lands for so long," commented Candida.

Mrs. Brewer muttered darkly, "Oh, don't you go wasting your sympathy on him! Not that I mean any disrespect, mind. But the one who's had the real hard time is Lord Berkeley. Funny, I can never accustom myself to calling him by such a grand title. I've known him since he was a boy, you see, and he was Master Greville to everyone then."

"You've been at Stratton Hall a long time then?" inquired Candida with a smile.

"I joined the staff as third scullery maid. Spent my first year with my hands the color of soot half the time from blacking the kitchen range, and red the other half from being in washing soap when I was cleaning the dishes. That was over thirty years ago, of course, when the old Duke and Duchess were alive." Her voice softened. "Oh, she was a lovely lady, the Duchess! All the staff adored her. We'd have done anything for her. Anything at all."

Candida placed her Bible on the oak bedside table, and quietly waited for Mrs. Brewer to continue. In her thirty years with the Berkeley family, clearly little had escaped the housekeeper's critical eye.

Months later, Candida was to remember that thought

and smile, wryly. How wrong she had been! For the most important secret of Stratton Hall had been kept from even the sharp eyes and ears of the faithful housekeeper herself.

"But, of course, the poor Duchess died not long after Master Greville's birth," recalled Mrs. Brewer, wiping a tear from her eye. "Ah, he's the one who has all my sympathy. It's a hard burden he has to bear."

"Why is that, Mrs. Brewer?" inquired Candida curiously.

"Because he is the second son, of course!" declared Mrs. Brewer. "It is his brother who has the title, and the Stratton fortune at his command. What's left of the fortune that is," she muttered bitterly. "Oh, Lord Berkeley has a good enough allowance from the estate. But it's his brother, the Duke, who's had the means to disport himself all over Europe for these past ten years, while Lord Berkeley has remained at home, managing the estate and overseeing the repairs to the house."

Candida pushed back a stray lock of golden hair beneath her demure governess's cap. "Has Lord Berkeley not ventured abroad at all?" she questioned.

"Yes indeed, he has traveled quite widely. He speaks four languages, you know, and is an extremely cultured man. But the shame of it was that he never had the means to travel in such style as his brother, the Duke."

Candida added thoughtfully, "And no doubt, now that the Duke has returned, Lord Berkeley finds his position here seriously undermined. For all these years he has been accustomed to making all the decisions, taking all the responsibility. But now he must take second place to his brother."

"That's it exactly!" sighed Mrs. Brewer. "Trouble is, they're both strong-willed men. And to own the truth, Miss Wilton, I've never seen two brothers who are as different as chalk and cheese. Well, you'll see for yourself. But one thing I will say: you'd never find Lord Berkeley insensible with drink and sprawled on the hall floor for all the servants to see. Oh, the shame of it!"

"Is this a frequent occurrence?" asked Candida with dread.

Mrs. Brewer pursed her lips. "It's the rule rather than

the exception I'm afraid, Miss Wilton. In my view, it's a crying shame that he inherited the title from his father at such a young age. Barely eighteen Young Lord Bart was then. He was always at odds with his father, and on the night of the old Duke's funeral, the new young Duke locked himself in the cellar with a hogshead of claret, and didn't come out for a week."

"Mercy me!" murmured Candida. "He must possess an extremely strong constitution to be able to absorb such quantities of alcohol."

"Oh, he's as strong as an oak barn door," said Mrs. Brewer.

And as thick, thought Candida, laying out her night attire on the bed.

Mrs. Brewer took the hint, and moved toward the door. "There is just one thing, Miss Wilton, while we're on the subject of His Grace's inbibing. Now I mean no disrespect to the Duke by saying this, mind, but if you hear that the Duke is drinking something called mahogany, then I would advise you to remove yourself immediately to your chamber and lock the door!"

Heavens, mused Candida frantically, this is going from bad to worse! Aloud she inquired, "Mahogany, Mrs. Brewer? But that is a type of wood, is it not?"

Mrs. Brewer laughed. " 'Tis also an alcoholic beverage, Miss Wilton, made of two parts gin to one part treacle."

"Ugh!" said Candida with a grimace. "How revolting!"

"Well naturally, a governess like yourself wouldn't be overly familiar with strong liquor," said Mrs. Brewer, blithely unaware that to fortify herself for the journey ahead, Candida had last night enjoyed a glass of brandy alone in her room at the inn.

Mrs. Brewer went on: "Mahogany is, I believe, a concoction enjoyed by Cornish fishermen. But it has a lethal effect on the Duke."

"Thank you for the warning, Mrs. Brewer," smiled Candida.

Mrs. Brewer regarded the slender girl standing by the bed and sighed. "Well, lass. You've a kind face and a willing air. I just hope you last a mite longer than your predecessors. Lady Lucy will be waiting for you in the schoolroom at ten tomorrow morning. I'll bid you goodnight then, Miss Wilton."

As the door closed behind the housekeeper, Candida moved across and quietly turned the key in the lock. She could well imagine the Duke of Stratton stirring from his drunken slumber, and recalling dimly that a new governess had arrived, setting forth for her chamber to make a personal inspection.

Candida sank into bed with a sigh of relief. She had been within the walls of Stratton Hall for just over two hours, and already she felt fatigued to the point of exhaustion.

It is worse, she admitted, far worse than I had anticipated. The Duke himself is a disgusting creature whom I fear will not improve upon acquaintance. And of course, he appears all the more appalling in comparison with his brother, Lord Berkeley.

Candida blushed for shame as she recalled her first sighting of Lord Berkeley, and her heady conviction that she had fallen instantly in love with him, believing him to be her future husband. You must put all such fanciful notions straight from your mind, Candida, she ordered herself firmly. Your purpose in masquerading as a governess is to inspect the Duke and determine whether you could live with him as his wife. There is, of course, no question of you falling in love with *him*. But you must give him a fair trial. You may find, over the coming month or so, that he has many redeeming qualities which would make him an admirable husband.

Such were the cool words issuing from Candida's head. But her heart was in violent opposition:

You cannot for one moment consider marrying the Duke, Candida! Your first instinct was the right one! It is Lord Berkeley whom you wish to marry, not his drunken brother!

Candida pressed a hand to her aching head, willing it to send forth a crushingly sensible reply, and soon the answer came, with a crisp, cutting conviction:

Lord Berkeley is an extremely handsome, cultured and

dashing man. He may not possess his brother's title or great wealth. But rest assured, there are scores of rich dowagers in this county who would like nothing better than to see their pretty grand-daughters wed to the distinguished brother of the Duke of Stratton.

Yes, Candida realized miserably, that is the stony truth. Lord Berkeley is an extremely attractive man. No doubt half the lovely young girls in the county are competing for his favors. And with all that to keep him occupied, why should he cast a glance at me, a lowly governess?

The word governess reminded Candida that tomorrow morning she would be plunged into her first danger-fraught encounter with the wilful Lady Lucy.

Lady Lucy will be waiting for you in the schoolroom at ten tomorrow morning Mrs. Brewer had said, somewhat ominously to Candida's ears.

But Candida's last thought, before drifting into sleep was that if nothing else, she must ensure that she got the upper hand in her first encounter with the Duke of Stratton's rebellious little ward.

Twelve-year-old Lady Lucy tripped happily along the corridor toward the schoolroom. Although it was scarcely half-past nine, there was a smile on the girl's perfect face and a lightness in her step. For there was nothing Lady Lucy enjoyed more than her first morning with a brand new governess!

Oh the thrill of watching the new lady walk into the schoolroom, to be deluged by a bucket of water over the door, or scared out of her wits by the sight of Lady Lucy hanging by her neck outside the window. (This last, of course, was just a life-sized doll dressed in Lady Lucy's clothes but it had been sufficient to cause two governesses to have uncontrollable hysterics.)

Today, Lady Lucy carried in her hand a jar containing a large and particularly ugly toad. She had risen especially early and selected the creature with great care from the vast Stratton Hall lake. Aware that all female adults were terrified of toads, Lady Lucy planned to place this one under her new governess's skirts.

But that was not all, for hidden in her pocket was a

huge black spider which Lady Lucy had ingeniously fashioned from black felt. Lady Lucy was purposely arriving early at the schoolroom this morning armed with a long length of string. Lady Lucy giggled, picturing the scene as the new harridan of the governess swept into the schoolroom and a horrid great spider descended onto her face!

As she approached the schoolroom door, she began to chant, "I shan't! I won't. Nothing will make me! Never, never *never!*"

Her piping voice rose to a crescendo as she swung open the door and marched in.

"Good morning, Lady Lucy," said a pleasant voice from the window. "You are early. I am delighted that you are so eager to begin your lessons!"

Lady Lucy stood open mouthed as she regarded the slim, pretty young woman in the dark blue dress. Her fingers closed around the furry felt spider hidden in the pocket of her smock. Oh, how infuriating of this new governess to arrive in the schoolroom before her! Now her practical joke was all spoiled!

Candida repressed a smile as she regarded the indignation on the young girl's face. She had achieved, then, her first objective with Lady Lucy. By ensuring that she arrived first, and was seated at her desk, looking totally in command, Candida had effectively pulled the rug from under her young charge's slippered feet. The next step, Candida knew, was to follow up her advantage.

Candida arose, and swept confidently forward. "My name is Miss Wilton. I am sure we are going to have a very happy time working together, Lady Lucy. Oh, and you have brought me a little toad to look at! How very sweet."

Lady Lucy watched aghast as her new governess took the jar, and encouraged the toad to hop out onto her desk.

"Are they not fascinating creatures?" exclaimed Candida. "I am delighted that you are so interested in Nature, Lady Lucy. I can see we shall enjoy many fascinating rambles around the estate together, looking at all the wildlife. Perhaps tomorrow morning you would be kind enough to bring me a little frog, and then we could compare him with the toad?"

Lady Lucy turned away, fearful that in a moment she would be violently sick. Heavens, it had taken all her courage to pick that horrid toad out of the lake. And now this dreadful governess was suggesting that she go and fetch a slimy frog as well! This was not at all what she had intended.

Desperately, Lady Lucy cast about for a different topic of conversation. "The . . . the schoolroom . . ." she stammered, "it looks different . . ."

"Oh, I am so pleased you noticed," smiled Candida warmly. "See, I have moved that big ugly cupboard from its original place in front of that window. Now the room is so much lighter, and we are both able to have desks under a window. But what I am really looking forward to is moving in a sofa."

"A sofa?" echoed Lady Lucy faintly. "In the *schoolroom?*"

"Why not?" queried Candida lightly, giving the atlas a playful twirl. "Oh, to be sure, when there are written lessons to be attended to, then you must sit straight-backed at your desk to attend to them. But when we are examining the wild flowers we have collected or the bird's feathers, or sea shells, how much more pleasant it will be to sit here side by side on the sofa and compare our treasures."

Lucy pouted. "You mean we are to go for walks to the sea?" she said dismally. "Oh, I should not like that at all. I hate the countryside!"

"Now I know that is not true," said Candida pleasantly. "Why, you have already taken the trouble to bring me this enchanting little toad!"

"But—but do you not think it is horrendously ugly?" demanded Lady Lucy.

"Surely we do not judge any creature in this world simply by its appearance," replied Candida. "A toad will not bite, nor poison nor maim us. So why should we think ill of it simply because it is not a very handsome creature?"

Sensing that she was in danger of being seriously outmaneuvered by this smiling young governess, Lady Lucy decided that there was only one thing to do. She would throw one of her celebrated tantrums. That would be sure to wipe the smile from this unpredictable Miss Wilton's pretty face!

With an ease bred of long practice, Lady Lucy took in a deep breath and held it until her pert young face turned red. Then she began to scream at the top of her voice:

"I don't want to go on country walks and collect beastly toads and frogs! I shan't! I won't! Nothing will make me. Never, never, *never!*"

And to emphasize her point, she seized the hem of her smock and tore it savagely into shreds.

Unfortunately, the effect was lost on Candida, who had turned her back and was gazing out the window. When Lady Lucy paused to draw breath, Candida said calmly, "Ah yes. I believe I heard you chanting that little refrain just before you entered the schoolroom. What were you doing, practicing your phrasing for your next spot of rebellion?"

Lady Lucy's blue eyes widened in disbelief. Caught off guard, she blurted the truth: "I make a point of being as disagreeable as I can to beastly Uncle Bart. Whenever he asks me to do something, I make an awful face, and jump up and down in front of him and shout never, never, *never!*"

Lady Lucy smirked as she waited for the inevitable reprimand from the governess for speaking of her elders so disrespectfully. Candida, however, merely replied in an interested tone.

"Mm. I should imagine that the shock element is completely lost on your uncle if you merely say the same words over and over each time. Tell me, have you thought of shouting it in French?"

"French?" faltered Lady Lucy, wondering if she were dreaming.

"Yes. You would have the benefit of catching him off guard, and surprising him. And the word for never in French has such a satisfying emphatic ring to it, don't you think?"

Lady Lucy bit her lip. "I can't remember what it is, Miss Wilton."

"Of course, you can," said Candida encouragingly. "Think about it. Just imagine how stunned your uncle will be when you devastate him with your French!"

"Is it . . . is it *rien?*" tried Lady Lucy. Heavens, however was she supposed to remember any French? She had never retained a governess long enough to get beyond the verb *to be.*

Candida moved casually across to the bookshelves on the far wall. "No, Lady Lucy. *Rien* if you recall, is what Cordelia said to her father, King Lear."

"I don't understand," protested Lady Lucy tearfully. "Who is King Lear? Is he French? Is my Uncle Bart acquainted with him?"

"*King Lear* is a wonderfully dramatic play by Mr. Shakespeare," said Candida, taking the leather-covered volume down from the shelf. "The King decides to divide his kingdom between his three daughters. But first he asks each of them how much they loved him. The two elder daughters declare that they love him excessively, but the third, Cordelia, when asked what she has to say replies—"

"Nothing!" cried Lady Lucy triumphantly, "I remember now. *Rien* means nothing! But why was Cordelia so stupid, Miss Wilson? Did she not want her share of the kingdom? What happened in the end?"

"Well, let us sit down together and find out," suggested Candida, opening the play. "I will take the part of the King and you must be the three daughters."

"Oh yes, I should like that!" cried Lady Lucy, clapping her hands. "I shall alter my voice for each one!"

Thus, to Candida's relief, her first morning as a governess passed most agreeably. With Lady Lucy in such good humor after her lesson, it would have been tempting for Candida to assume that she had succeeded in winning over the child. But Candida was aware that it would be fatal to rest on her laurels and congratulate herself that Lady Lucy was now a reformed character.

If I have assessed that young lady's temperament correctly, mused Candida in bed that night, then she will now be furious with herself for her good behavior in the schoolroom today. She will feel she has lost face, and tomorrow, no doubt she will be redoubling her attempt to shock me.

Sure enough, the red-haired minx bounced into the

schoolroom the following morning screeching at the top of her voice:

"Jamais! Jamais! JAMAIS!"

Restraining an urge to slap the girl into silence, Candida said calmly, "Very good, Lady Lucy. Excellent. I am glad you remembered at last the French word for never."

Lady Lucy stuck out her tongue. "I didn't remember. I asked my Uncle Greville. He speaks at least a hundred languages, you know. He's *very* clever. Oooh! I can't wait to go and shout *jamais* at Uncle Bart. He'll be so angry! At least I hope he will."

Once again, Candida refused to react to the girl's impertinent attitude toward her uncle and guardian. Instead, she inquired, with interest,

"Why are you so intent on irritating your Uncle Bart, Lady Lucy?"

"Because I want to go to boarding school, and he won't give his permission!" flared Lady Lucy, stamping her foot.

"Boarding school?" echoed Candida. "Dear me, they always sound like such austere, uncomfortable places."

"But you have such fun at school!" exclaimed Lady Lucy. "Uncle Greville was telling me that at Eton they'd play at cockfighting. Each boy had his hands bound and a broom handle placed behind his knees and then they'd fight one another with their feet, and all the onlookers would take wagers on the likely winner!" Lady Lucy clapped her hands with glee, and went on, "And they are always having excellent mutinies at boarding schools. Lord Brockway says that whenever King George encounters an old Etonian he always inquires, *had any good rebellions lately, eh?* Oh Miss Wilton, I should so much love to be ringleader of a rebellion!"

Candida pulled down the cuffs of her forest green dress, and said faintly, "That is all very well, Lady Lucy. But I would remind you that the antics of which you speak have all taken place at *boys'* schools. At academies for young ladies' life would be conducted in a far more genteel manner."

Lady Lucy's blue eyes glowed with triumph. "Not at all, Miss Wilton! Why, I have heard of one school where the girls are paying for their education through their winnings at Whist and Casino. It is strictly forbidden, of course, but they play under the covers at night. Now I happen to be extremely good at Whist. So I could make a fortune!"

"But my dear, there is no cause for you to be worried about paying for your own education, and earning money," said Candida.

Lady Lucy shrugged. "Oh, of course there is a huge amount in trust for me. But I am not allowed control of it until I am twenty-one!" She sighed. "I am sure I shall never, ever be as old as twenty-one years! But if I won some money at cards, then it would be all mine to spend as I like."

"And what would be your first purchases with your new-found fortune?" inquired Candida with a smile, confident that this strange child would have no truck with normal girlish delights like a new hooped petticoat or golden buckles for her shoes.

"First of all I'd buy some gunpowder," said Lady Lucy firmly, "and I'd blow up Lady Frances Brockway and Lady Angelica Kerr."

"Oh dear. And what have these two ladies done to offend you?" asked Candida.

"They are always here, at Stratton Hall," she explained with an impatient toss of her fiery curls. "Lady Frances moons around over Uncle Greville, and Lady Angelica obviously has her sights set on Uncle Bart." She giggled. "I'm longing to see her face when she learns that Uncle Bart is going to marry some awful girl from Hampshire!"

Candida knew it was wrong for her, as a governess, to discuss her employer's affairs with a twelve-year-old child. But Candida was human, and she could not resist murmuring,

"If the lady is so dreadful, I wonder why your Uncle is going to marry her?"

"Oh, for her money of course," said Lady Lucy with an airy wave of her hand. "I listened at the library door and heard him telling Uncle Greville all about it. Uncle Greville was shocked, and said—"

There was a crash as Candida, quite deliberately,

knocked over an inkwell to distract the child and prevent her from blurting further indiscreet revelations. Clearly, Lady Lucy was an eavesdropper and a tittle-tattler. It would never do for her to go running to her uncles to reveal that she had poured into her governess's fascinated ears details of the Duke's private conversation!

When the mopping up was completed, Candida abandoned all hope of conducting a formal lesson that morning as Lady Lucy was clearly in too restless a mood to settle down and study. So Candida said with a smile,

"You have not told me what else, apart from gunpowder, you would purchase with your fabulous winnings at cards."

"Well, having destroyed Lady Frances and Lady Angelica, I should then run away back to London," said the girl emphatically. "I hate living in the country. It's so quiet and boring!"

Candida leaned back in her chair. "You grew up in London, Lady Lucy? Tell me about it."

"My mother was very beautiful and my father was incredibly handsome and they both loved me dearly," began Lady Lucy, with shining eyes. "We had a big house in Park Lane and . . ."

"Yes, her mother was indeed a celebrated beauty. And the father, Lord Hawley, was an exceedingly dashing man. But as for loving little Lucy dearly, well, I am sorry to say that that is far from the truth. Lord and Lady Hawley were selfish creatures, interested only in their own pleasure, and I fear Lady Lucy was a sorely neglected child."

The speaker was Lord Greville Berkeley. At two o'clock, Lucy had left the schoolroom to join young Lord Rupert Brockway for a riding lesson. Candida, descending the marble stairs into the main hall, had found the handsome Lord Berkeley waiting for her.

From the anxious expression in his gray eyes, Candida realized that he was fully expecting her to resign her post. No doubt other governesses, wearied after drenchings of water, presents of toads, tantrums, and blatant refusals to attend to lessons, had come down these stairs and announced with understandable indignation that they were throwing in the towel.

But Candida greeted Lord Berkeley with a bright smile and the cheerful remark, "Good afternoon! Lady Lucy and I have had a most profitable morning in the schoolroom. She is an extremely intelligent and rewarding pupil, and we have made excellent progress today."

Lord Berkeley looked momentarily stunned. With relief in his voice he replied, "I . . . I am delighted to hear it, Miss Wilton. If there is anything you need, extra books, materials, do not hesitate to let me know."

"Thank you. As a matter of fact, I should be most grateful if a sofa could be moved into the schoolroom. Frankly, I see no reason why lessons should inevitably be conducted on hard, uncomfortable chairs."

"I will see to it that a sofa is installed first thing tomorrow morning," promised Lord Berkeley immediately. Good breeding prevented revealing any surprise he may have felt in his voice. But his gray eyes were glimmering with curiosity and interest as he regarded the demure new young governess.

"I am also a little perturbed that Lady Lucy regards the Sussex countryside in such an alien light," Candida went on. "With your permission, I should like to explore the estate a little, with the object of finding some interesting walks and rides with which to initiate my pupil into the delights of the countryside."

Lord Berkeley gave a gallant bow. "But of course. It will be my pleasure to escort you over the estate, Miss Wilton. I will order the horses to be saddled immediately."

Which is how Candida and Lord Berkeley came to be riding side by side on a glorious August afternoon across the lush South Downs, where cattle grazed peacefully in the meadows, and brilliant kingfishers darted up tree-shaded streams.

They skirted the glowing cornfields, and the beech wood, and as the horses were delicately picking their way up a chalk-ridged path, Candida brought up the subject of Lady Lucy's upbringing.

"So," said Lord Berkeley thoughtfully, absently fingering the scar on his cheek, "the little minx has given you the impression that she was utterly the apple of her parents' eye?"

"But it appears I have been misled," Candida added, tilting the brim of her plain straw bonnet to shield her face from the sun.

"As I understand it, the Hawleys' was an arranged marriage," said Lord Berkeley, "and from the moment they returned from their Wedding Tour, it was mutually agreed that they should lead separate lives. I understand that they both had many lovers, and I am afraid they regarded Lady Lucy as an intolerable nuisance."

Candida sighed. "Poor little girl. I expect the only way she could gain her mother's attention was by misbehaving."

"Yes, and ever since a rebellious attitude has become a way of life with her," muttered Lord Berkeley.

"Nevertheless, one cannot help feeling sorry for a child who is forced to fabricate a tale of parental affection," said Candida, softly.

Lord Berkeley smiled. "Clearly, you possess a kind heart, Miss Wilton. I just hope Lucy has the good sense not to take advantage of it."

"I fear she regards all governesses as enemies," remarked Candida. "She informed me that she dearly desires to go away to boarding school."

"Yes, I must own that I am to blame for that particular fancy," owned Lord Berkeley with a rueful smile. "I told her a gruesome story about young lads at Eton being forced to play cockfights with one another. I imagined, of course, that such a tale would deter Lucy but to my horror she found the notion vastly entertaining. Now she can speak of nothing else but the delights of boarding schools."

"If she is that set on attending such an establishment, I am surprised that the Duke does not give his permission," said Candida.

Lord Berkeley replied curtly, "My brother has decided

against sending Lucy to school. There is no more to be said."

Abruptly, he cantered on ahead, leaving Candida wondering what she had said wrong. But it was too lovely a day to brood over mere words, she decided. They had now ascended onto the top of Stratton Down. Far below, shimmering through a heat haze, was the Stratton Hall Home Farm, where the workers were just finishing their mid-day break. The horses had been given their nose-bags and led to a stream for water. Candida's sharp eyes picked out flames of red, the workers' cotton handkerchieves which had contained their bread, cheese, and bacon meal. She surmised that to quench their thirst they would have brought in tin bottles of that most refreshing of summer drinks—cold tea.

Noticing that Lord Berkeley had reined in his horse at the top of the next ridge, Candida cantered on to join him. As she drew level, she gasped with delight,

"Oh, the sea! I had not realized we were so close!"

It was indeed a magnificent view, with the sparkling blue sea forming a vivid contrast to the stark chalk white cliffs.

Candida threw back her lovely head, exulting in the salty air, and remarked, "Why, look Lord Berkeley, someone has built an enormous bonfire on the edge of the cliff. How very strange!"

He laughed. "That is no bonfire, Miss Wilton. It is the Stratton Down beacon. You will find such beacons all the way along this coast. It is lit only rarely, in times of danger, emergency, or invasion."

"I see. In the same manner, then, that the village church bell is rung," murmured Candida. "But Lord Berkeley, this area is completely uninhabited. Even if the beacon is lit, who is there to see it, and sound the alert?"

By way of reply, the handsome Lord pointed inland to the hill behind them. "See, there is another beacon on top of that hill, and a permanent watchman also. If ever he observes this clifftop Stratton Down beacon afire, then he sets light to his hilltop beacon. And that, in turn, is clearly visible from Stratton Hall."

"A chain of fire!" exclaimed Candida, most impressed.

Lord Berkeley nodded. "If we at Stratton Hall see the

beacon blazing, then we take to horse immediately and head for the coast to attend to the disaster."

"Naturally, I should not wish any tragedy to befall anyone—but those beacons must be a magnificent sight when they are afire!" commented Candida.

"I doubt if you will have the experience of observing such a sight," warned Lord Berkeley, turning back for home. "The last time they blazed was five years ago, when a ship went down. And please, whatever you do, don't mention the beacons to young Lucy. I'm sure nothing would delight her more than to creep out here with a tinderbox in her mischievous little hand!"

As Stratton Hall came once more into view, Candida courteously thanked Lord Berkeley for escorting her on the ride.

"Not at all, Miss Wilton, it has been my pleasure. It is well for you to be aware that we are, in many respects, an extremely informal household at Stratton Hall. When we are together, just as a family, we do not choose to stand on ceremony. With this in mind, my brother has indicated that it would please him if you would join us each day for our family dinner."

Candida was much surprised at this invitation. Yesterday, aware that the Duke and his brother were dining out at Lady Angelica's mansion, Candida had eaten alone with Lady Lucy in the child's private apartments. And she had assumed that even when Lady Lucy joined the men for dinner that she, as a mere governess, would take her meal separately.

As if reading her thoughts, Lord Berkeley went on. "You must understand that we live very quietly here, Miss Wilton. We see few new faces. So when we are fortunate enough to receive into our household an intelligent and personable governess like yourself, you cannot blame us for wanting to take advantage of your fresh outlook on the world."

Candida was not for a moment deceived by Lord Berkeley's graceful speech. What he means, she thought, is that the Duke has a mind to inspect the new young governess. I have no doubt that after all his years spent roaming around

Europe, he finds family dinners in rural Sussex excessively boring. But with a new young lady seated at his table, he will delight in the opportunity of bragging, and boasting and yes, baiting. For a mere governess would not, of course, have the temerity to answer him back, or slap him down if his hands began to wander under the table. Oh yes, there would be much sport to be had at the expense of the timid Jane Wilton.

Well, we'll see about that, my lord Duke, thought Candida, entering the Hall with the light of battle in her eye.

Chapter Three

Family meals at Stratton Hall were taken, Candida discovered, in the friendly atmosphere of the Morning Room. The imposing Eating Room, with its celebrated chandeliers and polished mahogany tables, was reserved for more formal occasions.

"Is Lucy not joining us for dinner?" demanded the Duke of Stratton as the footman held out the carved chair at the top of the rosewood table.

"No, Bart. Lucy is staying overnight with the Brockways, as usual after her riding lesson with the young Lord Rupert," replied Lord Berkeley, ushering Candida forward. "But as you requested, Lucy's new governess, Miss Wilton, is giving us the pleasure of her company at dinner."

The Duke of Stratton leaned back in his chair, his bloodshot blue eyes roaming freely over the face and figure of the new governess. Candida curtseyed, and stood before him in her burgundy red dress, with a deceptively demure expression on her countenance. She too was making her own appraisal of this man whom it had been decreed she should marry.

Being sober, he did not of course present such a revolting spectacle as on her first encounter with him. Candida was amused to note that he clearly considered himself as something of a dandy. His red hair was masked by a tightly curled wig, and his stocky frame was encased in a brocade waistcoat and a dark blue velvet skirt coat trimmed with gold. But to Candida's critical eye, the coarse, florid face seemed strangely at odds with the elegantly foaming lace at his neck.

The Duke leaned forward and pinched Candida's cheek in a familiar fashion. "Well, well! You're a pretty young thing and no mistake! How old are you, Miss Wilton?"

"I am nineteen years, Your Grace."

"Mmm." The Duke's hand reached out to touch her again, but deftly Candida moved aside and seated herself in the chair Lord Berkeley indicated for her. "Nineteen, eh? Rather young to be a fully fledged governess, are you not, my dear?"

Lord Berkeley interposed smoothly, "Miss Wilton may be young in years, Bart, but I assure you she has the authority of a woman twice her age. Why, Lucy came to me only this morning and actually expressed enthusiasm for her French lessons!"

The Duke roared with laughter, spluttering over his asparagus soup. "The little minx! She was all set to go off riding on that new chestnut that's far too frisky for her. I ordered her off it, and she brandished her whip at me, shouting, *jamis, jamis, jamis!* Best entertainment I've had all day. I admire a girl with a bit of spirit."

Observing the admiration in the Duke's pale blue eyes, Candida realized that poor Lucy was obviously employing the wrong tactic with her uncle. The child believed that by being outrageously rude to him, she would irritate him into sending her away to boarding school. Instead, the Duke was clearly fascinated by the wilful ways of his niece. What Lucy should do, Candida realized, is act the demure, prim and proper little miss with him. Then he'd be so bored, he'd be glad to see the back of her.

Over the excellent roast beef, the conversation between the two men centered on their various experiences in France. Lord Berkeley, it appeared, had greatly enjoyed his time there. To Candida's delight, he talked amusingly about the salons, balls, and hunting parties he had attended in Paris and Versailles. Candida could have listened to Lord Berkeley's reminiscences all night but the Duke called for more wine, and interrupted,

"Can't see what you find so fascinating about those damned Frenchies, Greville. Their food's disgusting, smothered in evil-smelling, garlicky sauces. And their horsemanship's a disgrace. When they're out hunting, y'know, the dashed Frenchies don't have the guts to take the fences. The entire proceedings are held up while their foreign lordships go *around* the hedges, and meanwhile, of course, old foxie is over the hills and far away!" The Duke was so indignant, he downed his wine in one gulp, spilling the dregs down his white lace ruffles.

"Have you travelled abroad at all, Miss Wilton?" inquired Lord Berkeley courteously.

"I fear I have not had that pleasure," smiled Candida, grateful for his gallantry in including her in the conversation. The Duke of Stratton had made no attempt to put her at her ease, although he was clearly conscious of her presence at his table. For while he had not addressed her verbally, his eyes were continually roving over her in a most lecherous manner.

The Duke, drinking twice as fast as his brother, was rapidly becoming loquacious and inebriated. His face was flushed, revealing a network of blue veins across his grainy cheeks. His wig was askew, and there was now an unappetizing mixture of soup, wine and gravy on the lace at his neck.

It was impossible for Candida not to compare this unsavory creature with the handsome civilized figure cut by Lord Berkeley at the other end of the table. As usual, he scorned the use of a wig, and his dark hair was tied naturally back onto the nape of his neck. Where the Duke was flamboyantly dressed, Lord Berkeley favored a plain, oyster silk waistcoat and a simple, immaculately cut skirt-coat, unadorned by foppish trimmings.

Replete at last, the Duke flung his monogrammed linen napkin down on the floor and cast a lecherous eye over Candida. "I must admit, Miss Wilton, it's a rare delight to have a pretty young governess tripping around the house. Can't say I'm sorry that those other women found little Lucy too much of a handful, Greville. They all irritate me excessively with their thin faces and spinsterish ways. But Miss Wilton here, in her pretty red dress, is just like a rose coming into bloom!"

As he spoke, his hand sneaked under the table and grasped Candida's leg, just above the knee. Deliberately, she jerked away, remarked with a calmness she did not feel,

"Lady Lucy is indeed fortunate to have such an influential and responsible person as yourself as her guardian, Your Grace. It is such a tragedy for a girl to be orphaned so young."

Lord Berkeley nodded gravely. "Her parents were fatally afflicted with the smallpox."

"Greville insisted on little Lucy having this new-fangled inoculation against smallpox. That thief of a physician sent me a bill for £42 for the inoculation," grumbled the Duke. "Damned waste of money. We'd have been far better off spending the cash on a lucky medallion of St. Hubert. He'd have warded off smallpox all right." The Duke turned to Candida. "St. Hubert, of course, is the patron saint of huntsmen, Miss Wilton."

"Indeed? I wasn't aware of that, Your Grace," murmured Candida, wondering if there were any subject under the sun which the Duke would not in some manner contrive to turn to horses and hunting. Heavens, had the man no other topic of conversation?

Lord Berkeley, certainly, appeared for the moment to have abandoned any attempt to know his brother from his imaginery saddle. "It was a good notion of yours to send Lady Lucy to accompany young Lord Rupert on his lessons. He is a year older than Lucy, and will no doubt spur her on."

The Duke grinned. "I've no fears for Lucy for by the time she's sixteen she'll be as good a horsewoman as Lady Angelica. Pity Lucy's not here to dine today, though. I do enjoy our verbal tussles. However, no doubt it'll be to her benefit to dine with the Brockways. Lady Frances may be an insipid wench but her mother will soon give Lucy a rap across the knuckles if she tries to be upperty."

Candida repressed a smile, imagining Lady Lucy in her

new beribboned blue dress, sitting at the Brockways' dining table and plotting to blow them all up with gunpowder purchased from her winnings at cards. But Candida's inner, wry smile lasted only a moment. For under the table, the Duke's hands were now becoming most insistent.

A blush stained Candida's cheeks. I must put a stop to this, she decided. If I do not make my position clear now, then this odious man will feel free to take liberties with me on our every encounter and will make my position at Stratton Hall quite miserable and untenable.

Had she been sitting at the Duke's table in her own right as Miss Candida Wellesley, Candida would have had no hesitation in delivering a sharp reprimand to the lascivious man. But in her guise as governess a degree of tact was called for. She must make her position perfectly clear—but at the same time she must not enrage her employer.

The servants were drawing the cloth now, and bringing fruit, nuts and salt biscuits to the table. Quietly, Candida arose and declared that with the Duke's permission she would retire to the adjoining drawing room, ready to pour tea when the gentlemen had finished their port.

The Duke, clearly disappointed at being thwarted of his under table sport, said thickly, "Oh, but will you not allow me to tempt you with a little fruit for dessert, Miss Wilton? Come, let me peel you a grape."

Candida saw her chance. Looking the Duke straight in the eyes she declared pleasantly, "Your phrasing reminds me, Your Grace, of the gentleman who took up residence at new lodgings, and inquired of the comely serving maid, *my dear, are you let with the house?* And she replied, *No, Sir, I'm to be let alone.*"

Swiftly Candida curtseyed and left the room, with Lord Berkeley's appreciative laughter ringing in her ears. As she closed the doors behind her, she heard Lord Berkeley remark,

"That'll teach you to keep your hands to yourself, Bart! I warned you this new governess is a cut above the others."

To Candida's relief, the Duke suddenly roared with laughter. *"I'm to be let alone!* That's capital! Wait till the fellows at boodles hear that one!"

It was an hour before the gentlemen entered the Blue Drawing Room. As Candida hastened to pour the tea for them, it was obvious to her that the Duke was now exceedingly drunk, while Lord Berkeley was excessively bored and irritated by his garrulous brother. The Duke had flung himself down on the blue velvet sofa and had begun a long, complicated story about two horses he and Lord Brockway had entered in the Derby. "Entry fee was fifty guineas, and the first prize was nine hundred. So I said to old Brockway, your nag hasn't half a chance, old chap, and Brockway turned furiously to me, and said . . . and said . . . dash it, what did the fellow say? You were there, Greville. It was that night at Brockway Hall when we spent so long over the after dinner port that Lady Brockway hustled Lady Frances off to bed, declaring that she wasn't having the girl shocked by the sight of her father senseless with drink. Ha! Do you remember, Greville? I kept refilling Brockway's glass and finally he ended up under the table giving a superb rendering of:

Comely Moll she went a-walking
But to a sailor soon was talking
And before the break of day,
Comely Moll had gone a-stray!"

"Bart!" cut in Lord Berkeley. "I would remind you that there is a lady present!"

The Duke wiped the spittle from his mouth, and muttered, "Oh, yes of course. Beg pardon, Miss Wilton."

Lord Berkeley crossed to the long window which overlooked the wide sweep of lawn. "May I inquire, Miss Wilton, if you play upon the harpsichord?"

Candida smiled. She had already observed the magnificent instrument in the corner of the Blue Drawing Room, and in truth had been itching to set her fingers upon the keys.

"I should be delighted to play for you and the Duke, if that would please you," she murmured.

"Capital!" shouted the Duke, slapping his thigh. "Nothing I like better than to listen to a pretty woman playing pretty tunes."

Candida crossed to the instrument and ran her fingers up

the keys. Lord Berkeley, behind her, was still standing at the window, gazing out into the gathering dusk. As she began to play, Candida was strongly conscious of his commanding, masculine presence. To her, he dominated the room, and it was for his pleasure alone that she sat herself to play more evocatively than ever before in her life.

After ten minutes or so, Candida was lost in the gloriously pure, golden sound of the harpsichord. She was aware of nothing but the music and her almost magical control, over each subtle phrase, each surging crescendo.

Yet when she finally lifted her hands from the keys, she was aware of a sudden emptiness of the room. She glanced around. Lord Berkeley had gone. She was alone in the Blue Drawing Room with the Duke of Stratton, who lay snoring on the sofa.

Tears of disappointment stung Candida's eyes. How cruel of Lord Berkeley to leave the room so abruptly! Had he not realized that she was playing purely for him?

Disconsolately, Candida rose from the harpsichord and forced herself to acknowledge the truth. Put yourself in Lord Berkeley's position, she ordered herself ruthlessly. He has sat at the dinner table and watched his odious brother become drunker and drunker by the minute. The conversation, being based on horses and hunting, could hardly be described as sparkling. With dinner, and the inevitable drinking session finally over, they repair to the drawing room where Lord Berkeley has the wit to urge the new governess toward the harpsichord. Now, Candida with your inebriated brother lulled by the music into a drunken slumber on the sofa, can you really blame Lord Berkeley for taking advantage of the situation, and stealing quietly away? Would you not have done the same in his situation?

Before Candida had opportunity to reflect further, the Duke awoke with a snort and a grunt.

"Where's Greville?" he demanded irritably. Then he went on, "Oh, up in those damned attics again, I suppose." He snapped his fingers at Candida, indicating that he wished her to pour him some brandy from the decanter. Seething, she did as she was bid.

The Duke swallowed the golden liquid at a gulp, and held out his glass for a refill. "Standing jest these days, Miss Wilton, Greville spending so much time up in the attic. At first I assumed he was wenching away with one of the housemaids, Mrs. Brewer, my indomitable housekeeper, insists that the lassies have their rooms up there y'know. Well away from the footmen who sleep down in the basement, Mrs. Brewer fondly believes that this arrangement keeps the housemaids pure. But I often retire well after the rest of the household, Miss Wilton, and I can tell you, the scurrying I hear on the back stairs certainly isn't caused by mice!" He bellowed with laughter, and lit a cigar, blowing the smoke into Candida's face.

"But it so happens, Miss Wilton, that all my brother is doing up there is sifting through old papers, paintings, all manner of rubbish thrown up there by my ancestors. A futile occupation for a strapping young man, wouldn't you say?"

The Duke staggered to his feet, a lustful gleam in his pale blue eyes. Candida realized that it would be timely for her to effect a speedy withdrawal.

"With your permission, Your Grace, I should like to retire now," she said quietly, but firmly. "I like to set a good example to Lady Lucy by arriving first in the schoolroom every morning."

To her horror, the Duke advanced toward her. For a dreadful moment, she imagined that his large hands were about to seize her around the waist. Then to her relief, she realized that she was standing between him and the brandy. Swiftly, she moved aside and allowed the Duke to lay his hands on the cut glass decanter.

"Must apol . . . apolo . . . sorry about falling asleep while you played," he stammered. "Quite delightful, I assure you. Brockways and Lady Angelica coming to dine tomorrow. Honored if you'd play for us after dinner, m'dear."

He swayed before her, his eyes glazed, his jowls loose. "Yes of course, Your Grace, I should be delighted." And bidding him a swift goodnight, Candida curtseyed, and made her escape.

As was the custom, they had dined at four. Candida was

hardly sleepy when she left the drawing room some four hours later. She went up to her chamber, and tried to read, but as the stableclock chimed nine, and ten, and the moon rose high in the sky, Candida finally flung down her book and acknowledged that tonight she was in a restless, unsettled frame of mind. The only solution, she knew, was to take a brisk walk, and attempt, thereby, to tire herself out.

Quietly, Candida left her chamber and slipped down the back stairs. In a few minutes, she was clear of the house, hurrying across the newly cut grass. Soon the lovely ornamental lake came into view, the water glistening silver in the moonlight, and ruffled by a light summer breeze.

Candida threw back her head, and impulsively snatched off her demure governess's cap. As she did so, a few stray locks of golden hair came loose. Joyously, Candida pulled out the pins releasing her glorious hair into a shimmering tumble on her slender shoulders.

Oh, that was better! How delicious to be free, just for a while, of all conventional restraint. Posing as a governess was certainly more exhausting than she had ever imagined. For every minute of every day, Candida was compelled to watch every word, every gesture to ensure they were in character with her role.

But it has been the most revealing experience, mused Candida, bending down to trickle her hands in the cool water. I had never realized before how difficult it is socially for any girl condemned to live her life as a governess, for she is not in society. Yet, she could not be considered totally outside it, either.

Take tonight. I was invited to dine with the Duke of Stratton. Yet it would be outside my station to have initiated any conversation. And when we were in the drawing room, he quite treated me as an ordinary servant, commanding me to fetch him brandy in that high handed manner. Again, had he been aware of me as Candida Wellesley, he would not have dared light that disgusting cigar without first requesting my permission. But because in his eyes I am a mere governess, then naturally he has no need to consider my sensibilities.

Candida sighed, and walked on. In the lake beside her

swam a large male swan, eyeing her warily as he protected his family.

What a contrast is Lord Berkeley to his brother, reflected Candida. He is at all times a perfect gentleman in his dealings with me. Oh, if only it were Lord Berkeley whom my mother had decreed I should marry, and not his oafish older brother!

This heartfelt thought brought Candida to the question she had been studiously avoiding for the past twenty-four hours. I came to Stratton Hall with the expressed purpose of inspecting my future husband, she thought. Well, now I have seen him, talked to him, observed him, and my first impression has not altered. I loathe the Duke of Stratton. Nothing and no one on this earth is going to compel me to marry him.

Why then, with this decided, do I not march straight upstairs, pack my box and leave immediately? What is the purpose of staying, and making myself more and more miserable by imagining myself bound for life to the drunken Duke? If I leave now, I could be safely half way across Europe before Uncle Montague discovers what has happened. There will be plenty of time for me to find a safe hiding place in Italy, there to stay until the Duke grows impatient and marries someone else.

But in order to leave the country, Candida would first be obliged to sell some of her jewels. For although she was an extremely wealthy young woman, most of her inheritance was, naturally, safely invested in stocks and bonds.

My jewels, thought Candida, are locked in my Uncle Montague's safe, and he, not anticipating my return, will have taken the key away with him on his grouse-shooting expedition.

Candida smiled to herself in the darkness. Come now, she admonished herself. If you were really determined to flee the country and the odious Duke, you are inventive enough to find a way. Cousin Clara in Guildford, for example, would not hesitate to lend you financial assistance.

No, the truth must be faced, Candida! You are reluctant to leave Stratton Hall because that would mean you would never again set eyes on Lord Berkeley. Admit it. You are totally in the thrall of the Duke's brother.

Yes, confessed Candida in anguish. He attracts me more than any other man I have ever met. Oh, it is not merely his rugged good looks and dashing air! There is more than that. When I am in his company I feel so joyously alive, so elated. When his gray eyes meet mine it is as if there are only we two in the whole world. No one else exists at all.

And yet, mused Candida, what can come of all this? Restlessly, she moved away from the lake, toward the long grass of the shrubbery. Remember what Mrs. Brewer, the housekeeper, told you about Lord Berkelcy having a small personal allowance, but no fortune. As the second son, it is imperative that he marry a rich heiress. Did not Lady Lucy mention that Lady Frances Brockway had her sights set on Lord Berkeley? No doubt from the point of view of both families, it would be an excellent match. The Brockways would be delighted to link their name with the illustrious Stratton line. And Lady Frances' sizable dowry would enable Lord Berkeley to free himself of his financial dependence on his brother.

Plans blazed around Candida's fertile brain, only to be rejected. Even if I revealed my true identity to Lord Berkeley, she mused, there is still the stumbling block of Uncle Montague. I need his permission to marry, and he would never agree to my wedding Lord Berkeley. He would lecture me again about poor mama and how it was her dying wish that I should marry the Duke of Stratton. In any event, on reflection, things are better left as they are. I should find it humiliating for any man to wish to marry me simply because I had inherited the vast Wellesley wealth. I wish to be loved for myself, irrespective of whether I be Candida Wellesley or Jane Wilton, governess.

Up in the trees, an owl hooted. He is mocking me, Candida decided. And rightly so. For here I am, arrogantly rejecting one suitor, and accepting a second—whereas in reality Lord Berkeley has not revealed a spark of romantic interest in me!

Oh, he has treated me with a gallant courtesy, fitting to my station in life as governess. But he has hardly swept me off my feet and declared undying love for me! Why, only this evening, he made a hurried withdrawal from the drawing room as soon as I began to play the harpsichord. How even the most besotted girl could hardly interpret that as the action of a man desperately in love with her!

Furious at herself for allowing her fanciful imagination to run away with her, Candida marched briskly through the moonlit shrubbery, slashing angrily at the laurels with a long hazel switch. Rounding a corner, there was a sudden rustle in the bushes, and a hard, masculine hand roughly seized her arm.

Candida screamed, and lashed out with the hazel.

"Calm yourself, Miss Wilton," ordered a familiar voice. "It is I, Lord Berkeley!"

Candida gasped as she gazed up at his tall, athletic figure. His gray eyes in the moonlight were blazingly angry.

"Oh, I beg your pardon," stammered Candida, uneasily aware of the sight she presented, with her long golden hair tumbling in such disorder over her shoulders. To be sure, no respectable, legitimate governess would be discovered wandering in such disarray around a shrubbery in the moonlight!

As if echoing her thoughts, he stared at her as if transfixed, and demanded, "What the deuce are you doing here at this time of night?"

At this point something in Candida snapped. Of course, she was perfectly aware that Jane Wilton, governess, would have answered Lord Berkeley with an apologetic, "I beg your pardon, I did not mean to wander so far from the house, pray forgive me!"

But tonight, thought Candida defiantly, I have abandoned Jane Wilton, along with that dull governess's cap. I have let down my hair, and just for one magic hour I am determined to be me, Candida Wellesley!

Accordingly, Candida tossed her head and replied boldly, "I am merely doing the same as you, Lord Berkeley. That is taking a quiet stroll before retiring." She laughed softly, and there was gentle mockery in her voice as she continued,

"I trust you do not belong to that breed of man who believe that the night air is harmful to the delicate female constitution!"

She held her breath then, fearful that she had overstepped the mark. But like Candida, the handsome dark-haired man seemed strangely affected by the moonlit night and the beguiling scent of honeysuckle in the air. To her relief, he seemed not at all surprised that a governess should speak in such a forthright fashion to the brother of her employer.

"Come with me," he said quietly, placing a guiding hand on her arm. "There are facts I must make plain to you, Miss Wilton."

He led her out from the shrubbery and back toward the lake, to a rustic elm seat screened from the house by a pretty bower of roses. When they were seated, Lord Berkeley said urgently,

"You must not walk alone at night, Miss Wilton. It is not safe."

"But surely here, within the house grounds—"

He cut short Candida's protest with a commanding wave of his hand. "I am at fault. I should have revealed the truth to you the instant you arrived at Stratton Hall. But I was . . . persuaded that if such intelligence was conveyed to you, you would take fright and depart back to Hampshire. And frankly, Miss Wilton, we at Stratton Hall are heartily sick of viewing the back of retreating governesses!"

Candida was burning with curiosity. Obviously, it had been the Duke who had *persuaded* Lord Berkeley to conceal certain facts from her. But what was this dreadful secret that meant no woman was safe, even when within sight of Stratton Hall itself?

Lord Berkeley's face was grave, with the moonlight highlighting the intriguing scar on his left cheek. He said grimly, "There have been several extremely unpleasant incidents in the Stratton Down area of late. It all began about six months ago when various wealthy families were robbed of priceless jewels and silver. This was bad enough; but a month ago, a dairymaid was missing from our own Home Farm. At first it was assumed that she had run away to London. Naturally, I made inquiries in the capital, but my agents could find no trace of the girl."

How typical of Lord Berkeley, thought Candida, to exhibit such concern and sense of responsibility for a lowly dairymaid. Someone like her Uncle Montague would merely have shrugged and declared they were best rid of the wench. But Lord Berkeley clearly believed in taking a personal interest in the welfare of his brother's employees and tenants.

"No sooner had I received this report from my agents in London," Lord Berkeley went on, "when another girl mysteriously disappeared, this time from Miss Bury's Academy for Young Ladies."

Candida's eyes widened. Miss Bury's Academy in the charming town of Lewes was one of the most respected girls' boarding schools in the south of England. "Was this then a titled young lady who disappeared?" asked Candida, aware that most of Miss Bury's pupils were daughters of peers of the realm.

"That's the rum thing," said Lord Berkeley slowly, absently twisting his gold signet ring around his finger. "The formidable Miss Bury is, of course, justly proud of her reputation as a teacher of the daughters of nobility. But once in a while, it pleases her to take as a pupil a girl from a good family, but reduced circumstances. One such was Verity Laine, the girl who is missing."

"I am surprised I have heard nothing of this matter," remarked Candida. "Surely Miss Bury and the girl's parents must have alerted the authorities? I am surprised that by now there is not the most noisy hue and cry."

"Verity Laine is an orphan," explained Lord Berkeley, "and as for Miss Bury, well naturally she is not anxious to draw attention to this *unfortunate incident* as she quaintly terms it."

Candida nodded. "Mmm. It would hardly be in her best interest to have anxious Dukes and Earls swooping on the academy to remove their precious daughters from danger. I imagine, then, that this is why the Duke has refused Lady Lucy permission to attend boarding school?"

"Exactly so," confirmed Lord Berkeley. "The nearest school to Stratton Down is Miss Bury's Academy. But there is of course no question of Lucy being sent there under the present circumstances. Which is a pity, as—without intending any disrespect to your own teaching—it seems to me that Lucy would greatly benefit from a school environment."

Candida leaned forward, and plucked a pink rose from the trellised bower. "Do not imagine that I underestimate the gravity of the situation," she said to the man who sat watching her in the moonlight. "But from what you have told me so far, I cannot see that there is any danger in my wandering alone within the very sight of Stratton Hall itself."

Lord Berkeley sighed, and said grimly, "It is bad enough that a dairymaid and a schoolgirl have strangely disappeared. But two days ago, Miss Wilton, an attempt was made to abduct Lady Frances Brockway when she was taking an evening stroll around her father's bowling green."

Candida gasped. "Oh, how dreadful! What exactly occurred? Is Lady Frances safe? Who was the man who made such an outrageous attack on her?" exclaimed Candida, by now thoroughly alarmed.

"Fortunately, a gardener was at hand when the attack occurred. He heard Lady Frances' scream and ran to her assistance. But he was only just in time, for the attacker was already dragging Lady Frances toward his waiting horse.

"I have not yet had the opportunity to speak to Lady Frances about the incident," replied Lord Berkeley. "Naturally, she was in an extreme state of shock, and since then her mother has insisted that she rest and speak to no one. But I gather from Lord Brockway that the villain was robed from head to foot, so unfortunately it was impossible for anyone to catch a glimpse of his face."

Candida sat in silence for a few minutes, stroking the soft petals of the rose in her hand as she digested this startling information. Then she sighed softly.

"It is so beautiful, so tranquil out here by the lake this evening. It seems impossible to believe that somewhere in the area lurks a robed raider with sinister designs on the young girls of Sussex."

"You see now why I was so concerned to find you wandering alone in the shrubbery," said Lord Berkeley quietly. "I apologize for addressing you so harshly, but the matter of these disappearances and the attack on Lady Frances has been much on my mind."

"I understand," murmured Candida, deeply touched that he should display such consideration for someone so new to the Stratton Hall household. She added thoughtfully, "I can see that the Robed Raider would have hoped to hold Lady Frances for a huge ransom from her parents. But what can have been his purpose in abducting the dairymaid and the school girl—if indeed it was the Robed Raider who was responsible for their disappearance?"

"Yes, that is exactly what is perplexing me," confessed Lord Berkeley. He crossed his well-muscled legs, and assessed the situation. "We know the Robed Raider began his career in crime by stealing jewellery and silver. Several servants at different houses reported seeing a robed man in the vicinity of their houses at the time of the crime. And as you say, his purpose in attempting to abduct Lady Frances was clear. But the dairymaid, and the school girl? It is all so worrying, Miss Wilton. The blackguard is totally unpredictable. One never knows quite where he will strike next."

Candida shivered. Instantly, Lord Berkeley leaped to his feet. "You are cold. How selfish of me to have kept you out so long. Come, I will escort you back to the house."

As he strolled back around the lake, Candida remarked, "I am deeply grateful to you for giving me the true facts. I promise you, I shall not venture out alone again at night."

"And you are not going to desert us and hurry away back to Hampshire?" he inquired.

Smiling, Candida shook her golden head. Her own future was confused and uncertain; but she knew that for the moment, nothing on earth would compel her to leave the house wherein resided the handsome Lord Berkeley.

As they paused by the garden door, Candida said, "Pray rest assured that I shall mention none of this to Lady Lucy. And when we leave the house, I shall not for one second let her out of my sight."

"I know I can rely on your discretion," said Lord Berkeley quietly. "As you know, Lady Frances is dining with us tomorrow so no doubt we shall then hear more details about this outrageous Robed Raider."

"Ah yes. I have been requested by the Duke to play the harpsichord for you all after dinner," said Candida, reaching for the handle of the garden door.

In the darkness his hand reached out and covered hers. Candida stood quite still, hardly daring to breathe, overwhelmingly conscious of his touch and the closeness of his body to hers.

He said softly, "You play the harpsichord quite exquisitely, Miss Wilton."

"I . . . I did not think I had pleased you," whispered Candida. "You left the drawing room so swiftly . . ."

His voice was suddenly harsh. "Your playing was too beautiful. It reminded me, so painfully, of many things which can never be. Goodnight, Miss Wilton."

Courteously, he opened the door for her, and stood with his eyes averted as she passed into the house. Trembling, she watched from the window as he strode away. But he did not return to the west door of the house, which led to his own apartments. Instead, he went back to the lake. And Candida knew with instinctive certainty that he was returning to the rose bower and the elm seat where they had sat together, not as governess and Lord . . . but simply as man and woman, enjoying a rare rapport as they shared the beauty of the silvered night.

Chapter Four

"Good day to you, Miss Wilton. Is it your opinion that the clement weather will hold?"

Candida, standing on the front steps of Stratton Hall, blushed as she regarded the dashing figure of Lord Berkeley striding up the drive toward her. He was dressed in old, but immaculately cut riding clothes, and Candida surmised that he had been out for a bracing early morning gallop across the Downs.

Instinctively, Candida's hand flew to her golden hair, which was neatly pinned this morning under her demure governess's cap. What a contrast to last night when Lord Berkeley had discovered her by the lake, with her hair flowing loose and free. How brazen he must have thought her! Yet this morning, there was nothing in the handsome lord's manner to remind her of the intimacy that they had shared by the moonlit lake. As they stood on the front steps discussing the weather, Lord Berkeley displayed the courteous good humor perfectly fitting for a conversation between a Duke's brother and a governess. It would be easy to believe, in truth, that the events of last evening had never taken place at all.

Candida smiled to herself. On waking this morning, the first sight to meet her eyes had been a wild pink rose, which she had plucked last night from the bower near the lake. She had put it in water, and placed it near her bed as a small memento of her unexpected encounter with a man she was beginning to suspect possessed an extremely complex character. What was that he had said about her playing the harpsichord, for example, *it reminded me, so painfully, of many things which can never be.*

Who would not be intrigued by such a remark, mused Candida. Yet, this morning, with the sun shining on his healthily glowing face, Lord Berkeley appeared to have shrugged off his melancholy mood.

He asserted cheerfully, "Now, Miss Wilton, my men are starting the corn harvest today. Do you think the weather will stay dry for them?"

"Being countrymen born and bred they are able to read the signs far better than I, I am convinced," protested Candida. She glanced up at the sky, and continued after a moment, "But I notice that the swallows are flying high today. In Hampshire we usually take that as a sign of fine weather."

"A sign of keen eyesight, too," laughed Lord Berkeley.

"I, too, am hoping the rain will hold off," said Candida. "As the house is abustle with activity for this afternoon's dinner, I thought it advisable to take Lady Lucy out on a country walk."

"Capital notion." Lord Berkeley approved. "A good dose of fresh air is just what she needs to dampen down all her natural exuberance. I seem to recall that the last time Lady Frances and her mother came to dine, we were all assailed by the most frightful aroma in the Eating Room. Naturally, the two Brockway ladies were too well bred to voice any complaint and it was only after Lady Frances swooned onto the floor that we discovered a dead, rotting fish nailed to the underside of the table."

"Oh dear," murmured Candida. "No need to inquire the name of the culprit. Well, I shall most certainly take her on a good, long walk. I make no promises, Lord Berkeley, but I shall do my utmost to ensure that by dinner time, Lady Lucy is too weary to do anything more strenuous than sit at the table and consume what is put in front of her."

Lady Lucy, of course, protested vigorously at the notion of accompanying her governess on a country walk. Patiently, Candida listened to the girl's predictable stream of assertions about the rutted paths, the thorns, the nettles, the wasps.

"I should much rather stay in the schoolroom," said the girl flatly. "I feel safer here."

"As you please," replied Candida calmly. "Indeed, it does occur to me that it would be a graceful gesture for us to offer assistance with the preparations for the Duke's dinner. Shall I tell him that we will attend to the flowers for the house?"

"Oh no, Miss Wilton!" wailed Lady Lucy. "I hate arranging flowers! They always topple out of the bowl, or else I thrust them all in so tight they look as stiff as soldiers."

"But, my dear, although you are so young, you are the lady of the house at the moment. It is only fitting that you should arrange the flowers yourself," murmured Candida. She was quite well aware that the capable Mrs. Brewer had, of course, already asked Mrs. Sewell, the head gardener's wife, to attend to the flowers.

"You don't understand how difficult it is," burst out Lady Lucy. "It isn't just a question of thrusting pretty flowers into silver bowls. You see, whenever there is a formal dinner, my Uncle Bart insists that the flowers be in yellow and green—his racing colors."

Of course. I should have guessed, thought Candida wryly. Heavens, is there any time of the day or night, any occasion or occupation when the Duke of Stratton is not obsessed with horseflesh?

Lady Lucy went on heatedly; "The green is easy, of course. But there aren't very many yellow flowers. Collecting them can take *hours!*"

Candida let this pass, aware that all the flowers for the house would have been cut this morning and brought up to the cool Stratton Hall flower room by Tom Sewell, the head gardener. Instead, Candida said gaily, "Why, Lady Lucy, how lacking in imagination you are! No yellow flowers indeed.

Have you forgotten the gallardias, the sun flowers, marigolds—why, Lady Lucy, where are you going?"

"To fetch a bonnet with a shady brim," declared Lady Lucy firmly. "I shall need it to protect my face on our country walk."

Candida smiled. My, what a wayward, contrary girl you are, Lady Lucy. And yet, despite your wilful ways, there is something quite captivating about you.

They walked out through the Home Farm, where the churns of fresh milk were being loaded onto carts ready to be conveyed up to Stratton Hall. Then, Candida led the way up to the top cornfield, where the men with scythes had been hard at work since sunrise. Much to her surprise, Lady Lucy greatly enjoyed her day. She chased the rabbits out of the corn, learned how to make a corn-dolly, held a tiny field-mouse in her trembling hand, and decorated her bonnet with brilliant red poppies.

She gazed at Candida in dismay when at two o'clock the governess said they must make their way back to Stratton Hall. "I'd much rather stay here than dress for dinner with Lady Angelica," pouted Lady Lucy. "And I'm so hungry! Do you think that fieldhand would share his apple tart with me? It looks so delicious!"

"Come along home at once!" said Candida firmly, hurrying the girl out of the field. "That young farmhand must have been up since dawn, and working all day. He'll be ravenous, and not at all pleased at the suggestion of sharing his food with you!"

On their return to Stratton Hall, Lady Lucy was hurried away by her maid to change. Candida went to her bedchamber, and completed her own toilette, slipping on a neat, green dress and matching cap. Then she sat in the window seat and waited with impatience for the carriages to arrive.

The Brockways were first. Lord Brockway, a pale, harassed-looking man, descended from the smartly painted carriage, and turned to assist his wife and daughter. These two ladies were dressed in exactly the same manner, in robes of figured silk. Lady Brockway, a tall, commanding woman, was in blue. Her daughter, Lady Frances had fussily dressed dark auburn hair, and a pink and yellow figured silk hooped dress.

Before they entered the house, Candida was amused to observe Lady Brockway issuing murmured last-minute instructions to her family. From her vantage point in the window seat it was, of course, impossible for Candida to hear what was being said. But Candida's lively imagination soon supplied the dialogue she could not hear.

"Now George, no lingering over the after-dinner port, if you please. I know the Duke is always insistent that you join him in his alcoholic excesses, but it is my opinion that as an older and mature man you should set him an example in moderation."

And to Lady Frances: "Be careful not to allow your eyes to roam too freely in the direction of Lord Berkeley, my dear. Remember it is your duty to be pleasant also to the Duke, your host."

"But he is so coarse and vulgar, Mama. And Lord Berkeley, why, he is so handsome, one cannot help but direct one's eyes in his direction."

"Then you must make a superhuman effort, Frances. I will have no daughter of mine behaving in a fast manner."

"Yes, Mama."

And with that the trio swept into Stratton Hall.

The fourth guest, Lady Angelica Kerr, did not arrive until a full twenty minutes later. As the mud splattered carriage creaked to a halt and the lady herself descended, Candida immediately sensed the reason for her delayed arrival. Clearly, Lady Angelica was anxious to make a dramatic entrance!

She was dressed in the very height of fashion, in a jaunty Polonese robe. Candida knew that even in London, only a few of the elite dared to appear in public in such an extravagant style of dress, with the over-skirt bunched up into the three exaggerated bustle shapes at the back.

Yet, in truth, Candida realized, such a style of dress flattered the tall, thin frame of Lady Angelica. Idly, as the lady rustled up the front steps, Candida wondered as to the true color of her hair. It was so elaborately dressed and powdered, that it could have been any hue, from pale gold to dark black.

Candida sat sadly in the window seat, imagining the merry gathering downstairs. How she longed to be part of it! How hateful it was to be a governess, condemned to wear dull, sombre dresses instead of the gay, frivolous styles of the ladies who were now going in to dinner. Lady Lucy would be joining them in the Eating Room, for the Duke found her abrasive company amusing.

Well, thought Candida with a sigh, I have done my best for you, Lord Berkeley. I have taken the girl into the fresh country air, and walked her off her feet. By now she should be only interested in eating as much as possible, then collapsing gratefully onto her soft goose down mattress.

The stable clock struck half-past seven before a footman tapped at Candida's door with the information that the Duke required her presence in the Green Drawing Room.

So he has chosen the formal Green Drawing Room in which to entertain his guests after dinner, thought Candida. How convenient. In my pine colored dress, I shall merge respectfully with the wall hangings.

But as she entered the drawing room, she noticed that the Duke, too, was clad in green. He wore an emerald frock coat trimmed with gold braid and large brass buttons, over an *eau de nil* waist coat in watered silk. It was a double-breasted mode, which Lady Angelica was admiring excessively.

"You have such fine taste, Bart! Not quite as exquisite as mine, true, but interesting all the same." She stood up, and twirled around in the middle of the carpet. "Now tell me true. Is this not the most amusing dress you ever set eyes on?"

"It looks to me rather in the nature of a meringue," declared Lady Brockway from her position at the copper tea urn.

Lady Angelica observed Lord Berkeley's smile, and lashed back indignantly, "Oh, you people who reside all the year in the country have no eye for what is fashionable. Why, look at Greville there. He must be the only man in England who refuses to wear a wig or at least powder his hair!"

"Angelica is right," nodded the Duke, accepting tea from Lady Brockway and lacing it with brandy from his hip flask. "It does not do to look so out of fashion, Greville. It makes people uncomfortable in your presence."

Lord Berkeley laughed and said easily, "I am my own man, Bart. I'll wear what I like, and look how I choose. I have no time for heavy, hot wigs or scratchy powder!"

Lady Angelica preened herself before the long mirror between the windows. "Oh, how ungallant, Greville. Surely you agree that my beautifully dressed hair presents quite the most alluring sight! The powder is so very fine, and the gold threads and bows twined through, so very pretty!"

"Ideally," replied Lord Berkeley, "a woman's hair should fall loose, and free. It should be untouched by powders, or adornments. That is the kind of hair a man longs to bury his face in, to breathe deep of its sweet natural perfume, and touch the silken strands one by precious one."

There was an aghast silence. Candida, still standing in the doorway, was aware that as he spoke, Lord Berkeley was gazing directly at her. Across the elegant room, his gray eyes held hers.

Do you remember our time together in the moonlight? he asked.

Yes. She smiled. *I remember!*

The Duke shambled to his feet. "Ah, Miss Wilton!" He directed a vague arm at the assembled company, and declared, "This is Lucy's new governess. She is going to entertain us on the harpsichord."

Candida crossed obediently to the instrument. She had noticed how Lady Frances had dismissed her with a glance. Lady Brockway was observing her deportment as she walked. And Lady Angelica's cold blue eyes were half-closed as if she was engaged on a private mental calculation. But about what, Candida could not fathom.

Candida ran her hands over the keys, and began to play a piece by Mr. Haydn she had recently perfected. No sooner were the melodious notes filling the air, than Lady Frances clattered down her cup and declared petulantly,

"Your Grace. I have been in your company for nigh on four hours. Yet, you have not voiced one word of inquiry into my fearful ordeal at the hands of the Robed Raider the other evening!"

"For the simple reason, my dear Lady Frances, that my ward Lucy was present with us at the dining table. Naturally, I have no wish to alarm the girl with such unpleasant tales. However, now that Lucy has retired for the night, naturally I am agog to hear the full story. You were, I believe, taking a twilight stroll around your father's bowling green?"

But Lady Frances was not to be hurried. First, there were the ruffles on her dress to be smoothed. A second cup of tea was accepted from her mother at the urn. The reason for her evening walk was explained at tedious length.

"Yes, yes," cut in the Duke impatiently, "your father left a cigar smouldering in the library, and the fumes overcame you. In need of fresh air, you ventured outside. Then what happened?"

Lady Frances glared at him, and continued in hushed, dramatic tones, "It all happened so quickly. I sensed a presence behind me. I whirled around and there he was! Robed from head to foot, his gloved hands reaching out for me!"

"Why did you not scream?" inquired Lady Angelica.

"He was too fast for me," whispered Lady Frances. "His hands closed over my mouth, and then he swept me into his arms and marched toward his horse which was tethered at the entrance to the green."

"What kind of horse was it?" asked the Duke, predictably.

"A hunter," said Lady Frances promptly. "Big, and strong, and clearly expertly trained. For when the Robed Raider flung me across the animal's back, he remained quite still and steady."

The Duke rubbed his chin, and asked keenly, "Any distinguishing marks on the horse? A blaize, perhaps?"

Lady Frances shook her beribboned head. "None that I could see. It looked completely black."

"The girl was terrified out of her wits," Lord Brockway reminded the party. "Ridiculous to expect her to remember details about the damned horse."

"It was probably dyed, in patches, anyway," said Lord Berkeley. "What happened then, Lady Frances?"

"As he threw me across the hunter, I kicked and screamed," a wide eyed Lady Frances told them. "He drew a cloth from his robe, and came to tie it around my mouth. But as we struggled," here she paused for a moment, and continued triumphantly, "I snatched the robe off his head!"

"By Jove!" declared the Duke, slapping his thigh. "That was brave work, Lady Frances."

"So you saw him!" exclaimed Lady Angelica, her hands clasped tight. "Oh, do tell us! Is he fearfully ugly?"

"I . . . I fear I did not see his countenance," admitted Lady Frances. "He twisted his head away, and at the same time pushed my head down so I was looking at the ground. All I can tell you is that he was not wearing a wig. And his hair was not of a light hue."

"Why, Greville, it was you!" laughed Lady Angelica, pointing an accusing finger at the man seated nearest to the harpsichord. "You are the only gentleman in Sussex who does not wear a wig!"

Lord Berkeley smiled. "Did the Robed Raider speak at all, Lady Frances? Were you able to deduce anything from his accent?"

Lady Frances shook her head. "It was so sinister. He did not utter one single word but I did notice brandy on his breath."

Observing the Duke's speculative glance at his port decanter, Lady Brockway cut in hastily, "At which point, fortunately, the gardener heard Frances' cry of distress and rushed to her aid."

"The Robed Raider threw me off the horse and rode off hell for leather into the night," said Lady Frances breathlessly.

"Churning up my bowling green in the process," muttered Lord Brockway indignantly.

"The question is, Bart, what is to be done about this Robed Raider?" demanded Lady Brockway, clutching the sapphires at her wrinkled throat. "Brockway here is all in favor of calling in the Lewes constabulary, but they are all such plodding, half-witted creatures."

"Obviously, it is quite appalling to have our women permanently under threat in this fashion," said Lord Berkeley, leaning forward. "It seems to me that we should mount our own investigation, set up watchguards on strategic roads—"

The Duke banged down his teacup and leaped to his feet. "Kindly leave these decisions to me, Greville! I am the one who should decide such matters. It so happens that I have decided to place myself at the head of an investigatory force." He turned to Lady Brockway, and executed a clumsy bow. "Rest assured, Madam. Before long the villain will be apprehended, and the ladies of Sussex will sleep easy in their beds once more."

"Oh, bravo, Bart!" applauded Lady Angelica. "If anyone can bring the Robed Raider to justice it is you!"

Candida repressed a smile as the Duke's chest expanded visibly under this flattery. Lady Angelica continued, with a wave of her jewelled hand,

"Well, Lady Frances, I do hope your dreadful ordeal has not sapped your strength for the annual Harvest Supper play. I have composed a thrilling drama, and would earnestly entreat you to accept the role of the heroine."

"Why, Lady Angelica," simpered the girl in figured silk. "I am most honored! But surely as the writer of the play, the role of heroine should by right be yours."

The Duke roared with laughter, "Come now, Lady Frances. I seem to recall that as children, we once allowed Lady Angelica to play the leading role. Now as you know, by tradition, we perform the play to the farmworkers and tenants immediately before the Harvest Supper. But Lady Angelica spent so long arranging her costume, her hair, and her jewels, that the play was not over till midnight, and we had a riot on our hands from the ravenous audience!"

While Lady Angelica and the Duke argued good humoredly over this episode, Lord Berkeley quietly crossed to the tea urn, and then brought a cup across to Candida at the harpsichord.

"You have earned some refreshment, Miss Wilton," he said softly. "You have sat here playing so beautifully. I am sad that tonight your melodies are falling on unappreciative ears."

Candida smiled her thanks, and sipped her tea appreciatively. The wrangle over the Harvest Supper play was still continuing.

"No, no," declared Lady Angelica firmly, "I insist that you accept the role of heroine, Lady Frances. There are not many lines to learn. In fact, she spends most of the play swooning over one thing or another."

Lady Frances colored with indignation but was clearly intimidated by the older girl, and dared not voice a retort. Lady Brockway, however, was not that easily cowed.

"Just imagine," she cooed sweetly, "next year, Angelica, you will have the bigger cast for your play. For by then Bart will be married. I am sure the new young Duchess will be delighted to accept a role."

Angelica's cold eyes narrowed and she dug her nails into the soft green velvet of the sofa. "Ah yes, Bart," she remarked acidly, "what a surprise you gave us with the announcement of your engagement! Do tell. Did you fall in love with this Miss Wellesley at first sight? Or have you harbored a secret passion for her for years? Oh, my dear! How wonderfully romantic!"

The Duke scowled. "Don't be absurd, Angelica. You know perfectly well I've been enjoying myself in Europe for the past ten years. I've never even set eyes on my fiancée."

"But have you not requested her to send a portrait?" exclaimed Lady Frances.

"No!" growled the Duke.

"But my dear Bart," trilled Lady Angelica, "she's probably pig ugly, pock-marked, and toothless. Don't you *care?*"

"Not a straw," said the Duke dismissively. "Miss Wellesley happens to be extremely rich, and that's *all* that matters."

"Ah," murmured Angelica knowingly. "Do I take it that those indulgent years in Europe have proved somewhat costly?"

"Frankly, I'm fair cleaned out," said the Duke bluntly, heaving himself to his feet and heading for the port. He poured himself a generous measure, then waved the decanter in Lord Brockway's direction. The graying Earl shot a nervous glance at his wife, and reluctantly made a gesture to decline the port.

Well satisfied with the outcome of this silent exchange, Lady Brockway adjusted her quizzing glass and remarked, "Now the story I heard, Bart, was that this marriage between yourself and Miss Wellesley was something ordained long ago. A fervent wish, in fact, of both your mothers."

"Yes, I believe they were childhood friends," replied the Duke carelessly, quaffing down his port.

"But what I don't understand," pursued Lady Brockway, "is why you have waited all these years before offering for her hand."

The Duke seemed not at all put out by Lady Brockway's bold questioning. "Because Miss Wellesley is a good ten years younger than I, and it was necessary for me to wait until she was out of the schoolroom."

"Fiddle, faddle!" exclaimed Lady Angelica with a mocking laugh. "Own the truth now, Bart. You had no interest in Miss Wellesley whatsoever until her father and brother died in a fire, and left her an extremely wealthy young woman. There is no point in denying it. You have yourself admitted that you care not a bean what she may look like, for it is only her money you are interested in."

The Duke shrugged. "My dear Angelica, if she is really as wealthy as I have been led to believe, then believe me, in my eyes she will be truly beautiful." He snapped his fingers at

Candida. "Miss Wilton! Why have you stopped playing? Pray recommence without delay."

"Yes, Your Grace," murmured Candida. It took every ounce of Candida's self-control not to crash her hands discordantly over the keys.

How dare he, she raged, her eyes a stormy blue. How dare he speak of me, Candida Wellesley, in such a dismissive manner. I suspected, of course that he was only marrying me for my inheritance. But I had not dreamed that even such an oaf as he could talk of his future bride with such callous indifference.

A movement caught Candida's eye as she played. It was Lady Frances rising from her seat to stand beside Lord Berkeley in the window arbor. During the discussion about the Duke's marriage, Candida had noticed that Lord Berkeley had taken no part. He had quietly withdrawn to the window arbor and gazed onto the night, to all intents and purposes immersed in his own thoughts. Yet to Candida's observant, and loving eye, there had been something about the set of his head and his broad shoulders which convinced her that he was, in truth, fully alert to the conversation taking place behind him.

She sensed now, as Lady Frances approached him, that he was reluctant to have his solitude disturbed. But if a flicker of annoyance crossed his gray eyes as she touched his arm, it was gone in a second, replaced by a disarming smile so dazzling that it caused Lady Frances to sway as she gazed up at him. Oh Heavens, thought Candida wryly, no doubt our delicate damsel is preparing to swoon. And how convenient, that Lord Berkeley's strong arms should be there to save her!

As Lady Frances swayed dangerously a second time, Candida took action. She switched from the gentle, lilting melody she had been playing to a jaunty, lively tune which soon had everyone's feet tapping. The Duke beat time with the port decanter, spluttering, "Deuced good, Miss Wilton! Nothing I like better than a jolly tune. Tell me, can you play *The Huntsman's Song?* That's a long time favorite of mine."

I should never have guessed, thought Candida, sliding into the pom-pom rhythm of *The Huntsman's Song.*

"Heavens, I do hope Miss Wellesley takes an interest in hunting," murmured Lady Angelica. "Else her life will be excessively tedious!"

Lord Brockway frowned. "Hardly a seemly activity for a lady, Lady Angelica, especially a Duchess!"

"It matters not a buckle to me what interests or bores her," declared the Duke. "The only time I shall set eyes on her is during the hunting season. Once I have control of her money. I shall spend most of my time in London."

"*Spend* being the key word," murmured Lady Angelica with a flick of her long eyelashes.

Lady Brockway sat ramrod-straight in her chair, and said severely, "Now, Bart. That is not at all a dutiful attitude. Your place is here, at your family seat, by your wife's side."

The Duke spluttered, "Why so? Apart from her great wealth, I have no interest whatsoever in the future Duchess of Stratton. It is unfortunate that my family seat is sited so deep in the Sussex countryside. On this matter I agree entirely with Mr. Horace Walpole." The Duke stood up, and declaimed, thickly, "*I see no difference between a country gentleman and a sirloin. Whenever the first laughs or the latter is cut, there run out just the same streams of gravy!*"

"Stap me, Stratton!" protested Lord Brockway, rising indignantly to his feet.

The Duke pushed him back into his velvet covered chair. "Present company excepted, Brockway! No cause to take offense."

Irritated at being thus treated, Lord Brockway inquired, "You affect to despise the countryman, Stratton. But who, may I ask, will supervise your estates while you fritter away your wife's fortune in London?"

The Duke raised a mocking eyebrow. "Why, all those tedious details will be attended to by my dear young brother . . . under my direction, of course."

Lord Berkeley stood with one hand resting on the

harpsichord. It was as if his handsome face was carved of stone. Not by the slightest flicker of a muscle did he reveal what fury he must be feeling at his older brother's provocative remark.

Candida burned in sympathy for him. For ten years Lord Berkeley had managed the vast Stratton estates. From her talks today up in the cornfield with the farmhands, she knew that Lord Berkeley was one of the most respected employers in all Sussex. Each of the workers had recounted a different, and always flattering tale about him.

When storm clouds gathered and the harvest was in danger, Lord Berkeley had stripped off his shirt and joined the men, scything corn as if his life depended upon it, to get it to the threshing barn before the rain fell.

During that bad snowfall in the lambing season, Lord Berkeley had personally combed the Downs, listening for the tell-tale bleat of a ewe marooned with her new born young.

And when one of the herdsmen had put a dairymaid with child, and refused either to acknowledge the babe or marry the maid, Lord Berkeley had taken a horsewhip to the rogue, lashing his back to a pulp before evicting him from Stratton village.

"But did he not force the man to marry the dairymaid?" Candida had questioned.

The farmhand bit on an ear of corn, and chewed it thoughtfully. "No, he did not, Miss Wilton. Lord Berkeley told the dairymaid that a man who married under dur—dur—"

"Duress?" Candida smiled.

"Ah. That were the word. Well, he would never make her a kind, considerate husband. She should marry a man who loved her, Lord Berkeley said. And until she found such a man his lordship promised to provide for herself and her child."

Remembering all this, Candida longed to stretch out an arm and cover his hand with hers, in a quiet gesture of sympathy. But even as the thought occurred to her, Candida rejected it. Lord Berkeley was one of the proudest men she had ever encountered. He would not tolerate sympathy from anyone.

The Duke, meanwhile, was fully launched on his favorite topic. "Tell me, Angelica, have you corresponded with your Cousin Hugh of late? I'm deuced anxious for him to join our first hunt of the season."

Lady Brockway raised her eyebrows. "Why I had no notion you possessed any cousins on the male line?"

Lady Angelica patted her high, powdered hair and remarked in a bored tone, "Oh, Hugh! He rides over from Guildford to hunt with the East Sussex. But he's so tedious to entertain, because he has absolutely no conversation at all! Heavens, Bart here is arid enough, but at least he's interested in all aspects of horseflesh. Poor Hugh can never summon enough energy to make any remark whatsoever!"

The Duke laughed uproariously. "Blister me! I do relish your acid tongue, Angelica! But you must admit, Sir Hugh Legatt is the most admirable horseman! Hunts like a demon, never flags, never shirks a fence, always in for the kill. Just the kind of man I admire."

And of course, thought Candida, her hands floating demurely over the keys, you appreciate Sir Hugh's silence because it enables you to fill the void with vacuous conversation of your own. Oh, how I despise you, Duke of Stratton!

Lady Angelica said vaguely, "Well, if I can summon the energy, I will write to Hugh and extend your invitation, Bart," she sighed. "Oh, how I should love to ride to hounds."

"Absurd!" declared Lord Brockway. "Quite unseemly."

"It was not considered improper of Queen Anne to follow the hunt in her chaise," retorted Lady Angelica.

"I have a notion that Queen Anne and I would have been utterly in accord," mused the Duke, paying no need to Lady Brockway's affronted coughing as he lit up a cigar. "We would have agreed, Her Royal Highness and I, that the only good thing about the countryside is its horses."

Candida repressed a sigh. Goodness, she was beginning to suspect that the Duke had been born in a loose box.

But Lady Angelica, at least, did not appear fatigued by the Duke's choice of conversational fodder.

"Do you remember that marvellous hunt last September, Bart," she asked enthusiastically, "when we tore across a corner of the old maze?"

"Deuced fox got us tangled up in the undergrowth, and we lost him," recalled the Duke with a laugh. "Really, something will have to be done about that old maze."

"I had not heard of such a thing," said Lady Frances, looking inquiringly at Lord Berkeley. "A maze! How romantic!" Her eyes, as she gazed on the dashing lord, were as large and as soft as pansies.

"We were fond of playing there when we were children," said Lord Berkeley with a smile. "It is situated on a far corner of the estate and was grown, I believe, under the orders of the first Duke of Stratton. But now, of course, it is wildly overgrown which is a pity. I have half a mind to send the men up there tomorrow and set them to cutting the hedges and clearing the paths again."

The Duke of Stratton leaped up, his face scarlet. "You've half a mind indeed! I would remind you, Greville, that it is *I* who am Duke. *I* who have control. *I* who make the decisions! If you wish to make any changes on the Stratton estates, you will come to me *first* and ask *my* permission! Is that clear?"

Lord Berkeley's face was ashen. Candida's hands trembled on the keys as she ruminated on the inward turmoil he must be experiencing as a result of this public humiliation. Oh, how low, how crass of the Duke to make such a remark! But even now, though his eyes blazed with fury, Lord Berkeley retained his dignity. With matchless control, he arose from his chair and gravely bade the assembled party goodnight. Then without a word, or a bow to his drunken brother, Lord Berkeley strode from the room.

It was Lady Angelica who broke the embarrassed silence. "Tut, tut, Bart dear," she said lightly, tapping him on the arm with her mother of pearl fan. "You put your ermined hoof right in it that time, did you not?"

The Duke scowled. "Hold your tongue, Angelica! It's about time Greville learned his place. Trouble is, while I've been away, he's been accustomed to acting Lord of the Manor in these parts. But now that I'm back at Stratton Hall, Greville must learn to take second place!"

"But Bart, you have already admitted that you loathe country life," protested Lady Brockway. "Why not be content to leave the running of the estate to your brother, who clearly enjoys it. And he is highly respected by all the county, you know."

"He must learn to accept that I am his superior!" said the Duke stubbornly, reaching again for the port. "I am the firstborn, therefore, he must bow to me in all matters. That is the natural way of things."

Lady Angelica yawned behind her fan. "Ah, me! I must be away home, Bart. It has been a delightful evening, but you must excuse me if I leave now. I have a vital fitting for my new ball dresses tomorrow. If I am tired I shall droop, and then the stupid modiste will get the line of the dresses all askew."

No sooner was Lady Angelica's carriage heard rumbling off down the drive, when Lady Brockway turned to the Duke and remarked,

"Strange, Bart. I had always assumed that you and Angelica would make a match. She appears to be the only woman, apart from little Lucy, who is outrageous enough to make you laugh."

The Duke shrugged. "Of course I am fond of Angelica. She is a spirited girl, and I adore her extravagant dress. However absurd the latest fashion, one can rest assured that it will be adorning Angelica! But," he sighed, "I fear that Angelica is not wealthy enough to make me a bride. Her father had all those gambling debts, y'now, and left her in very dire straits."

Lady Brockway added in hushed tones, "One hears that Lady Kerr will scarcely leave the house for shame. Now *I* think it is appalling that she permits Angelica to go out to dine without a chaperone—"

"Oh Mama, Angelica is safe enough at Stratton Hall," interrupted Lady Frances impatiently. Her little face was pinched with pique as she went on, "What I do not understand, is that if Lady Angelica is alleged to be so poor, how is she able to afford all these new fashions, and to be fitted with new ball dresses tomorrow?" She turned to her father and waited. "Papa!?"

"Of course you shall have new ball dresses," he said soothingly. "As many as please you. But on one matter I am adamant. You are not to imitate Lady Angelica to such an extent that, like her, you are obliged to sit on the floor of the carriage in order to accommodate your high head-dress. That, Frances, would be plain absurd!"

Lady Frances giggled, and ran across to whisper in his ear. Candida, still seated at the harpsichord, felt sickened by this overt display of girlish innocence. Poor Lord Berkeley, she thought. If Lady Frances has her way and succeeds in becoming your bride, what will your life be like with her? Will you enjoy stimulating conversation, shared laughter, a lively exchange of views? I fear not. You will be obliged to suffer one long round of Lady Frances becoming petulant about another lady's fine carriage, new clothes, London house, sweet blackamoor. She will pout, and sulk, and swoon until at last you consent to her current whims, and then she will run to you and whisper in your ear that you are the most divine, most understanding, most generous husband in all the world . . . and she loves you dearly . . . until the next day, and the next whim.

To Candida's relief, the Brockways now made their departure. The Duke lurched out into the hall to bid them farewell, and Candida took advantage of his absence to slip from the Green Drawing Room and escape to her bedchamber.

With relief, she plunged her aching hands and wrists into a basin of cold water on the marble topped washstand. She felt as if she had been playing the harpsichord for three days, instead of three hours.

When she had dried her hands, Candida pulled back the curtains and sat for a while on the window seat, gazing out on the peaceful gardens, and lake. After an evening filled with other people's voices, it was pleasant to savor the tranquil serenity of the scene outside.

Candida was just musing that the only sounds she could hear were those natural to the countryside at night—the hoot of an owl, the bark of a fox, the wind sighing in the trees—when her sharp ears were alerted to another noise. It was the soft clip-clop of a horse, passing somewhere near her window.

And then she saw him. Not too clearly, for there was no moon tonight. But the man leading the hunter around the lakeside path was unmistakably Lord Berkcley. His stride was brisk. His shoulders purposefully set. Candida surmised that Lord Berkeley was using the lakeside path as a shortcut to the sweeping Downlands beyond. If he intends enjoying a night gallop across the Downs, he will need all his wits about him, Candida thought, for with no moon it is dark tonight. But then, Lord Berkeley grew up in this countryside. He must be totally familiar with every hollow, dew pond, and blade of grass on those Downs.

Candida's heart went out to the handsome, dark-haired lord. Instinctively, she understood why he sought the freedom of the Downs. His position here at Stratton Hall is untenable, Candida realized. How shamefully the Duke treats his brother! It did not escape my notice that he offered port to Lord Brockway, his guest, but none to Lord Berkeley, his own kin! And how one was put to the blush, listening to the Duke's pig-headed orders to Lord Berkeley over the management of the estate. *It is I who am Duke. I who have control. If you wish to make any changes you will come to me first and ask my permission!*

This from a man who boasted openly that his interest in the country, and his estate, was limited to horesflesh! The Duke seizes on every available opportunity publicly to make Lord Berkeley feel inferior, the second son, the underling, thought Candida, her eyes blazing. Just as he snaps his fingers at me, the lowly governess, and silently orders me to play on the harpsichord, so he verbally snaps orders at Lord Berkeley.

Candida smiled as she considered the irony of the situation. How little you realize, my lord Duke, that things are not as they seem. By your every gross action, you are damning yourself. Each time you leer at me, or treat me with contempt you reinforce my determination never to marry you.

And the principle is exactly the same with Lord Berkeley. You imagine that because he is the second son, your power over him is absolute. But you would do well to look deep into your brother's gray eyes. For there burns within them the fierce light of independence. Lord Berkeley is a proud and a determined man. A man you cross at your peril, Duke of Stratton!

Chapter Five

"Oh, Miss Wilton, may we go up to the cornfields again today?" asked Lady Lucy as she burst into the schoolroom. "It is such a lovely sunny day, and I did so enjoy our excursion up there!"

Candida smiled, and thought for a moment, considering it not a wise notion to pay another visit to the cornfield. While the farmhands had been extremely patient yesterday with the exuberant Lady Lucy, Candida appreciated that harvesting the corn was an extremely serious business. It was work which must be completed with the utmost speed, unhindered by the antics of a twelve-year-old girl.

"I thought we'd do something different today," Candida said encouragingly. "How would you like to ride out over the Downs, and then take a walk along the beach?"

The pert young face looked troubled. "I do not know . . . I have never been on the seashore . . ."

Candida raised a surprised eyebrow. "But I recall your telling me that you paid a visit to Weymouth with your dear mama."

Lady Lucy twisted up the red skirt of her smock. "Yes . . . but Mama would not allow me to venture near the sea. She was afraid a big wave would come and wash me away. She loved me dearly, you see," said the girl defiantly, "and she would have been heartbroken if any tragedy had befallen me!"

Fimble-framble! thought Candida, turning away from Lady Lucy to conceal the anger in her eyes. The truth is that your dear mama could not summon the energy to take you for a stroll beside the sea. No doubt she was far too busy receiving her devoted male admirers to be bothered entertaining her own daughter. Poor little Lucy. How humiliating it must have been vying with a brace of beaux for your own mother's affection.

"I give you my word that no big wave will wash you away today," Candida promised. "See how still it is outside—there is hardly a breath of wind. That means the sea will be beautifully calm. Now you run down to the stables and arrange for our horses to be saddled, and I will advise Mrs. Brewer of our destination."

With the Robed Raider in mind, Candida sensibly made a point of never taking Lady Lucy from the house without leaving word with the housekeeper of their intended whereabouts.

Candida and Lady Lucy enjoyed an uneventful ride up over the Downs, and before long were in sight of the sea. Although the wind had freshened along the coast and the waves were tipped with white, Lady Lucy forgot her fears in her excitement at all the new sights and sounds around her.

"Oh, look at the sailing boats scudding across the sea!" she cried. "Do you imagine they are going all the way to France? Uncle Bart and Uncle Greville have been to Paris, you know. That's where Uncle Greville got that scar on his cheek. Heavens, Miss Wilton, what noisy birds! What are they?"

"Seagulls," replied Candida, intrigued by the girl's careless reference to Lord Berkeley's scar. Naturally enough, Candida was burning to know the rest of the story. But it would have been most improper for her to quiz her twelve-year-old charge on the matter.

Candida had begged some bread from Cook. She stood on the grassy clifftop and threw pieces into the air. Lady Lucy clapped her hands in delight as the shrieking seagulls wheeled down, adroitly catching the bread in their large beaks.

"See, they are settling on the chimney pots of the coastguards's cottages down there," Candida pointed.

Lady Lucy laughed. "What silly birds they are. There are four chimney pots, yet all the seagulls are squabbling over the right to sit on the end one." She tugged at Candida's arm. "There are some steps here. May we go down onto the shore?"

It was a happy morning. Although the sun gradually clouded over, Lady Lucy was happy as a lark. She hoisted up her skirts and scrambled through rock pools, chasing crabs and trying, vainly, to catch the tiny darting fish. The tide was going out, leaving the flinty rocks grassed by glistening green seaweed. Candida seated herself on a dry, bleached-white rock and watched a group of children further up the beach, busy with their shrimping nets.

She was so absorbed, that it came as a shock when she stood up and realized that she felt quite chilled. The sun had disappeared, and the sailing ships were hidden behind a thick haze.

Candida looked around for Lady Lucy, and saw her up near the cliff, using a sharp piece of flint to carve her initials in the chalk face. "Come back to the steps now, Lady Lucy," she called. "We must make our way home."

The girl pouted. "I won't come yet. I like it here!"

Candida began to move toward her, but her progress was impeded by the line of rock pools. Defiantly, Lady Lucy ran toward the sea and shouted,

"Promise we can stay for another half-hour. If you don't, I'll fall in the sea and get all wet and then Uncle Bart will scold you for not taking proper charge of me!"

Candida was furious. What a little monster you are, she thought, scrambling across the rocks toward the girl. But if I give in to your blackmail now, I shall never regain my authority over you.

The red-haired girl waited until her governess was within

ten feet of her. Then, grinning broadly, she ran up the beach and veered off toward the cliff.

"Lady Lucy! Come here this instant!" shouted Candida. "Can't you see the weather has taken a turn for the worse? You foolish girl! Look at the mist rolling in from the sea—"

But Lady Lucy was in the wrong direction to hear Candida's plea. The wind snatched her words away, while the red-haired girl jumped on a rock and declaimed:

"I'm a witch!
And I never stitch
And I never bake nor sew
But I have the way, Heigh Ho! Ho-Heigh!
To learn what I want to know!"

Gasping for breath, Candida ran toward her. But the lethal mist moved faster. Thick, gray, and damp, it mantled the coastline, blotting out landmarks, rock pools—and little Lady Lucy.

For a moment, Candida stood stock still, frozen with horror. Then she stumbled on up the beach, frantically calling Lucy's name. The swirling mist was so thick that she almost ran straight into the looming chalk cliff face. Grateful for its reassuring solidity, she inched her way along beside it, keeping one hand on the face for guidance. Every moment she expected to see the bright red of Lady Lucy's smock signalling through the mist. But after ten minutes walking and searching, Candida was forced to admit defeat.

She stood with her back to the cliff, her heart pounding with fear. She remembered that not far away, in the next bay, lay a wrecked ship. Candida closed her eyes in panic, imagining Lady Lucy falling headlong over the broken mast, lying trapped and helpless amid jagged, splintered wood.

"How *am* I to explain this to the Duke and Lord Berkeley?" whispered Candida in anguish. "They will accuse me of gross negligence. And they will be right! I was warned that Lady Lucy was a wilful child. It was my responsibility to ensure that she was kept on a tight rein. And I failed!"

Almost faint with despair, she rested for a moment on a smooth, bleached rock. Afterward, she was to bless that sudden impulse which led her to sit down. For if she had continued blundering through the mist, she would surely have missed the sight of the small red handkerchief lying on the edge of a rock pool.

With beating heart Candida snatched up the handkerchief and examined it. There was no doubt that it belonged to Lady Lucy: it was exactly the same color and material as her smock. But where could Lady Lucy have disappeared to?

Carefully, Candida moved in a direct line back from the rock pool toward the cliff. She was searching for a hidden cave, or perhaps a deserted fisherman's hut. With her mischievous sense of fun, Lady Lucy would no doubt consider it great sport to make her governess play hide-and-seek for an hour or two.

But at the cliff, Candida found no cave. Instead, there was a crumbling flight of steps, leading up, up into the mist. Candida felt chilled, frightened and thoroughly alone. It is akin to a situation in a fairy tale, she thought, where the heroine stumbles across a mysterious flight of steps which appear to lead straight up into the sky. Who, or what, will be at the top? A dragon? A pot of gold? Or Prince Charming himself?

With a wry smile, Candida began to climb. The steps, which had been roughly hewn out of the chalk, were worn with age and extremely dangerous and made Candida's progress very slow. She tore her nails, ruined her stockings, and roundly cursed little Lady Lucy every inch of the way. At last, with a sigh of relief, she flung herself down on the damp, springy grass at the top of the cliff.

"Co . . . ld!"

Candida started to her feet at the sound. What was it? A shrieking seagull? Or a person—a child? And from which direction had it come?

"Oh, a pox on this wretched mist," muttered Candida angrily. "It distorts sound to such an extent that it is almost impossible to tell from whence a noise is coming."

She stood quite still, straining every nerve, waiting for the sound again.

"I'm *cold!*"

This time there was no mistaking the complaining tone of a twelve-year-old girl. Blindly, Candida ran forward into the mist, following the sound as best she could. But who, she wondered, was Lady Lucy talking to?

And then, quite suddenly, she ran straight into them. Lady Lucy and Lady Angelica.

"Ah, there you are at last!" snapped Lady Angelica. "A fine thing! Allowing your charge to run off in such a manner! If I had not happened to be taking a stroll along the clifftop—well, I dread to think what might have befallen Lucy!"

Candida was so relieved to see Lady Lucy safe, it did not cross her mind to wonder what Lady Angelica was doing wandering alone across a misty clifftop.

"Lady Lucy, how dare you disobey me when I tell you it is time to go home," Candida scolded the girl. "I've been so worried about you! For all I knew, you could have been snatched away by the—by anyone!" she finished hastily, remembering just in time that the name of the Robed Raider was not to be mentioned in front of Lady Lucy.

Lady Lucy shivered. "I didn't realize this horrid mist was going to come. I'm so cold, Miss Wilton!"

"Heavens, if you say that again I shall scream," muttered Lady Angelica, delicately brushing down her elegant emerald green riding habit.

At that moment, the mist lifted a little, and Candida exclaimed, "Oh, I am sure I noticed the lights of a cottage not far away. Let us go there, and take shelter until the mist clears."

"Oh yes," agreed Lady Lucy, drawing close to Candida. "Perhaps they will have some hot chocolate for me to drink."

Candida doubted it. The cottage was probably inhabited by a poor fisherman who would not be able to afford costly beverages like chocolate. However, there was no point in voicing such thoughts just at the moment. The essential thing was to find the girl some shelter.

Candida put her arm around Lady Lucy's shoulder with the intention of hurrying her to the cottage. But a furious Lady Angelica barred the way.

"Don't be absurd!" she shouted. "I am the Lady Angelica Kerr. I will not have it known all through Sussex that I went begging for shelter at a common fisherman's cottage!"

Lady Lucy's teeth were beginning to chatter. "The child is cold and tired," said Candida firmly. "She needs warmth, and shelter. I am taking her to the cottage. If you do not choose to accompany us, Lady Angelica, that is your affair."

But Lady Angelica stood her ground. "Far better to get the girl home straightaway," she declared. "Sometimes these mists don't lift for days. Even if you do take shelter at the cottage, it may be a long time before the mist clears enough for you to return home."

"Lady Angelica," said Candida impatiently, "how can I possibly take Lady Lucy home when the mist is so thick that I cannot see a yard in front of my face?"

"I will guide you," said Lady Angelica confidently. "I grew up on these Downs, you know. I am familiar with every inch of land. Now, can you remember where you left your horses?"

"They are tethered near the main cliff steps," replied Candida.

Lady Angelica nodded. "Then the quickest way will be to walk along the cliff's edge."

Observing Lady Lucy's eyes widen with fear, Candida said quickly, "But in this mist, Lady Angelica . . . would not a cliff-top route be extremely dangerous?"

"To the uninitiated, yes," agreed Lady Angelica, retying the ribbons of her pretty plumed bonnet. "But I assure you, I know every inch of the way. And you will note, as we walk, that the cliff's edge is marked by large white stones. Even in this mist they are clearly visible. Come. Follow me!"

Such was the authority in her tone that Candida and

Lady Lucy followed her without question. Lady Angelica set a brisk pace, and after a few minutes Lady Lucy's teeth stopped chattering and she began to feel warmer once more.

Candida was much taken with Lady Angelica's bold attitude. What a strange person she is, mused Candida, her eyes firmly fixed on the figure in emerald green striding on before her. On the one hand, she would not dream of being seen in public unless she were dressed in the most extreme version of the current fashion. Why even today, for a simple ride across the Downs, she has chosen to wear a riding hat more suited to the rarefied environs of Hyde Park. And yet, on the other hand, Lady Angelica seems totally fearless. Last night she was positively scornful when the Duke suggested that one of his footmen should accompany her home.

"If the Robed Raider dares to lay a finger on me, I'll give him a black eye and twist his nose off!" she declared. "It's about time that rogue learned that not all the women of Sussex are pathetic, milksop creatures!"

Lady Frances had taken this remark personally (as of course it was intended to be) and sulked for the remainder of the evening.

On the clifftop, Lady Lucy uttered a scream of delight as the faithful horses suddenly came into view. Lady Angelica's chestnut was also tethered nearby, and before long the trio were passing through the village of Stratton Down, and the house itself was looming reassuringly out of the mist.

At the gates, Lady Angelica paused and said to Candida, "In view of your negligence with Lady Lucy today, Miss Wilton, it would be best if you mentioned this incident to no one. You may rest assured, that no word of it will pass my lips."

Candida smiled, but said nothing. As she bade farewell to Lady Angelica, Candida reflected that it would be impossible for Lady Lucy to hold her tongue about her adventure. Before long, thought Candida ruefully, the tale will be all around Stratton Hall. And I, no doubt, will be called into the library for an extremely unpleasant interview with the Duke!

But days passed, and the dreaded summons to the library did not come. Lady Lucy, meanwhile, was confined to bed with a severe chill. Candida attended her each morning, with books and games and any diversions she could muster. But by early afternoon, Lady Lucy's eyes were unusually bright, and her cheeks flushed, whereupon Candida would slip away, and leave the girl to sleep.

Candida took advantage of her unexpected leisure time to ride out and explore the two thousand acre Stratton estate. As she rode around the fields of waving hay, beside tree-shaded rivers, and surveyed the farms, cottages, and rolling hills that stretched as far as the eye could see, a wry smile touched Candida's lips.

"I could be mistress of all this," she whispered. "As Duchess of Stratton, I would be the first lady of Sussex."

Her eyes misted as she dreamed of the perfect life she could live here. For she knew she had fallen deeply in love with the countryside of Stratton Down. She thought of her sons, fine, strapping boys, enjoying a morning's fishing on the river, returning home in triumph with a brace of tench. There at the door to greet them was Candida's daughter, with the same golden hair as her mother, her young face flushed with excitement as she told of her exploits on her new pony.

And there, striding out of the library, was the children's father, Candida's husband. His dark hair gleamed in the sun, and his gray eyes . . . .

Here Candida's dream shattered into a thousand fragments. Firmly, she gathered up the reins and set off at a furious gallop across the Downs.

You must not continue to think thus about Lord Berkeley, she scolded herself. Face facts, Candida! If you wish to become mistress of Stratton Hall, you will be obliged to marry the Duke—your betrothed.

No! gasped Candida, spurring on the horse. A thousand times no. I would die rather than spend my life with that oaf. *I shall never marry him!* Oh, if only I had the courage to turn my back on Stratton Hall and Lord Berkeley! The sensible thing would be to pack my box, and quietly run away to a secret address in Europe. For surely, the longer I delay, the more difficult it will be for me to slip the net and avoid marrying the Duke.

But I cannot leave yet, Candida admitted. I love it so much here it would break my heart to leave a moment sooner than was necessary. I will stay another few weeks, she compromised, until the hot weather breaks. In September, there will be a cooler, crisper tang to the air and then I shall feel more inclined to take some positive action. At the moment, with the sun shining, and all the Downs drowsed with heat, I cannot make decisions of a positive and irrevocable nature.

One afternoon, Candida was surprised to find Lord Berkeley himself deep in discussion with the head groom in the hunters' stables. He was carefully examining each animal, and rubbing over its glossy coat with a cambric handkerchief. The head groom watched anxiously, aware that if Lord Berkeley found his handkerchief to be soiled, it would indicate that the horses had not been groomed properly.

However, Lord Berkeley seemed well satisfied, and remarked, "Mmmm, I see you've put the Duke's Black Knight in a separate stall. Is he unwell?"

The head groom nodded. "The Duke had him out in that heavy mist of a few days ago, m'lord. Seems he stopped at a tavern for refreshment, and forgot to put a saddle cloth on Black Knight. Now he's taken a chill."

"The best remedy I know for that is a drink of liquorice, horehound, aniseed and despente," said Lord Berkeley, "boiled in a quart of ale, with honey added."

"Mmm. Sounds very tasty, m'lord." The head groom grinned. "I'll have one of the boys make it up at once."

"Good. I want you to let me know immediately if Black Knight takes a turn for the worse," ordered Lord Berkeley quietly. He glanced around and noticed Candida leading out her dappled gray. "Taking advantage of this glorious afternoon? Hold still, a moment, Miss Wilton, I'll accompany you on your ride—if you have no objection?"

Objection! As always when she was in the presence of Lord Berkeley, Candida's blood felt turned to liquid fire.

As they rode out together through the pretty village of Stratton Down, Candida inquired, "May I ask if any further information has been received about the Robed Raider?"

Lord Berkeley frowned. "I regret not, Miss Wilton. As you know, my brother has placed himself at the head of the investigation. But there are many people to be questioned as discreetly as possible of course, for we do not wish to spread undue alarm among the people. I'm afraid it is going to be a long business . . ."

Tactfully, Candida did not pursue the subject. Obviously, it would not be proper for Lord Berkeley to utter a word of criticism against his brother, the Duke. He could not express his concern that instead of mounting a thorough investigation into the movements of the Robed Raider, the Duke of Stratton was idling his time away in taverns—and neglecting in the process to ensure that his hunter, Black Knight, was properly protected against the chilling Sussex mist.

With his uncanny ability to follow her train of thought, Lord Berkeley remarked, "No doubt you find it strange how the weather in these parts can change so suddenly. It must have been most alarming for you when Lady Lucy disappeared the other day."

He saw the governess's blue eyes cloud with dismay, and went on quickly: "Lady Lucy told me the full story. Do not distress yourself over the incident, Miss Wilton. You were certainly not to blame for her prank. I recall once, when she was in my charge, the little minx disappeared for an entire afternoon. I searched high and low, and eventually ran her to earth in a windmill."

Candida laughed. "She is an incorrigible girl. But I am loath to scold her too severely for her misadventures. I am ever mindful of what you told me about her upbringing and the shameful manner in which her parents neglected her."

They stopped at the road's fork to allow a shepherd to

guide across his flock of sheep. Raising his hand in a friendly greeting to the weatherbeaten shepherd, Lord Berkeley remarked to Candida, "I must confess, I greatly admire the manner in which you handle our rebellious young filly. Lucy appears quite fascinated by her new governess. Tell me, Miss Wilton, what is your secret?"

Candida smiled, sorely tempted for a moment to tell him the truth. For the fact was, that as a child, Candida, too, had been wilful and unmanageable. Lacking the benefit of a mother's gentle guidance, Candida had run wild and had been the despair of a positive fleet of governesses. Then at last, a desperate Lord Wellesley had hired a certain Miss Bone.

Candida had never forgotten her first encounter with Miss Bone. The wilful eleven-year-old Candida had entered the schoolroom in the same style as Lady Lucy, determined to create havoc and break the new governess on her first day. Concealed in her hand was a heap of pepper which she intended to spread in liberal fashion across the governess's desk.

But Miss Bone was already present in the schoolroom. She was not seated timidly at her desk, but instead sat boldly astride the old rocking horse in the corner. And she was giving forth with a loud and lusty version of *Greensleeves*. The young Candida was so surprised, she rubbed her blue eyes in amazement. But she had forgotten the pepper in her hand!

The new governess continued with her song, ignoring Candida's frantic fit of sneezing. At last, when the girl had dried her streaming eyes, Miss Bone changed her song, and began to chant:

Sneeze on Monday, you sneeze for danger,
Sneeze on Tuesday, kiss a stranger,
Sneeze on Wednesday, sneeze for a letter,
Sneeze on Thursday, something better,
Sneeze on Friday, sneeze for sorrow,
Sneeze on Saturday, see your sweetheart tomorrow!

Candida's childish blue eyes widened. "But today is Monday!"

"Sneeze for danger!" shouted Miss Bone excitedly. "The schoolroom is under attack. Quick! We must gallop to safety!" and she whirled Candida up onto the rocking horse and rocked her until they were both quite breathless with laughter.

After that hilarious introduction, Candida had come to adore Miss Bone. So much so, that she had quite dreaded her sixteenth birthday, and the end of her fascinating days in the schoolroom.

But it was, of course, the eccentric Miss Bone whom Candida used as a model in her dealings with Lady Lucy. Right from the start, Candida had determined to disarm the child by continually surprising her, and presenting her with the unexpected.

Yet, Candida could reveal none of this to Lord Berkeley. It would be fatal for him to inquire too deeply into the past and background of the demure Miss Wilton. So in reply to his question about her success with Lady Lucy, Candida merely smiled and remarked,

"One of the most satisfactory things about life, I find, is that occasionally one strikes up a rare rapport with a person with whom at first sight it would appear that one had little in common at all."

He turned to look at her, and for a long moment his gray eyes held hers. "Yes," he murmured. "I understand exactly what you mean, Miss Wilton."

Oh, thought Candida with a longing, how I wish this day could go on forever! Up here, on the topmost ridge of the Downs, it is as if Lord Berkeley and I are the only two people in the world. How easy it is now, to forget about the menace of the Robed Raider and the decisions that I will have to make if I am to avoid marriage with a man I detest.

Lord Berkeley sat with his face turned to the sun, the wind ruffling his thick black hair. Slowly, he turned and surveyed the Stratton estate, his gray eyes proud, yet tinged with sadness.

"My God, I love this land," he murmured. "I have

travelled widely across Europe, Miss Wilton. Yet this place has captured my heart. This is where I belong."

How well Candida understood the conflict raging within him. For the past ten years he had managed the Stratton estates in his brother's absence. He had been lord of all he surveyed. His word had been law, and he had proved himself. The farms were flourishing; the land was lush; the tenants were content. Yet now, with the Duke once more in residence, Lord Berkeley was obliged to take second place. Oh to be sure, the indolent Duke was only too happy to leave all the hard work to his brother. But at the same time he was insisting that Lord Berkeley should consult with him over decisions concerning the estate. Which would be perfectly fair, mused Candida, if the Duke were an equal authority on estate management. But he cannot rouse himself to take the slightest interest in the land, or the welfare of the tenants. He obliges Lord Berkeley to consult him, and then vital decisions are made out of pique, or in a drunken stupor.

And these are critical issues which affect the livelihood of hundreds of tenants and their families.

Desperately, Candida sought a topic which would divert Lord Berkeley from his painful thoughts. Her eye alighted on the thatched rooftops of Stratton Down village, dotted beneath them.

"How well kept the village is," she remarked. "I'm sorry to say that in Hampshire, many landowners allow their villages to fall into dreadful states of disrepair."

Lord Berkeley sighed. "You have touched on a very sore point, Miss Wilton. My brother has it in mind to demolish the village."

"Oh, but that's scandalous!" cried Candida, turning her anguished eyes to his. "For what reason? And what will happen to the villagers? They will lose their homes . . ."

Lord Berkeley said flatly, "My brother is of the opinion that the straggling village spoils the view from the house. He intends to rehouse the villagers at a point further up the valley."

"But there is no road further up the valley," protested

Candida. "Those poor people will be completely cut off! It is bad enough in summer, but what about in winter when the heavy snow falls?"

"I know, Miss Wilton, I know." Lord Berkeley wearily rubbed his eyes. Suddenly, he turned to her, with passion in his voice. "I have known you so little time, Miss Wilton. And yet I feel that between us—"

"Greville! Good day to you!"

Candida realized she had been holding her breath, waiting for Lord Berkeley's next words. Now, to her dismay, she saw Lady Angelica cantering toward them on her frisky chestnut. Candida could cheerfully have pushed the elegantly dressed Lady Angelica off her horse. That she should choose this, of all moments, to interrupt her conversation with the handsome Lord Berkeley. What had he been about to say, Candida wondered frantically. Could it be that her feelings for him were reciprocated?

Oh, curse you, Lady Angelica, raged Candida inwardly. But violent though her inner thoughts were, Candida was careful to reveal no trace of them in her demeanor. Demurely, as was fitting to her station as governess, she urged her horse a few paces away from the lord and lady, so as not to be observed to presume on their conversation.

Lady Angelica expertly reined in her chestnut, and fussed with the ribbons on her peacock blue hat, which was set at a jaunty angle on her thickly powdered hair. Although Candida was heartily sick of the plain dresses she was condemned to wear in her role as governess, she was glad that her lowly position relieved her of the obligation to powder her hair in the fashionable mode. It seemed to her particularly absurd to veil the hair in itchy powder when one had come out expressly to enjoy the benefits of good clean air!

"I have just come from Brockway Hall," Lady Angelica informed Lord Berkeley. "Lady Brockway was in such a stew over the Duke's dinner today. *Now see here, Brockway,*" mimicked Lady Angelica, "*you know I don't approve of these all-male dinners. If you come home drunk I'll throw you into the lake, d'you hear?*"

Lord Berkeley laughed. "No doubt she will, too! And how did Lord Brockway respond?"

"Bad form not to put in an appearance, m'dear," said Lady Angelica gruffly. *"Besides Stratton's only got a few more months of freedom left. When he's wed, his new bride won't take kindly to boisterous all-male dinners."*

Irritated though she was at this unwitting reference to herself, nevertheless, Candida could not repress a smile at the devastating accuracy of Lady Angelica's imitation of the portly Lord Brockway.

Lord Berkeley said quietly, "Strictly between ourselves, Lady Angelica, I cannot but feel sorry for the Duke's young bride. They are to be wed at the end of the year, but he has put in hand no refurbishing of the major apartments. Nothing has been planned for the new Duchess's special comfort and convenience."

No doubt, thought Candida wryly, the Duke intends to accommodate me in the stables.

"If your brother is as spent up as he alleges," declared Lady Angelica with a shrug, "then he is probably waiting until he has taken possession of her great wealth before ordering redecorations to Stratton Hall. But frankly, Greville, knowing your brother, he will probably spend Miss Wellesley's inheritance not on improving his home but on an expensive string of racehorses."

Too true, Lady Angelica, agreed Candida, the color burning high in her cheeks. Oh, thank heavens I had the resolution to come here and pose as a governess! Imagine, if I had been a less spirited girl accustomed to obeying without question the dictates of my guardian! I should have arrived here in December and found myself wed to a drunken pig who cared more for my money than for me. And no doubt my wedding tour would have been not to the gracious capitals of Europe, but a thorough exploration of the race courses of England! Candida shuddered.

"Are you feeling the effects of the wind, Miss Wilton?" inquired Lady Angelica. "I am in total agreement with you.

Its abrasive action is positive death to the complexion." She raised her whip. "Good day to you Greville!"

As she galloped away, Lord Berkeley reluctantly turned his horse toward home. "Dash it. I had forgotten about this cavalier dinner my brother is giving today. We had best return without delay, or I shall be late."

"Who are the other gentlemen attending the dinner?" asked Candida, as they descended onto the combe.

"Well, Lord Brockway will be there of course, and is sure to make an ass of himself. He is let off the marital leash so seldom that when he is set free for an evening, he goes completely wild. Then there's Sir Gerald Hawkshead and Lord Micklesham. I swear if they were blindfolded, and placed in a field with their horses and their women, it would be their precious hunters they would recognize before their own wives."

Candida's eyes danced with laughter, and Lord Berkeley smiled. "I am being dreadfully indiscreet talking to you thus, Miss Wilton. But we understand each other, do we not?"

Candida whispered, "Yes, Lord Berkeley, I believe we do."

She returned to Stratton Hall that day with a song in her heart. How she had enjoyed her afternoon ride with Lord Berkeley. And what a strong rapport had been established between them! He appreciated her company; that was plain. But he felt sufficiently at ease with her to pass familiar remarks on his dining and drinking companions for that evening. They were the kind of comments, mused Candida, which would normally pass between an engaged or married couple . . . people who had known one another for many years, and understood each other completely.

Her eyes were bright as she climbed the stairs to Lady Lucy's apartments. I have no notion, she thought, how this extraordinary tangle of commitment and emotional involvement is to be unravelled. I am betrothed to the Duke, but my heart inclines toward his brother. Yet, Lord Berkeley, whatever his feelings for me, regards me as a humble governess.

As the second son, with no great wealth of his own, he must marry an heiress.

I am an heiress! Surely if I went to him, and revealed my true identity, all our problems would be resolved!

And yet, mused Candida, as she strolled through the long gallery hung with portraits of Stratton ancestors, there is something perverse in me which insists that marriage should not be a question of *you are rich, therefore I love you!* If Lord Berkeley really, truly cares, it will matter nought to him whether I be wealthy or a waif. He will love me regardless of whether he knows me as Candida Wellesley, one of the wealthiest young women in Hampshire. Or Jane Wilton, with only four dresses and a silver cross to call her own.

Still in a buoyant mood, Candida dined with Lady Lucy in the girl's bedchamber, and then retired to her own apartment for the night. But at ten o'clock there came a tap on the door: it was the housekeeper, Mrs. Brewer.

"I am so sorry to disturb you, Miss Wilton, but could you possibly come and see to Lady Lucy? She's feverish and fretful, and keeps calling out for you."

Candida threw a wrap over her nightgown and hurried across the long gallery which overlooked the flight of stairs leading from the ground floor, toward Lady Lucy's room. From the noise below, it was evident that the gentlemen had long past finished their dinner, and were now ensconced in the library, drinking strong spirits.

Inevitably, it was the Duke's voice which could be heard above all others:

"Dash it, Brockway, you can't leave now! The evening's only just begun! It's bad enough being deserted by one's own brother. Greville was so different in Paris, y'know. Then he'd drink till the small hours. Oh, the tales I could tell about my young brother! But of late he seems to have lost the taste for it. Oh, well if you insist, Brockway. Footman! Attend his lordship to his carriage. Yes of course you'll have to carry him, you dolthead! Now then, Hawkshead! I want to hear all about that hunter you sold to good King George III for two hundred guineas! Footman! Bring some mahogany, I say! I'm tired of these milk and water brews. Mahogany is the drink for true lusty men!"

Candida shivered, recalling Mrs. Brewer's warning about the potency of this strange drink, which was two parts gin to one part treacle. To be sure, thought Candida, I shall lock my door tonight!

Lady Lucy was sitting up in bed, her blue eyes unnaturally bright, her lips dry and her skin damp. Candida immediately rang for Mrs. Brewer, and asked if a housemaid could be roused at this late hour to change Lady Lucy's bedlinen, which was soaked with perspiration. While this was being done, Candida sponged down the girl's face and arms with cool, rose scented water, and talked to her all the while about the Downs, and the blue butterflies fluttering among the long grass.

At last, the girl's eyelids began to droop. Candida nodded to Mrs. Brewer, and together the two women assisted the girl back to bed. The fresh linen smelled of lavender. Candida stayed at the bedside until she was sure Lady Lucy was sleeping soundly, and then she crept away.

She hurried back to her own bedchamber. Below, in the library, she could hear male voices raised in contention. Clearly, the Duke was beginning to feel the full lethal influence of the powerful mahogany brew.

Candida hastened toward her bedchamber, and slipped quickly inside. With a sigh of relief she turned the key in the lock. Let them revel to their hearts content, she thought. At least I am safe tonight from the after-effects of the dreaded mahogany.

She groped for the tinderbox, and lit a candle. And it was then that she heard a familiar male voice say thickly,

"My, you think of everything, my dear. You have lit a candle that we may see our pleasure. And you have locked the door, that we may not be disturbed. How thoughtful, Miss Wilton. But rest assured. You shall have your reward!"

Chapter Six

Candida gasped in horror. The Duke of Stratton was sprawled across her window seat, clutching a large tankard of a strong smelling, browny colored brew.

The dreaded mahogany, thought Candida with hammering heart. The drink which she had been warned was reputed to drive the Duke to disgusting depths of lechery and lust.

Quickly, Candida turned, to unlock the door and make her escape, but the Duke, though thoroughly drunk, was still possessed of an animal cunning and a fast turn of speed.

He shot across the room and wrenched the key from Candida's trembling fingers. "No, no!" He smiled glassily, waving a reproving finger at Candida. "I want to have a little talk with you, Miss Wilton. A *private* talk, if you understand my meaning?"

Candida understood only too well. The Duke was standing familiarly close to her. His wig was askew, his breath was sour, and the fastenings of his wine stained jade green waistcoat were half undone.

Candida knew she would need all her wits if she was to emerge intact from this encounter. Trembling, she stood with her back to the door, watching the Duke's pale blue eyes roam suggestively over her figure. Swiftly, Candida assessed the situation: what should I do?

The worst tactic, she realized, would be to scream or shout at the Duke. That would only have the effect of antagonizing him, and might besides, goad him to turn more aggressive with her.

The Duke grinned at Candida, and took a long draught of mahogany. The best approach would be to humor him, Candida decided. Somehow, I must endeavor to be pleasant, while at the same time keeping my distance. The Duke has imbibed such vast quantities this evening, that surely it is only a matter of time now before he drops unconscious to the floor.

Forcing herself to smile, Candida murmured, "Naturally, I am honored to be accorded a private interview with Your Grace." She slipped sideways out of the Duke's grasp, and drifted across to the window. "I hope you are satisfied with Lady Lucy's progress under my instruction. She is a dear girl, and I have become extremely fond of her."

The Duke blinked, and drew the cuff of his coat across his mouth. "Lucy's a good lass," he murmured, "but I didn't come here to talk about her."

Naturally not, thought Candida acidly. It is difficult to conduct a seduction, is it not, when one is being douched with cold water reminders of one's responsibilities?

"Time you and I got better acquainted," slurred the Duke, lumbering toward Candida. "I've had my eye on you, you know. Don't pretend you haven't noticed. I'll tell you straight, Miss Wilton: you're the prettiest governess I ever set eyes on. Wasted in the schoolroom you are." He seized her around the waist and pressed his wet lips to her neck.

Candida felt almost physically sick at his touch. She clutched her wrap tightly around her, desperately conscious that underneath she was barely protected by a thin nightshift.

Frantically, Candida sought for a topic with which to divert the Duke. Anything to keep him talking until he lapsed into unconsciousness. What she said didn't have to be true, she realized, it just had to be fascinating enough to still the Duke's repulsive advances!

"Of course, as a mere governess I have never had the opportunity to travel," she whispered, guiding the silver tankard to the Duke's eager mouth. While he is drinking, he cannot be kissing, she reasoned, and the more he drinks, the more speedily will he become insensible.

She went on in an encouraging tone: "Do tell me about Paris, Your Grace, and the life you led there. It must have been so exciting!"

The Duke hiccuped, and staggered a little. "Paris would be a splendid city, if only they could rid themselves of the French! They boil their meat to rags, y'know, and they don't know the first thing about hunting!"

Candida could have kicked herself for not remembering before. Of course! The one and only topic certain to divert the Duke was horses and hunting. Sure of her ground now, she sat on the window seat and inquired, "Do tell me, Your Grace, what was the most exciting hunt you ever attended while in Europe?"

The Duke roared with laughter, and took another gulp of mahogany. "The most exciting, Miss Wilton? Oh, I remember it well. It took place at the *Chat Bleu*, a very exclusive gentleman's club in Paris."

Candida wondered if he had misheard her question. "We were talking of hunting, Your Grace," she murmured.

"I know that, woman!" he roared. "I may be drunk, m'dear, but I am not stupid. You would do well to remember that!"

Candida shivered at the menace in his tone. Casually, she moved the lighted candle into the middle of the window seat. The curtains were drawn back—perhaps someone will look up, and witness the difficulties I am in, she prayed. It was a slim hope, but all she had to cling to for the present.

Again, Candida willed herself to smile. "What happened at the *Chat Bleu?*" she asked persuasively.

"Ten women we had in there that night," grinned the Duke. "No one of any consequence. Just common girls we dragged in off the street. D'you know what we made them do? We forced them to stand on their hands, so their skirts fell over their heads. Oh, such a pretty sight, believe me! Then we got out our whips, and made the girls run all around the club—up and down stairs, along the corridors, through the saloons—my, it was great sport! No man who was present has ever forgotten it."

Avoiding his lascivious eye, Candida was furious that her plan had misfired. She had sought to divert him onto the subject of hunting, but he had skirted that fence, and doubled back to the topic of women!

Candida was seated on the window seat and the Duke stood, swaying, before her. He took a final draught of mahogany, and flung the tankard violently across the room. Candida saw his eyes begin to gleam. Then he licked his lips, and took a step toward her.

She flung herself to one side, and screamed as he caught hold of her. Furiously, he slapped her face, and hissed;

"No point in screaming, Miss! Greville's disappeared for one of his moonlit rides across the Downs, and none of the servants would dare appear in my presence without my permission."

"Let me free this instant!" Candida demanded. "Your behavior is outrageous!"

By way of an answer he snatched the pins from her hair and pulled the golden tresses loose over her shoulders. "Beautiful," he murmured thickly. "I have a notion that all of you is beautiful, Miss Governess!"

His clammy hands wrenched aside her wrapper, and tore at the bodice of her thin nightshift. Frantic, Candida clawed at his hands, kicked his shins and finally, in desperation, sank her teeth into his fleshy neck.

"You pig, you oaf!" she shouted forgetting in her fear the constrained vocabulary fitting to a governess. "How dare you force your way in here and attempt to take advantage of me!"

She clawed his face, and drew blood, but the Duke was so inflamed with alcohol that his sense of pain was completely numbed. Taking a firm grip on her slender shoulders he pushed her back toward the bed. Candida writhed and struggled and screamed, sending the bedside table crashing to the floor.

Candida fought him with every ounce of strength she

possessed. But she was powerless against this big, crazed man with but one thought on his mind; to force her to submit to him.

Ruthlessly, he ripped the bodice of her nightshift from neck to waist. With tears of fury misting her eyes, Candida delivered a stinging blow to his cheek. Employing all the might of a maddened wild animal, he held her down with one hand, and wrenched aside the tattered bodice with the other.

"Fight me, would you?" he gasped. "You forget your place, my girl. I am the Duke, remember—and you are my servant. Like all the women in my household, you are there to be taken by me, if I choose. It is my right!"

"I shall never submit to you. *Never!*" spat Candida writhing in vain to escape from his hot, exploring hands.

He grinned as he gazed down on her white bosom. "I was right," he said thickly. "You *are* very lovely, Miss Governess. Come, let me kiss you!"

He fell on her then, his hands on her bosom, his mouth searching for hers. Candida felt breathless with terror, and her heart was hammering so loudly she thought it would deafen her.

It was then that she realized that the banging she heard was not her heart—it was a fist, crashing imperiously against the locked bedchamber door.

Dizzy with relief, she heard the furious tones of Lord Berkeley. "Bart! Open this door this second, you blackguard! Or you'll have me to answer to!"

The Duke raised his head and laughed. "Run away, little brother! I am the Duke, and I am engaged in man's work!" He seized Candida's long hair, and pulled her toward him. She screamed, digging her nails into his back, twisting this way and that to avoid his sour kisses.

For a moment there was silence, and Candida was cast down into the depths of despair. Had Lord Berkeley deserted her? Was he, like everyone else at Stratton Hall, powerless to defy the Duke's authority?

A loud crash, followed by the unmistakable sound of

splintering wood provided her answer. The Duke pushed Candida aside, and staggered to his feet. His coarse face was a picture of horrified disbelief.

"Why . . . the impudent rogue is breaking the door down!" he stuttered.

Another crash, as Lord Berkeley once more put his muscular shoulder to the door. His eyes bulging with rage, the Duke picked up the bedside table and advanced toward the door.

Suddenly, the door burst open, and Lord Berkeley roared into the room. The Duke lunged with the table. Scornfully, Lord Berkeley raised his booted leg and kicked the table from his brother's hands. As the Duke fell back, off balance, Lord Berkeley marched purposefully toward him, swung his fist and delivered a single crushing blow to his brother's jaw. The Duke's eyes glazed, and he fell heavily to the floor, quite unconscious.

Without a word, Lord Berkeley bent and dragged his dishevelled, drunken brother out of the room, and into the corridor. He returned, picked up the Duke's wig, and threw it through the door onto the supine body of the Duke.

Then, and only then, he turned his gray eyes upon Candida.

Candida, white faced, knelt on the bed, with the bedcurtain wrapped around her shoulders to conceal her nakedness.

Lord Berkeley said quietly, "On behalf of my brother, I apologize from the bottom of my heart for what happened here tonight. I must advise you that you will receive no word of regret from the Duke. From long and bitter experience I know that by tomorrow morning, he will have absolutely no memory of his shameful actions. But I am distressed beyond words, Miss Wilton, that you have been placed in such a humiliating situation."

"Thank heavens you were here," whispered Candida. "I believed you to be out riding . . ."

"No, I was up in one of the attics, sifting through some old papers and portraits. When I heard the commotion I realized at once what was happening. Thank God I was not too late!" His mouth tightened into a grim line as he reflected on the tragedy which had only just been averted.

Candida sat still on the bed, drawing strength from his reassuring presence. Lord Berkeley picked up the fallen oak table, and placed it near the bed. Then he fetched the candle from the window seat, and after drawing the window curtains, set the candle on the oak table.

Candida watched him, saying nothing, but feeling immensely comforted as he performed these simple actions. Then he turned to her, and something in his expression made her whole being feel afire. She knew she should ask him to leave. It was improper for her to be with him thus, alone in a bedchamber with the curtains drawn. She was sharply aware of her tousled, loose hair and her nakedness thinly veiled by the bed curtain wrapped around her. And from the look in his gray eyes, she knew that he was equally aware of her state of disarray.

And yet, Candida realized with a sharp intake of breath, my state of undress matters not between us. In the sight of this man, I do not appear immodest, or wanton. Here, now, at this moment, I am neither humble governess, nor wealthy Candida Wellesley. And he is not a lord, and brother of a Duke. Our positions in society are irrelevant.

He is a man. And I am a woman. And we are fiercely, uncontrollably, unashamedly attracted to one another! Whatever happens now, will occur because it is right. I love him! With all my heart and soul, I love him. And I shall regret nothing!

He came toward her, and with infinite tenderness laid his hands on her shoulders. Gently, he lifted her to her feet, and drew her into his arms. After a trembling, hesitant moment, she returned his embrace, heedless that the bed curtain had fallen away revealing her white bosom under the torn nightshift.

Her blood ran molten through her veins as his hands caressed her silken, golden hair and traced the delicate line of her face.

Kiss me! she willed him. *Kiss me! Take me. For I belong only to you!*

His gray eyes burned into hers. He bent his dark head and kissed—not her waiting lips, but the smooth white skin of her forehead.

Then he suddenly put her from him, and said in a voice burning with anguish and passion, "My God! If you knew how much I wish the cruel lottery of life had dealt us different cards!"

Before Candida could collect her shattered wits to reply, he had turned on his heel, and strode from the room, slamming the splintered door behind him.

For a long moment Candida stood stunned, too shocked scarcely to breathe. She felt so numb, it was as if she was not part of this world. But gradually, painful reality returned.

Candida caught sight of herself in the long glass. Her hair was dishevelled, tumbling over her bare shoulders. Blushing, Candida hastily threw on her wrapper, not daring to look at herself any more. Although the blush soon faded from her cheeks, Candida felt as if her entire body was on fire with shame.

She flung herself down on the window seat. How could I, she thought with anguish. Oh, what madness caused me to behave so shamelessly? Lord Berkeley's last passionate words to her were branded on Candida's mind:

"My God! If you knew how much I wish the cruel lottery of life had dealt us different cards!"

Candida shivered, imagining the scene as it must have appeared to Lord Berkeley. Hearing that the Stratton Hall governess is in distress, he gallantly rushes to her rescue. Then, with the drunken Duke safely removed from the room, Lord Berkeley realizes that the governess is gazing at him with something more than schoolmistressy gratitude in her eyes. He is a red-blooded man. For a moment he is sorely tempted to take advantage of her. Take advantage? Nay, hardly so. For clearly, she is surrendering to him of her own free will.

But as he draws her into his arms, Lord Berkeley

remembers that he is a gentleman, and a man of honor, and it is not honorable for the brother of the master of the house to engage in dalliance with someone whom he believes to be a governess. For Lord Berkeley to succumb to such an impulse would, Candida knew, in his mind, place him on the same despicable level as the Duke of Stratton. The Duke, clearly, had no scruples about seducing members of the Stratton Hall female staff. In fact, he regarded it as his sovereign right to bed whomsoever he wished in his employ. But Lord Berkeley would never attempt to take such advantage.

Scalding tears burned Candida's cheeks. Oh, whatever must he think of me, she wept. To stand as I did, so shamelessly before him! How foolish I was to believe that there existed between us a rare affinity which transcended all traditional codes of behavior. I believed that he returned in full measure the love which I have felt for him since that day when we first met. But of course, the cold truth is that he feels nothing of the kind for me. He would not allow himself to. No, while I gazed at him tonight with love in my eyes, he looked at me and saw nothing more than an amorous governess, a frustrated spinster, a wanton.

"How am I to face him?" whispered Candida. "Oh, never again shall I be able to meet his gaze with equanimity. Just to be present in the same room with him would be enough to put me to the blush!"

I could go to him and reveal the truth about my identity. I could . . . but I shan't, and for two very good reasons.

Candida paced her bedchamber, ticking off her reasons on her fingers. First, because I should feel so embarrassed about my shameless behavior here in this bedchamber tonight. I would far rather draw a veil over the entire incident, and never have it referred to again.

And secondly, the Romantic in me counsels against telling Lord Berkeley the truth about myself. Surely, if he really loved me, it would not matter a buckle whether I was a laundrymaid or a Lady? Love should conquer all. And when I marry, I am determined that it shall be to a man who loves me for myself, not my title, my position, or my wealth.

It was after midnight when Candida finally fell into bed. Her mind was still awhirl with the events of the night, and the embarrassing encounters to be endured tomorrow with both the Duke and his brother. But on one matter Candida was firmly decided.

I must leave Stratton Hall, she resolved, tossing restlessly between the sheets. For my own peace of mind, I must quit this place without delay.

"Such dreadful goings on last night, Miss Wilton," clucked Mrs. Brewer, drawing Candida into the privacy of the Housekeeper's Room. "Do come and sit with me awhile—here in this chair by the window."

Candida allowed herself gently to be urged onto the hard-backed chair. She knew that Mrs. Brewer, like the rest of the Stratton Hall staff, was agog for more details of last night's drama with the Duke. While Mrs. Brewer rang the bell, and instructed one of her housemaids to bring refreshment, Candida appraized the housekeeper's domain.

It was only a small room, tucked away near the China cupboard, but into it a writing desk, two chairs, and a small chest of drawers were set. The desk was covered with lists, which Candida surmised were housemaid's duty rotas, the linen inventory, and suggestions from the cook for next week's menus.

When the housemaid had set down the hot chocolate and departed, Mrs. Brewer intoned, in the hushed voice one uses with an invalid, "Of course, we all heard the commotion, Miss Wilton. We knew exactly what was taking place. To own the truth, every governess who's set foot in this house has endured a similar fate." She sighed. "If it's not Lady Lucy's wilful ways that drive her governesses away, then it's the Duke with his lecherous nature. My, if his poor mother could see him now, why she'd turn in her grave for shame."

Candida sipped her hot drink, wishing the housekeeper would change the subject and talk about something else. The last thing Candida desired was to relive the horror of last night!

But Mrs. Brewer was determined to say her piece. "I do appreciate that it must have been a dreadful experience for you, Miss Wilton! But I do hope you won't be leaving us because of it. Lady Lucy is a quite changed girl when she's in your charge."

"I . . . I have not yet made up my mind what to do," said Candida evasively. She had determined to tell no one of her decision to quit Stratton Hall. Far better, she resolved, simply to slip away from the house at midnight, saddle a horse and disappear into the night. She would leave a note for young Lady Lucy, wishing her well and explaining her hurried departure with a white lie about a sick aunt. As for her governess's clothes, they could stay and rot at Stratton Hall for all Candida cared. When she left this house, she wanted to set eyes on neither her sober governess gowns, nor the occupants of the house ever again.

"You are angry with us!" Mrs. Brewer burst out, misinterpreting Candida's long, reflective silence. "You are blaming the Stratton Hall staff for turning a deaf ear to your cries for help! But you must understand, Miss Wilton, that we are all in an extremely difficult position. We dare not risk being dismissed by the Duke, for where else is there for us to go?"

"Do not distress yourself, Mrs. Brewer," murmured Candida. "I assure you, there is no resentment in my mind against the Stratton Hall staff. I do understand, believe me."

Candida spoke sincerely for she was well aware that the Duke of Stratton was the major landowner in this part of Sussex. And everyone who worked at Stratton Hall had a relative somewhere on the Stratton estates who was employed by the Duke. Their livelihoods depended on this man. It would be asking too much of any servant to expect them to incur the Duke's wrath by interceding in his attempted seduction of a governess. The situation was totally unjust, but it was one that every man, woman, and child on the Stratton estates was forced to accept and live with.

Although she gave Mrs. Brewer a reassuring smile,

inwardly Candida was seething. How appalling, she raged, that all these hundreds of people should be subject to the whims of their drunken, irresponsible employer! A man who cares so little about them that he is seriously considering ordering their village to be moved, lock, stock and barrel, to an inconvenient site further up the valley. And why? Because this village, the place they call home, is spoiling the ducal view from the Stratton Hall windows!

Mrs. Brewer leaned forward and said in a conspiritorial tone, "It was that gentlemen's dinner the Duke gave last night that triggered it all off. The footmen tell me that Lady Brockway is beside herself with rage over Lord Brockway's behavior last night. She says it will be all around the county in no time, and she will be the laughing stock of all Sussex."

"But as far as I recall, Lord Brockway did not stay very late," queried Candida. "He was mightily drunk, of course, but—"

"Ah, that was the cause of it!" exclaimed Mrs. Brewer, brushing a speck of dust off her starched white cuffs. "Lord Brockway was so drunk, he clambered into the wrong carriage. Sir Gerald Hawkshead's carriage had drawn up outside the door, but Sir Gerald had collapsed into a laurel bush. Lord Brockway came rushing out of the house, fell into Sir Gerald's carriage, and was whisked away to Hawkshead Manor in Lewes."

"Heavens, how alarming!" cried Candida.

"*That* wasn't the end of it," said Mrs. Brewer. "Lord Brockway, believing himself to be at home, crept in through the garden door, went upstairs and then, overcome with a fit of drunken lust, entered what he believed to be his marital bed."

Candida's eyes widened. "Not Lady Hawkshead's bedchamber?" she gasped.

Mrs. Brewer nodded. "Her ladyship awoke, and well, you can imagine the ruck when she discovered Lord Brockway, full of amorous intent, beside her!"

Candida struggled with herself. But it was impossible to maintain a suitable grave countenance at this astounding intelligence about Lord Brockway and Lady Hawkshead. Candida threw back her head and laughed, and soon Mrs. Brewer, too, was wiping tears of mirth from her eyes.

"Oh dear," gasped Candida, "poor Lord Brockway. I should not be at all surprised if Lady Brockway has banished him from the house and has chained him to a kennel."

"I gather that it's the Duke's blood she's after," remarked Mrs. Brewer, tucking her handkerchief back into the sleeve of her black dress. "It was he, she considers, who led her husband astray last night."

The smile faded from the housekeeper's worn face, and she muttered bitterly, "If I were ten years younger I'd quit this place, Miss Wilton, and look for another position. Trouble is, I've served at Stratton Hall since I came here at fourteen as a scullery maid. I don't know of any other place, or any other way of life. And then there's Lady Lucy. With respect, Miss Wilton, it is my experience that governesses tend to come and go somewhat speedily at Stratton Hall. If I resigned my post, it would mean leaving her alone in this house with no married woman to protect her. Now that wouldn't be right at all, would it, Miss Wilton?"

"I assure you, I do appreciate your difficult position," said Candida, rising to her feet and smoothing down her apron. "Now if you will excuse me, I will go and wait on Lady Lucy. I have been out this morning collecting lumps of chalk. I thought I would teach her how to make chalk carvings." She paused by the door and inquired,

"I trust Lady Lucy was not disturbed by last night's events?"

Mrs. Brewer shook her gray head. "Bless you no. The lassie slept soundly enough until three in the morning. Then she had us all awake with demands for tea, and cake and gingerbread biscuits."

"Oh dear. The housemaids must be dreadfully tired today," sympathized Candida.

"No, they're cheerful enough girls. Besides, today's a special one for all the staff, as it's the *beating the bounds* ceremony. Lord Berkeley always relieves us of our duties and tells us to come and watch the lads learning their boundaries."

Candida smiled. She understood, of course, that it was essential for every country lad to know exactly where his parish ended and the next began. But it did seem hard on the boys that they should be marched around the perimeter of the parish, and at strategic intervals held upside down, and bumped by their heads on the boundary line. The argument was that for the rest of his life, that boy never forgot his bumping, or where his parish ended. Nevertheless, witnessing the scene had always made Candida secretly glad that she had been born a girl!

"Will not the Duke be in charge of the ceremony today?" asked Candida.

Mrs. Brewer shook her head. "No, he's not interested in our country rituals. He's away shooting today."

Candida made her way up to Lady Lucy's apartments. She found the girl fast asleep, her cheeks flushed and her red hair spread out across the lace pillow. Candida returned to the ground floor, and slipped into the library. The great old house was hushed and still, with all the servants away at the *beating of the bounds* ceremony. Candida was relieved, so far, not to have encountered the Duke or Lord Berkeley.

The Duke, having slept off the excesses of the night before, had arisen early and set off with his gun dogs. Candida had no doubt that if their paths did cross this evening, he would be ebullient with tales of the day's shoot, with his shameful behavior of last night completely erased from his mind.

No, it was not the Duke whom Candida dreaded encountering—it was Lord Berkeley whose eyes she feared to meet. I must not think of him, Candida resolved. It is fruitless to torture myself about the events of last night. What is done cannot be undone. By midnight tonight, I shall have quit this house, and I never again shall set eyes on Lord Berkeley.

Determined to turn her mind to other realms of thought, Candida selected a morocco bound book from the shelves, and left the library, intending to sit and read by Lady Lucy's bedside until the child awoke. As she approached the impressive marble staircase, Candida noticed a flash of white at the top of the first flight.

"Who's there?" she called, suddenly alarmed. Surely all the servants should be at the *beating of the bounds* ceremony by now? Candida had believed herself to be alone in the house.

But as Candida stared upward, she saw it: a white robed figure, standing in a gloomy corner behind a beautifully carved statue of Apollo.

Candida's mouth felt dry. Surely, she thought, Stratton Hall is not possessed of a ghost? Heavens, having a drunken Duke in residence is blight enough, without a ghost complicating matters as well.

Well, thought Candida, marching boldly toward the stairs, I am the Lady Candida Wellesley, and no ghost is going to frighten me!

But she stopped, and hesitated ten yards from the bottom of the stairs. The figure in white was moving, emerging from the back of Apollo and advancing to the top of the stairs.

Candida gazed up and almost shouted with relief. "Lady Lucy! Whatever are you doing out of bed?"

The girl in the white nightrobe stared down at her governess with bright, strangely unseeing eyes. She swayed on the top step and began to shiver.

Candida's blood ran suddenly cold. Lady Lucy was sleepwalking, she realized. Her eyes may be open, but she cannot see me. The crucial question is: can she see the stairs? Does she realize she is standing at the top of a marble staircase? Oh Heavens! I must reach her. And soon!

Candida ran forward, but it was too late. The red-haired

girl had taken a step into mid-air, her nightrobe tangled around her feet. She twisted sideways and began to roll, with increasing terrifying speed, down the long, red carpeted, marble flight of steps.

Chapter Seven

For an agonizing moment, Candida stood as if paralyzed. At the bottom of the stairs, in a direct line with Lady Lucy's head, was a large brass statuette of the goddess Diana with her bow.

If I don't act *now*, thought Candida in a panic, Lady Lucy's head will smash against the statuette, and at the speed she is travelling, it will mean certain death!

Galvanized into action, Candida fled toward the stairs. Lady Lucy, awake now, white-faced, screaming and helpless, was but four steps from the bottom.

Afterward, Candida was to bless her impulsive intention to teach Lady Lucy how to make chalk carvings that day. To save her dark blue governess's dress from becoming powdered with chalk, she had donned an enveloping apron, and it was this which the kneeling Candida now held out before her at the bottom of the stairs.

Wild-eyed with terror, the red-haired girl hurtled down, and rolled safely into the apron. Candida staggered back under the impact, cradling the girl's head in her arms to shield her from contact with the brass Diana. For a second or two, Lady Lucy and her governess sat in a tangled heap on the floor, each breathing hard and atremble with fright at what might have been. Then Lady Lucy took a deep, shuddering breath and burst into hysterical tears.

"There now, you are safe, Lady Lucy," murmured Candida, gathering the sobbing girl into her arms. "It is all over. There is nothing to be afraid of."

"It was so horrible!" wailed the red-haired girl. "I was having a lovely dream, where I was floating along a long corridor toward my mother. She was calling to me and telling me she loved me, and then I awoke—" her blue eyes filled again with tears—"and I was falling down those horrid stairs!"

Candida held the girl close, stroking her hair and murmuring soothing words. But inwardly, Candida felt murder in her heart for the irresponsible, butterfly beauty who had been Lady Lucy's mother. How dare she bring a child into the world and then proceed to neglect her so shamefully, raged Candida. Poor Lady Lucy has been so starved of affection that when she is ill, her feverish brain envisages wonderful dreams of a kind and loving mother, with time to spare for her cherished daughter. The reality, of course, was a harsh and far cry from the rosy illusion of the dream.

Candida was suddenly aware that they had been sitting for a considerable time on the hall floor. It would not do at all should some of the servants return early from the *beating of the bounds* ceremony and find Lady Lucy and her governess in such an undignified situation. But Lady Lucy was still in an extremely distressed condition, and in no fit state to move far.

When Candida gently raised the girl to her feet, she noticed an insignificant sidedoor tucked away behind the statuette of Diana. Placing a supporting arm around Lady Lucy, Candida opened the door and guided the girl into what at first sight appeared to be a room set aside for general lumber that would eventually be transferred to one of the attics.

Here were broken benches and stools from the servants' hall. Bent fishing rods, a dented hip flask, and discarded game bags lay heaped in a corner. The floor itself was littered with old dust cloths, and it was onto these which Lady Lucy and Candida subsided. Candida pushed the door shut. There was something oddly comforting about this strange, out of the way room, filled with the debris and unwanted articles of Stratton Hall. Most of the house was so grand, so imposing, with its impressive statues, sweeping staircases, and graciously spacious saloons.

Yet, how safe and secure I feel, tucked away in this cosy, cluttered room, thought Candida. Her curious eyes roamed around the heaps of discarded fishing tackle, a grinning, peeling rocking horse, a crate full of chipped china, the old rough hooded robe hanging on the back of the door....

Candida sat transfixed, in a state of horrified disbelief, as if her bosom friend had just stabbed her in the back. She found it impossible to remove her eyes from the robe on the door. With all her heart she longed to touch it, examine it, scrutinize every inch of the cloth. But Lady Lucy, though calmer now, was in no mood to be moved from the comfort of her governess's arms. Candida's face was as white as the dust sheets on which they sat. Her lips moved soundlessly:

The Robed Raider! The villain who had terrorized Sussex by abducting innocent young girls was here, *here* within the very walls of Stratton Hall!

Instinctively, Candida hugged Lady Lucy all the closer as she considered the implications of her unexpected discovery. There was no doubt in her mind that the brown, woollen garment hanging on the door was the disguise of the Robed Raider, as it was of a length to fit a tall grown man. And this room, quite obviously, was rarely entered by any of the Stratton Hall staff. Indeed, if anyone had any cause to place any discarded object in here, in all probability they simply opened the door, threw in the broken article and made haste away. They would certainly not linger here. And they would definitely not concern themselves to glance behind the door.

Candida's hands and feet were beginning to tingle. Though whether with fear, or with pins and needles from sitting so long in one position she was at first uncertain. In any event, she decided, in view of what I have discovered, Lady Lucy and I must make ourselves scarce from this place—and without delay! To be caught hiding in here could result in the most dire results from the enraged Robed Raider.

Accordingly, she urged Lady Lucy back upstairs to her bedchamber where she rang the bell for the reliable Mrs. Brewer, and arranged for the housekeeper to bring Lady Lucy a soothing tisane of lemon balm. Before long, exhausted from her ordeal and lulled by the deliciously scented herb tisane, Lady Lucy had drifted into a peaceful sleep. Candida remained at her bedside for two hours, until she was certain that the girl was no longer in a feverish condition, and then she returned to her own bedchamber.

From the window seat she was able to observe the first party of servants returning from the *beating of the bounds* ceremony. They walked arm in arm, laughing, joking, and clearly delighted with life. But Candida's lovely face was grave as she regarded their innocent high spirits.

"If they but knew," she whispered, "that they are returning in such jubilation to a house which harbors the most evil villain that Sussex has known for centuries!" The Robed Raider.

"The Duke of Stratton!" breathed Candida, giving voice at last to the terrible thought which had tormented her since she first set eyes on that brown wool robe hanging on the back of the door.

It must be he, Candida realized, pushing open the window to allow a buzzing wasp to escape. Abducting young girls is just the kind of sport which the coarse ruthless Duke would find highly entertaining. There is the thrill of the chase, the hounding of the quarry, the final triumphant gallop of glory with the innocent girl strapped helpless to his horse.

It all fits, Candida realized. Lady Frances, during her encounter with the Robed Raider was certain that the villain had been riding a black hunter. And there is one such animal, Black Knight, in the Duke's own stables.

"But oh, what impertinence for the Duke to attempt to abduct Lady Frances!" murmured Candida. "Why, he dines frequently at her mother's table! To think that he partakes liberally of the generous Brockway hospitality, when all the time he is planning to make off with the daughter of the house. Why, it is quite outrageous!"

Thank heaven, Lady Frances is safe at Brockway Hall, Candida mused. But two other girls have fallen into the Duke's ignoble hands. By now they are probably in London, enduring the most unspeakable physical degradations. And, of course, the Duke would no doubt have been paid handsomely for delivering up these Sussex damsels. He makes no secret of the fact that he is extremely short of funds. Until the happy day when he marries Miss Candida Wellesley, and secures her considerable fortune, an income derived from selling young women is obviously very welcome.

Candida tossed her golden head. Well, my lord Duke, you have miscalculated! For there will most definitely be no marriage between yourself and Miss Wellesley. By midnight tonight, Miss Wellesley will have quit this house, and in three days' time, with Cousin Clara's assistance, Miss Wellesley will be across the Channel and safe from the threat of the Duke's sour marital embraces.

First, however, one delicate and difficult task lay ahead of Candida. She knew that in all conscience, she could not leave Stratton Hall without advising Lord Berkeley about the brown robe she had unwittingly discovered.

Her heart went out to Lord Berkeley. It was embarrassing enough for this noble, upright man to live with the knowledge that his brother was a dissolute winebag who had squandered the family fortune and cared not a snap for the welfare of his tenants, or the preservation of his heritage. Now, it seemed, the Duke was hell bent on destroying his good family name also. For if it became publicly known that the Duke himself had been unmasked as the Robed Raider, then the Berkeley family name would be besmirched not just in Sussex, but throughout all England. They never again would be able to hold their heads high in society.

And the final irony, mused Candida in despair, is that the Duke himself was allegedly leading the county-wide search for the evil Robed Raider! Oh, how he must have laughed to find himself in such an entertaining situation! My, what dupes he has made of us all.

Over the past hour, the entire Stratton Hall party had passed beneath Candida's window on their way back from the ceremony. Lord Berkeley among the last, had paused for a moment in the drive, a smile touching his lips as the servants clustered around, voicing their heartfelt thanks to him for providing them with a break from their routine labors and such a merry few hours' diversion. Then with a courteous wave of his hand, Lord Berkeley strode into the house. There was no sign of the Duke. Candida surmised that he must still be out on the Downs with his gun dogs.

Candida knew that she must go immediately and tell Lord Berkeley what she had discovered. Yet, she lingered in her chamber, retying the girdle on the dark blue dress, pushing wayward fronds of golden hair back under her demure cap, smoothing invisible wrinkles from her stockings.

Finally she admitted the truth to herself: *I am afraid to face him.* Her entire being was still seared with the memory of her encounter last night here in this very bedchamber with Lord Berkeley.

"How could I have acted thus?" she whispered. "To reveal myself to him in such a wanton, shameless manner? Whatever possessed me?"

And oh, to have suffered thus the indignity of the firm noble manner in which he had put her from him and left the room! To face him now, to endure the contempt in his steel gray eyes, would be the hardest act of Candida's life.

Yet, I must be strong, Candida told herself resolutely, I am a Wellesley, and our family have never evaded its duty. Is not our family motto *Duty Unto Death?* Lord Berkeley must be told the truth about his brother. For me to leave him in ignorance would mean that the innocent young girls of Sussex would remain in perpetual peril from the evil Duke. It would be ever on my conscience that by cowardly keeping silent, I had placed others in danger.

Gathering up all her courage, Candida left her chamber

and ran down the main staircase. She encountered Mrs. Brewer, who informed her that Lord Berkeley was in the library. As Candida tapped on the library's double doors, she felt some of her fears recede. After all, her own personal embarrassment at this meeting was secondary in importance to her revelation about the identity of the Robed Raider. Naturally, Lord Berkeley would be horrified at what she had to tell him. But at the same time, there would be an underlying feeling of relief that the mystery was solved at last. And this mutual relief over the Robed Raider, thought Candida, will surely be sufficient to veil our uneasy memories of the scene between us in my bedchamber.

Receiving no answer to her knock, Candida opened the doors and entered the library. Lord Berkeley was seated by the window, one immaculately breeched leg crossed over the other. The latest London newspapers and a glass of brandy were on the sidetable beside him.

He glanced up, and said coolly, "I believe I gave orders that I was not to be disturbed, Miss Wilton."

Candida dipped a curtsey, and with an effort, controlled the tremble in her voice. "I beg your pardon, Lord Berkeley, but while you were away from the house, something came to my attention which I thought best to advise you of without delay."

He raised a dark eyebrow. "Indeed?"

Candida found it impossible to meet his eyes. Her carefully prepared speech fled from her head, and she found herself blurting, "In the sideroom at the bottom of the stairs . . . behind the door . . . there is a robe. Dark brown, with a hood. It occurred to me that it must be—"

With a controlled, yet angry movement, Lord Berkeley had leaped to his feet. "What were you doing in that room?" he demanded curtly.

His tone astounded and unnerved Candida. "I . . . Lady Lucy was feeling unwell. It was the nearest place for her to lie for a moment and recover . . . and then when I closed the door I saw—"

"What is more to the point," interrupted Lord Berkeley icily, "is that I see that you would do well not to meddle in that which does not concern you, Miss Wilton. Now, would you kindly return to your duties with Lady Lucy and leave me in peace!"

His eyes were glacial, his knuckles white as they gripped the arm of the brass studded leather chair. Stunned, Candida turned and fled from the room.

In her chamber, she flung herself down on her bed and shook with rage. Rage at Lord Berkeley, and at herself also. How dare he speak to me in such a contemptuous tone, she stormed. Why, it was as if he were refusing to listen to a word I uttered! He would not take me seriously. He brushed me off as if I were a fly that had dared to land on his arm.

And I, how did I respond to such treatment? With courage, and fearless resolution? No! I lowered my eyes, and stammered, and ran from his presence like a gauche schoolgirl. Yet, even a schoolgirl, even Lady Lucy would have displayed more spirit than was evident in me!

But I love him, she sobbed, burying her face in the pillow. That is why the interview was such torment for me. When the man you love treats you with such callous disregard, it is like emerging from a warm house, expecting sunshine and encountering instead a harsh east wind. Oh, I had expected him to be distantly polite to me. But I had not anticipated such arctic disdain!

Well, if nothing else, the episode has taught me a lesson, thought Candida, sitting up and drying her tears. Never again must I allow Lord Berkeley to throw me off balance in such a humiliating manner. From henceforth, I shall behave toward him with the utmost reserve. In fact, I shall endeavor to avoid his presence as much as humanly possible. For although I love Lord Berkeley with all my heart and soul, being near him causes me too much pain. Yes, the less I see of him, the easier will my agony be to bear.

Candida had realized that it was now impossible for her to carry through her plan to quit Stratton Hall at midnight.

I cannot go, she reasoned, until the Duke has been well and truly unmasked as the Robed Raider. It would be unforgivable of me to leave young Lady Lucy here in such circumstances. Oh, if only Lord Berkeley had listened to me! But he was so curt and unyielding, he did not allow me a proper opportunity to explain fully my fears about the dark brown robe hanging on that door. Clearly, he was as embarrassed as I about our encounter, and only wished to bring the interview to a speedy end. Why, I doubt if he even heard a word of what I said. But I cannot allow the matter to rest there. I shall wait a few days, and then when the atmosphere between us seems more tranquil, I shall broach the subject again. Then, and only then, will I be free to leave Stratton Hall.

"Which of my suitors shall I marry?" demanded Lady Frances Brockway, laughing merrily. She held in her hands a tattered, slim volume entitled *The Oracle of Life and Love.* "You ask it questions," Lady Frances informed the assembled company, "and the book provides you with amazingly truthful answers."

Lady Brockway raised her eyes to heaven. "Will it advise me how to deal with an errant husband?" she inquired tartly.

The party was gathered under a magnificent spreading oak tree which dominated the sweeping lawns of Brockway Hall. The occasion was Lady Frances' twentieth birthday, and the Duke and Lord Berkeley had ridden over that morning to give her presents, and their best wishes. Lady Lucy, now fully restored to health, had insisted on accompanying the men—not because she had any desire to be in the company of Lady Frances, but in order to go riding with Lord Rupert, the young Brockway heir.

Lady Lucy had been accompanied by her governess, who was seated now on a stool a few feet from the main group under the oak tree. As she bent demurely over the sampler she was embroidering, a glimmer of a smile touched Candida's lips as she recalled the hilarious sequence of events which had resulted in Lord Brockway climbing into Lady Hawkshead's bed! Clearly, Lady Brockway had neither forgotten nor forgiven the incident and was determined to make all involved do penance for their bibulous misadventures.

Haughtily, Lady Brockway turned to the Duke who was sprawled in a wicker chair, mopping his perspiring face with a large, lace-edged handkerchief. "The whole disgraceful episode was entirely your fault, Bart. You led poor Brockway astray, and encouraged him to worship too long at the shrine of Bacchus."

Not at all upset, the Duke slapped his thigh and roared, "If you mean that we were mightily drunk, madam, why not say so? Of *course* we were drunk." He raised his glass, and the bright August sunshine sparkled on the fine crystal. "Have you never been drunk, Lady Brockway?"

"Don't be absurd," she snapped, glaring at her husband who sat miserably fanning himself with a spray of oak leaves. "And if I have my way, Bart—which I shall for I always do—Brockway here will never again be allowed within ten miles of your gentlemen's dinners at Stratton Hall."

Candida could not help feeling sorry for the downcast Lord Brockway, and she was glad when Lord Berkeley changed the subject by inquiring of Lady Frances, "You seem absorbed in your book. Is the Oracle providing the answers you hoped for?"

Lady Frances fluttered her eyelashes at the handsome man seated beside her. "I have not dared ask anything yet. I am in fear and trembling lest I receive the wrong reply!"

My, what a pathetic little creature you are, thought Candida scornfully, wrenching at a knot in her thread. It was agony for Candida watching Lord Berkeley and Lady Frances seated less than a foot from each other. Lady Frances, evidently, was still totally enamored of Lord Berkeley. Each of her remarks were directed at him, and whenever he spoke, she listened with a rapt and flattering attention.

"Who gave you the *Oracle* book, my dear?" inquired Lord Brockway.

Lady Frances smiled, and her brown eyes were luminous. "Lord Berkeley brought it for me, for my birthday."

"I found it upstairs in one of the Stratton Hall attics," explained Lord Berkeley. "It is probably all foolish nonsense, but I thought it might amuse Lady Frances for an hour or two."

"No, no, of course it is not nonsense!" exclaimed Lady Frances. "See how old the book is! The printing is strange and hard to read, plus the pages themselves have clearly been well thumbed. I do believe that in the past, the Berkeley ladies used this book frequently, and consulted it on all the important issues of their lives."

The Duke snapped his fingers at a waiting footman, and held out his glass for more wine. "Deuced hot in this heat," he explained, observing Lady Brockway's baleful glare upon him. He leaned across, and playfully pulled undone the ribbons of Lady Frances' large brimmed straw sunbonnet. "Come along then, m'dear. Let's put the book to the test. I'll ask the first question if you like."

"You shall not!" said Lady Frances petulantly. "It is *my* book, and I shall ask the first question." She gave a coquettish laugh. "I shall ask the *Oracle: Which of my suitors shall I marry?*" She flashed a sideways glance at Lord Berkeley as she spoke, but he was too occupied in observing the flight of a striking orange butterfly over the lawn.

"This is the procedure," explained Lady Frances. "You ask the question aloud, then shut your eyes and place your finger over these strange ancient symbols on page one. See, the symbols represent a heart, an axe, crossed swords, a circle, and a flower. Depending on the symbol you choose, this leads you to another page of the book, and the answer to your question. So, I have asked the question and I am shutting my eyes, and the symbol under my finger is . . . a circle."

Excitedly, she turned to the allotted page, and in a trembling voice declared, "It says that I shall marry *him whom I deserve!*"

Again, the brown eyes flickered momentarily toward the

dark-haired man at her side. But the moment was destroyed by a raucous burst of laughter from the Duke.

"My turn now, Frances! We'll test the *Oracle* by asking it something we know the answer to already. Now, I'm to be wed to a wealthy young woman before long. That's an undisputed fact. So I'm asking you, *Oracle: May I hope to receive a fortune?*"

He closed his eyes and stabbed his finger over the symbols, remarking, "The answer must be yes, for all England knows Miss Wellesley to be in possession of a splendid fortune."

Confidently, he turned the pages, read the answer, then flung the book down in disgust. "Bah! Stap me, Greville's right! The book is a heap of airy fiddle-faddle!"

"Well, out with it man," demanded Lady Brockway. "What did it say?"

"I asked, *May I hope to receive a fortune,*" said the Duke indignantly, "and the idiot book replied, *it would be folly to depend upon it.*"

Lady Brockway hooted with laughter. "Priceless, my dear Bart! Why, I have not enjoyed myself so much for years! Now, who shall be next?"

"Greville!" snapped Lady Frances promptly. "You must take your turn. After all, it was you who placed the book in my hands in the first place."

She favored him with a winning smile which made Candida so furious she pricked her finger with her embroidery needle.

Lady Frances thrust the book into Lord Berkeley's strong hands. "Here is the list of questions to choose from," she instructed, her white hand brushing his over the yellowed pages of the *Oracle.*

In good humored vein, Lord Berkeley entered into the spirit of the occasion. He declared in a firm bold tone, "I ask the *Oracle: That which I most desire: will it come to pass by day or by night?*"

Lady Frances pouted as she watched Lord Berkeley turning to the relevant page for his answer.

Clearly, mused Candida, she is disappointed that Lord Berkeley did not inquire of the *Oracle* whether he was to be honored with the hand of Lady Frances in marriage.

"Greville is frowning!" declared the Duke triumphantly. "No doubt his answer is as absurd as the one I received!"

Lord Berkeley shook his dark head. "It is a strange answer, to be sure. It appears that that which I most desire will come to pass *By night, by fierce heat and blazing light.*"

Inevitably, it was Lady Brockway who gave voice to the thought in everyone's heads: "Well only you can be the judge of the perspicacity of that answer, Greville. Since only you are aware of that which you most desire!"

"I think someone else should now take a turn with the *Oracle,*" suggested Lord Brockway.

To Candida's alarm and surprise, Lord Berkeley declared, "Miss Wilton! Will you not join in the fun with the *Oracle?*"

He was holding the book out to her. For the first time in many days, Candida allowed herself to meet the eyes of the man she loved. They were deep gray, their expression unreadable.

Hastily, aware of all faces turned toward her, Candida shook her head. "No, really, there is nothing I wish to know!"

"Nonsense!" declared Lady Frances, seizing the book from Lord Berkeley. "There is not a single woman on this earth who does not desire to know when, or if she shall marry." She thumbed through the list of questions, and murmured, "Now there is no point in asking the *Oracle,* on behalf of Miss Wilton, *Which of my suitors shall I marry* for the poor governess probably has no beaux at all!" She giggled at her own joke, and went on, "So we shall ask it simply, *Shall I marry?*"

She beckoned Candida across, compelling her to close her eyes and place her finger on the page of symbols.

"Ah, crossed swords is your symbol," announced Lady Frances. "That sounds highly significant to me!" She looked up the reply, and then informed the party in an astounded voice, "Well! It appears that Miss Wilton is *not* intended to remain a spinster all her life. For the *Oracle* says, Miss Wilton, that you will marry *He whom destiny has chosen for you.*"

"How exciting!" exclaimed Lady Brockway, waving her arms so vigorously that her parasol fell to the ground.

During the ensuing commotion, a footman rushed to lift the parasol and brush off the grass. Candida was strongly conscious of Lord Berkeley's gray eyes upon her. Although it was a searingly hot day, Candida felt suddenly chilled to the bone.

It was foolish in the extreme, she told herself, to be so affected by the absurd words of Lady Frances' *Oracle.* It was merely intended to provide a diversion, a little light entertainment. The questions and answers were never meant to be taken seriously.

Even so, the splinters of ice still stabbed at Candida's heart. She could never forget that her mother had declared, on her deathbed, that she desired Candida to marry the eldest son of the Duchess of Stratton. However much Candida fought against the notion, as she looked on the coarse, dissolute figure of the Duke, she could not ignore the harsh reality of the fact that this was the man her mother had chosen for her. This was the man destiny decreed she should marry.

Candida shivered. Can it be, that despite all my efforts, I shall in the end be forced to marry this man? Oh, surely Fate could not be so unkind?

Lady Frances, however, was still clearly enamored with the *Oracle.* "I cannot resist asking the book another question! Now let me see, which shall it be? Well, as it is my birthday, I do believe I have a right to indulge myself a little. So I shall ask the *Oracle: Am I considered pretty?*"

Confidently, she turned to the appropriate page, ready to read aloud the flattering reply, and then demure modestly as the gentlemen of the party chorused their assent to the *Oracle*'s perceptive reply.

But it was the Duke, leaning over Lady Frances' shoulder, who read out the answer to Lady Frances' question. "Am

I considered pretty? *Yes, on a moonless night when the candles are out!"*

In a rage, Lady Frances flung the book down on the grass. "Oh, it is silly to waste so much time on such nonsense!"

Smiling Lord Berkeley arose. "May I escort you for a turn around the garden, Lady Frances?"

"Why, that would be delightful!" trilled Lady Frances.

"Good notion, Greville. I'd like your opinion on the new turf on my bowling green," said Lord Brockway, levering himself out of his chair with the intention of accompanying the pair. Lady Brockway, however, hastily slapped him down again, muttering, "Stay where you are. No cause to exert yourself in this heat."

As Lord Berkeley and Lady Frances moved out of earshot, the Duke, never the most subtle of creatures, inquired of Lady Brockway, "Well, Madam, do you think you'll soon welcome Greville here as a son?"

Lady Brockway sighed, and narrowed her eyes as she regarded the girl in pale blue drifting across the lawn on the arm of the tall, handsome man.

"Naturally, if he asks for Frances' hand I should be more than delighted. But frankly, I doubt if he will. Frances is a dear, sweet girl, but I doubt if she possesses enough backbone to attract a man like Greville."

Candida, bent over her embroidery, was listening intently, her opinion of Lady Brockway rising in leaps and bounds.

"I don't agree with you at all," put in Lord Brockway, snapping his fingers to call back his dogs who were teasing his prize peacock on the far lawn. "A delicate little flower like Frances needs a strong man like Greville as a husband. I'd be proud to welcome him here as my son."

Lady Brockway gave him a glance of withering contempt. "Heavens, Brockway, do you never listen to a word I say! Of course, I should be the happiest woman in Sussex if Greville approached you for Frances' hand. But my own feeling is that she is not spirited enough to stand up to him."

The Duke grinned. "What about me, Lady Brockway?

Do I, too, require a strong-willed girl to match my impetuous temperament?"

"You are a weak, lazy creature, Bart," Lady Brockway informed him calmly, "and what you require is a girl with a will of iron, to keep you under control. Lady Angelica would have been perfect."

"But she's got no money, dash it," growled the Duke, kicking at a turf of grass with his boot. "So I'm stuck with this Wellesley girl from Hampshire. Her fortune will be most welcome, of course. But I know I shall loathe the very sight and sound of her."

That emotion, thought Candida tartly, is entirely mutual, my lord Duke!

"And what do you intend will happen to Greville once you are wed?" Lady Brockway inquired, brushing a fallen leaf from her green silk dress.

"Happen?" queried the Duke. "Why, everything will continue as before. I shall be spending most of the year alone in London, of course, so it will be convenient for Greville to continue running the estate."

Lady Brockway sighed. "Don't be absurd, Bart! You can't marry Miss Wellesley then leave her to rot at Stratton Hall while you rush off to London and squander her fortune! And the situation would be most unsatisfactory for Greville. It was all very well for him to manage the estate while you were living a carefree bachelor's life in Europe. But soon you will be a married man with responsibilities. Your place, Bart, is here in Sussex."

"Doesn't do for land to have two masters," said Lord Brockway with unaccustomed firmness. "If Bart stays in Sussex life will be untenable for Greville. They can't both manage the estate."

"That is precisely what I said about half an hour ago!" exclaimed Lady Brockway.

The Duke stood up and muttered irritably, "Oh, everything will shake down into place. You'll see."

"Typical!" snapped Lady Brockway. "As usual, you're refusing to face facts and make proper decisions!"

"One thing I have decided is that I'm not prepared to tolerate any more of your interference in my life!" shouted the Duke.

Candida watched, fascinated, as Lady Brockway shot to her feet—a tall, commanding woman with her hair brushed up, who gave the appearance of towering over the red-faced Duke.

"Now you listen to me," she rapped, prodding the Duke of Stratton in the chest. "I've known you since you were a yowling infant bandaged from head to foot in birth clothes. I took one look at you then and told myself, *that one is going to be a trouble-maker all his life*. And I was right. But I promised your poor mama that I would watch over you, and give you the best advice I could. If you don't want to listen to me you can pull your wig down over your ears. But you still won't stop me telling you what's right and what's best for you!"

The Duke roared with laughter. "My, there is no one like you, Lady Brockway! I declare, if I could only marry you, what a model citizen I should soon become!"

He raised a hand in greeting to Lady Lucy who had returned from her ride with Lord Rupert. Then it was time to leave.

Riding home across the springy turf of the Downs, the two men cantered on ahead, and Candida and Lady Lucy followed at a more leisurely pace. Candida asked the girl about her earlier ride with Lord Rupert, but it was soon evident that Lady Lucy's thoughts were elsewhere, for she inquired,

"Miss Wilton, what's that word beginning with p . . . it means you're absorbed in your thoughts and you don't notice what's going on around you."

"Preoccupied?" suggested Candida.

Lady Lucy nodded. "That's what I was thinking of. Well, Uncle Greville is very preoccupied at the moment. We've just passed two broken fences, as well as a haycart lying overturned in a field. Normally, Uncle Greville would be remarking on these things, ready to have them set right tomorrow, but he's just ridden straight past without even looking at them."

Candida smiled, musing on how Lady Lucy had changed of late. At one time, this town-reared and town-loving girl would not have recognized a haycart if it had run over her foot. But now she was developing a healthy curiosity about the sights and sounds of the countryside.

In answer to the girl's remark about her Uncle Greville, Candida commented casually, "No doubt Lord Berkeley is preoccupied thinking about the important work still to be done on the estate farms before the winter sets in. For although the harvest is now safely gathered in, the corn has still to be threshed."

Vigorously, Lady Lucy shook her head. "I don't believe he was thinking about the estate at all! His thoughts were on Lady Frances Brockway."

Candida laughed. "What fanciful notions you have, Lady Lucy!"

"It is not fanciful at all," retorted Lady Lucy hotly. "When I came back from my ride this afternoon, I heard him declare his love for Lady Frances. He gave her a ring, but asked her to keep their betrothal a secret until Uncle Bart has married Miss Wellesley!"

Chapter Eight

Up on the Downs, the line of flames blazed orange against the night sky. With the harvest in, the farmers were now burning off the stubble.

Through her open bedroom window, Candida watched the glowing flames, burning bright at first and then over the hours, dying gradually away leaving only the faint sooty smell of decay in the night air. For the farmers, the ritual of the burning of the stubble marked the end of the summer.

"And for me," whispered Candida, "it is the death of all my dreams. Any last lingering hopes I may have harbored that Lord Berkeley loved me as I do him, must now like the corn stubble, be smouldering ashes."

On their ride back from Brockway Hall, it had been impossible for Candida to prevent Lady Lucy from prattling indiscreetly about what she had overheard between Lord Berkeley and Lady Frances.

"I didn't mean to eavesdrop," she assured Candida with an impish smile. "I was behind the hedge near the bowling green, you see, and had I tried to move out of earshot, I should immediately have been observed and Lady Frances would have been furious with me. So I deemed it best to stay where I was."

Which was no great hardship, mused Candida wryly to

herself, as no doubt the little minx was quite enthralled by the romantic drama enfolding before her eyes.

"You know I have loved you dearly for many months, now, Uncle Greville told Lady Frances," said Lady Lucy excitedly. *"But until my brother is wed, we must be discreet, and keep our love a secret from the world."*

"In which case," said Candida firmly, "you should not be repeating all this to me."

But Lady Lucy had never in all her life been able to keep a secret. "Then he gave her the ring! I could not see it very well, but Lady Frances was delighted with it. *Why,* she cried, *it is the most exquisite thing! There is a diamond, an emerald, amethyst, ruby, epidote, sapphire, and a turquoise—and the initial letters of each jewel spell Dearest! Oh, how wonderfully romantic of you . . . my dearest!*"

Lady Lucy's imitation of Lady Frances' swooning tones was so cutting that Candida had been obliged to bite her lip hard to prevent herself bursting into laughter. Yet ironically, merriment had never been further from her heart. The ride home had seemed endless, and on their arrival at Stratton Hall, Candida had pleaded a headache and retired to her chamber. Mrs. Brewer had tapped on her door to inquire if she would like a tray of supper sent in, but this Candida had politely refused. She wanted only to be alone, to nurse her grief, and gather her courage to face what would now undoubtedly be a loveless future.

There can be no other man in my life, she told herself, gazing out at the glowing hillside. I knew from the moment I first set eyes on Lord Berkeley that he was my one true love. I have never been in love before. I am not the kind of giddy girl who whirls mindlessly from one beau to another. When I give my heart, it is forever.

A gust of wind got up, and for a few seconds the flames licked high against the horizon. Candida wondered if Lord Berkeley were somewhere on the hillside, watching the blaze. She remembered the question he had chosen to ask Lady Frances' *Oracle:*

That which I desire, will it come to pass by day or by night?

And the answer: *By night, by fierce heat and blazing light.*

A rueful smile touched Candida's lovely lips. Absurd to believe in the *Oracle* . . . and yet, at this moment he may be watching the stubble burn, knowing that his future is now assured.

Candida realized that from a practical point of view, the match with Lady Frances made sound sense for Lord Berkeley. For included in her handsome dowry was a magnificent house and estate owned by Lord Brockway in Derbyshire. By marrying Lady Frances, Lord Berkeley would solve in one stroke the delicate problem of what his role in life was to be after his brother wed Miss Candida Wellesley.

Except, of course, that such a wedding is most definitely not going to take place, thought Candida. But neither the Duke not Lord Berkeley are yet aware of that.

A chill stole over her as she recalled what the *Oracle* had decreed for her: that she would marry *him whom destiny has chosen for you.*

Don't believe it! She ordered herself fiercely. Uncle Montague is a stern, hard man; but even he would not be so cruel as to force you to marry a man who repels you so utterly. Tears misted Candida's blue eyes. "Yes," she whispered, "out of loyalty to my mother who gave her life for me, he would make me marry the Duke. Wherever in the world I hide, he will drag me back and compel me to accept the Duke's ring, and the Stratton tiara."

Candida turned away from the window, feeling numb with despair. But as she drew breath to blow out her candle, she heard the church bell in the village begin to ring.

Candida froze. It was well past midnight, she calculated. Who could be ringing the bell at this hour? And why? Could it be another girlish prank of Lady Lucy's?

She ran down the corridor to Lady Lucy's apartments. But the girl was lying innocently in her bed, fast asleep. And still, insistently, the sound of the church bell rang out over the Sussex night air.

Candida didn't stop to think. She flew downstairs, running instinctively to answer the summons of the church bell. Since time immemorial country folk had rung the bell to warn of danger, plague, floods, fire, and invasion. Not for a second did it occur to Candida that it was dangerous for a girl like herself to run alone through dark country lanes into the village. She did not stop to reflect that it would be safer for her to remain in the house, and let others go down to the church in the village and investigate what was wrong.

No, it was as if she were responding to some primitive, ancient call—the call of someone in distress. A call which must be answered without delay.

Candida was halfway down the drive when she heard the furious thunder of hooves behind her. In the darkness, she recognized Lord Berkeley's splendid gray. Wasting no time on questions or scoldings with respect to Candida venturing out alone, Lord Berkeley reached down, seized her around the waist, and in one easy movement lifted her up onto the horse in front of him. And together, they galloped on toward the village and that mysteriously ringing church bell.

Behind them, Stratton Hall was gradually coming awake as servants lit the lamps and went in search of the master of the house. Despite her anxiety about what awaited them at the church, Candida felt a rush of exhilaration as the surefooted gray sped them toward the village. Lord Berkeley's strong arm was around her, and her head was thrown back, resting against his broad shoulder. For a short, joyous while, all thoughts of Lady Frances and his future with her were driven from Candida's mind. She was conscious only that she was so close to the man she loved that she could feel the warmth of his breath on her cool cheek.

Then the village lay before them. Although it was one o'clock in the morning, the streets were crowded as if it were market day. But there was no laughter, no merry quips. Every man, woman, and child was running toward the church, their faces grim in the light of the flaring torches carried above their heads.

As the gray cantered into the village square, Candida heard a murmur of relief from the waiting crowd.

"It is Lord Berkeley!"

"I told you he'd be first to come from the Hall!"

Yes, thought Candida as the dark-haired man swung her down from the horse. Of course Lord Berkeley would be the first to answer the distress call. No doubt at this moment the Duke is lying snoring in his bed, feeling aggrieved that the clanging of the church bell is disturbing his drunken dreams.

At the door of the old Norman church, they were met by the tall figure of the Rector. "Thank heavens you have come," he said quietly to Lord Berkeley. "The villagers are enraged. There was talk of them marching in a body on Stratton Hall itself . . ."

"Something must be done!" shouted an angry voice from the crowd. "We won't tolerate this any longer."

The ringing of the bell suddenly stopped. With grave authority, Lord Berkeley addressed the Rector. "Tell me quickly what has occurred here tonight?"

The Rector answered, "It was not I who rang the bell, my lord. I awoke—"

"I rang it!" screamed a red-haired woman, pushing her way out of the church. "I rang the bell because my daughter, my innocent young Hannah, has been snatched away by a man in a robe! I saw him! I saw him take her!"

The woman broke down and began to sob hysterically. Impulsively, Candida ran forward and drew the weeping woman into her arms.

"It is Mrs. Sewell," Lord Berkeley quietly informed Candida. "She is the wife of the head gardener at Stratton Hall. My God! That such a thing should happen . . ."

He turned to the villagers, who were now seething with anger. "Hannah Sewell isn't the first young girl to go missing! There's been others!"

"Why has nothing been done? Why has this Robed Raider not been brought to justice?"

A young woman elbowed her way forward and shouted, "Our daughters are no longer safe! Every mother in this village now lives in fear and trembling of what might befall our girls. If the Duke won't take action against this Robed Raider, then I assure you, we, the women of Stratton, will take matters into our own hands! We'll search every house, cottage, and farm in the county until we unearth that villain, and when we find him we'll have him hanged, drawn and quartered!"

Lord Berkeley raised his hand. Despite their fear and fury, Lord Berkeley had over the years earned their loyalty and respect, and they fell immediately silent.

"I want all of you to know that both my brother and I are deeply distressed by what has happened here tonight. And I give you my word of honor that the Robed Raider will be brought to justice—and soon. I promise you, I shall not rest until Hannah Sewell, and the other unfortunate girls who have fallen prey to this evil man—all of them *will be found.*"

There was a short pause, and then a burly blacksmith, who was the Head Man of the village, stepped forward. "We know you to be a man of your word, my lord. We trust you to keep your promise."

Lord Berkeley nodded. "Go back to your homes now. I shall return here tomorrow and talk to each and every one of you. In the meantime, I want you all to give thought to the question of who this Robed Raider might be. If you have any information, however slender, concerning his possible identity, you must reveal this to me tomorrow. But first, I must go and talk to poor Mrs. Sewell."

The murmuring crowd dispersed, and Lord Berkeley walked through the church to the vestry, where Candida had tactfully taken the sobbing Mrs. Sewell. Gradually, Candida had quieted the head gardener's wife, and drawn from her the full story. When the grim-faced Lord Berkeley entered the vestry, Candida told him what she had learned.

"Mr. Sewell is away tonight, visiting his brother in Lewes. I gather that Hannah arose in the night to attend to her new puppy which sleeps under the apple tree in the garden. I think it must have been taken away from its mother too young, because it tends to whimper a great deal in the night."

"I woke up," wept Mrs. Sewell, "and looked out of the window. There was Hannah, kneeling under the apple tree. There was a full moon, so I could see everything well. Then I heard the garden gate creak, and there *He* was!"

She buried her head once more in her hands. Candida murmured soothingly, "Come now, Mrs. Sewell. Try to tell Lord Berkeley exactly what you saw. The more you can tell us, the easier it will be to catch the villain, and bring Hannah home safely."

"He was wearing this long dark robe with a hood that all but covered his face," stammered Mrs. Sewell. "Hannah was so absorbed with the puppy, she didn't see him till he was right upon her. I called out—I was frantic—but he acted so fast. He had a long scarf, or handkerchief in his hand which he wrapped tight around her mouth. Then he dragged her out of the garden. The puppy was barking blue murder, but he was tied up. I ran downstairs to give chase, but by the time I'd got through the garden, they were nowhere in sight."

"Did you see his horse, Mrs. Sewell?" asked Lord Berkeley gently.

She shook her head. "The garden wall is high, you see. I couldn't see anything beyond it. Oh, my poor Hannah! Whatever is to become of her?"

Candida and Lord Berkeley exchanged a grave glance across Mrs. Sewell's head.

"She cannot be far away," said Lord Berkeley reassuringly. "And I have given my word to everyone in the village that the Robed Raider will be run to the ground in the very near future."

"I am convinced that the best thing would be for you to return home and rest now, Mrs. Sewell," said Candida. Then, observing the drawn expression on the older woman's face, she suggested, "Would you like me to stay with you for the night?"

Lord Berkeley nodded. "That is an excellent notion, Miss Wilton. With Tom Sewell away in Lewes, it would be understandable if his wife felt nervous of being on her own in her cottage tonight."

"I could do with some company right enough," admitted Mrs. Sewell, who looked now on the point of exhaustion.

"I shall take you home immediately," said Candida, "and you shall have a soothing hot drink in bed."

Lord Berkeley escorted them through the deserted village streets to the flint stone cottage that was the Sewells' home. While Mrs. Sewell fumbled with the latch, and felt for the tinderbox to light the door candle, Lord Berkeley laid a hand on Candida's arm. In the moonlight, his countenance was clearly visible to her. A smile softened the hard lines of his face, and his gray eyes gleamed with a warmth and affection which made Candida's heart beat suddenly faster.

"Thank you," he said simply.

"Have no fear, Mrs. Sewell will be well looked after," Candida replied, thinking how tired he looked, and how she longed to reach up and kiss away the blue shadows under his eyes.

"No." He smiled. "That is not what I meant. I am grateful to you for being there with me tonight . . . for answering with me the summons of the church bell. It meant a great deal to me to have you by my side, Miss Wilton."

And before Candida could utter another word, he quickly bade her goodnight and disappeared into the dark streets of Stratton Village. Candida immediately turned her mind to Mrs. Sewell, who was beginning to fuss that her kitchen was not tidy enough for a lady like Miss Wilton to enter.

"There now, you see I told Hannah to wash up our supper plates—we had a tasty bit of bread and cheese, as you can see—and she didn't do it and I scolded her, and now, oh mercy me, what do you think has happened to her, Miss Wilton?"

Observing that Mrs. Sewell was on the verge of hysteria, Candida adopted a kindly, but firm tone. "Now leave those plates alone, Mrs. Sewell, and get yourself up to bed. One thing's certain: wherever Hannah is at this moment, you are not going to help her by becoming agitated. We must all try to secure a good night's sleep so we are fresh to assist Lord Berkeley in the morning."

After a while, Candida climbed the rickety stairs and gave Mrs. Sewell a soothing drink of hot honey and lemon. As the older woman sipped from the earthenware cup, Candida remarked, "Tomorrow your husband will be back from Lewes. Oh dear, I hope he will be so upset by the news that he insists on mounting a personal search for the Robed Raider."

"My Tom does what I tell him to do," Mrs. Sewell said curtly. "He may be head gardener at the Hall, with a staff of twenty doing his bidding, but in this cottage, *my word is law.* And I've decided that if anyone can find my Hannah it's Lord Berkeley. He's a good man, you know, Miss Wilton, which is more than can be said for that so-called brother of his."

Candida took the cup from Mrs. Sewell's hand, realizing that the older woman was becoming increasingly drowsy.

"What I want to know is," murmured Mrs. Sewell, "where was the Duke tonight? Why did he not answer the distress call of the church bell?"

"Oh . . . er, unfortunately the Duke is suffering from a mild fever at the moment," lied Candida. "Nothing serious, I'm happy to say, but the doctor has confined him to bed."

"You're pulling the wrong pig by the ear," muttered Mrs. Sewell. "He's confined to bed right enough, in a drunken stupor, I'll be bound. He's a bad 'un, that one. Blood will out, you mark my words. Blood will out . . ." Her head drooped onto the pillow, and she fell fast asleep.

Bone weary, Candida climbed up into the attic, and laid herself down on Hannah's simple straw mattress. It smelled of fragrant herbs, and by the light of her candle, Candida noticed that although the tiny room contained nothing but the mattress and an embroidered kneeler, it was scrupulously fresh and clean.

Poor Hannah, thought Candida as she stretched out on

the mattress. Where are you now, I wonder? How terrified you must be, by now so many miles from your home, and with only the dreadful Robed Raider for company.

But at least Hannah has one advantage over us, Candida mused. By now she must be aware of the true identity of the Robed Raider. Is he someone she knows, I wonder? When he pulled away the hood of his robe, did Hannah gasp to find herself looking into the familiar face of the Duke of Stratton?

Where was the Duke tonight? Candida wondered. Having pleaded her headache, and confined herself to her bedchamber, Candida had no notion of the Duke's movements during the evening. Certainly, there had been no sound of carousing from the saloons of Stratton Hall. Presumably, then, the Duke had been out at a tavern, or drinking and dining with his rumbustious companions.

Tomorrow, Candida vowed, I will talk to Lord Berkeley once more about the robe I found at Stratton Hall. Painful though it may be, I must voice to him my suspicions that the Robed Raider is none other than his own brother. Did not Lord Berkeley himself implore everyone in the village to come to him with any evidence they may have which would help to bring the Robed Raider to justice? Admittedly, last time I approached Lord Berkeley on this matter, there was a strained atmosphere between us. But now all has changed. Tonight, as we stood before the hollyhocks framing the door of this cottage, it was as if, once again, all titles, all social conventions were stripped from us.

Our positions in the world (whether real in his case, or assumed in mine, for I am not the Jane Wilton he believes me to be) were suddenly irrelevant. Once again it was purely a matter that he was a man and I was a woman. And between us, there was such a deep mental understanding, that no words, no actions were necessary. Together, we had come to the church, and done what was required of us.

Candida sighed. Naturally, her heart went out to poor Hannah Sewell, at this moment so frightened, and so alone. And yet, thinking selfishly, mused Candida, how satisfying it was to act thus in total concert with Lord Berkeley. Oh, if only it could be that he and I were free to wed, free to live together at Stratton Hall!

Closing her eyes, Candida indulged in her favorite, and most impossible dream.

How wonderful it would be, she thought, if the miracle happened, and Lord Berkeley and I found ourselves master and mistress of Stratton Hall! Oh, how happy I should be. The house would be filled with flowers, music and laughter . . . there would be balls, with the garden lit by a thousand lights and the cream of Sussex society invited.

But it would not be one long selfish round of pleasure. For there is the estate to be managed. It would be my duty to know each and every one of the tenants by name . . . to be familiar with their families . . . to give advice, help, and encouragement to these loyal citizens who have served so faithfully before the illustrious Stratton crest.

Candida fell asleep that night with Lord Berkeley's last words echoing in her ears . . . *It meant a great deal to me to have you by my side.*

But as always, the harsh light of dawn brought cold reality. Throwing aside the coarse woollen blanket, Candida scrambled to her feet and went down into the garden. There had been a heavy dew, and the spiders's webs strung across the branches of the old apple tree were frosted with moisture. The puppy sat forlornly under the tree, his velvety eyes mourning the absence of his young mistress.

Candida bent and stroked the puppy's ears. Your mistress has been snatched away, she silently informed the forlorn puppy. And my love, too, is now lost to me. For the man I love is betrothed to Lady Frances Brockway. It is she, not I, who will stand by his side. And at the end of the day, it is she whom he will take into his arms; she whom he will hold and caress, far into the night . . . .

The thought was unbearable. Swiftly, Candida returned to the house. Mrs. Sewell was already in the kitchen firing the range with bundles of dry birch twigs. She reached into a net hanging out of reach of any insects on the floor, and produced a loaf of crusty bread.

"May I offer you some breakfast, Miss Wilton? I've only bread and cheese but you're welcome to share with me."

In truth, having missed her supper last night, Candida was ravenous. Gladly, she sat down at the scrubbed kitchen table, and enjoyed a large chunk of delicious bread and mellow, crumbly cheese.

As she took her leave, Mrs. Sewell suddenly took Candida's hand, and said awkwardly, "I was in a right cabobbled state last night, Miss. But I'm recovered now. My husband will be home soon, and I've every faith that Lord Berkeley will find my Hannah for me."

Candida smiled reassuringly. "I know he will, Mrs. Sewell."

The woman gave Candida a direct glance. "It was good of you to stay with me, Miss Wilton. I want you to know that if there's anything, at any time, that I can do for you—well, don't you hesitate to ask."

Candida walked slowly back through the village, and up the winding road to Stratton Hall. With her mind in a turmoil over recent events, she found it most relaxing simply observing the early morning sights and sounds around her. There was the creak of chains as the first buckets of the day were lowered into the deep water wells . . . the soft, welcoming whinny of the horses grazing in the fields . . . the lowing of the cows as they waited for the milkmaids . . . and above in the trees, the birds sang joyously, bringing an answering smile of pleasure to Candida's lovely face.

As Candida entered Stratton Hall, she was met by the housekeeper, who drew her into her room and demanded to know all the details of the midnight drama in the village.

"Poor little Hannah Sewell," said Mrs. Brewer, with a shake of her gray head. "She's barely seventeen years old. My heart goes out to all those who are mothers in that village of Stratton. As if they hadn't got enough to worry about, they won't dare to let their daughters out of their sight now."

Candida knew she was referring to the Duke's intention to raze all the present village dwellings to the ground. The thought of the Duke prompted her to inquire, with an indifferent air,

"The Duke . . . was he in residence when the church bell began to peal last night?"

Mrs. Brewer shook her head. "No, he did not return until the early hours of the morning, and what a ruck he caused too, throwing his saddle through the Blue Drawing Room window, smashing both the glass and a beautiful figurine that's been in his family for generations."

So, it is just as I suspected, thought Candida. The Duke *is* the Robed Raider. Oh, I must speak to Lord Berkeley without delay!

But Lord Berkeley, Mrs. Brewer informed her, had left the house early and was not expected back until midday. Meanwhile, there were other matters claiming Candida's attention. She must change the crushed dress in which she had slept all night. There were Lady Lucy's lessons to be resumed. And also, most unexpectedly Candida found she had received a letter.

"It came by the night mail," said Mrs. Brewer, handing Candida a package on which she recognized her cousin Clara's seal.

But it was midmorning before Candida had the opportunity to peruse her cousin's letter. Having refreshed herself and changed into a clean dark green dress, Candida took Lady Lucy down to the lake, and set her to paint a watercolor of the elegant swans gliding across the water. Inevitably, the restless red-haired girl took some time to settle to her task, but at last she set to work, and Candida eagerly broke open the seal..

She quickly discovered that there were in fact two letters. But it was her dear cousin Clara's which Candida read first.

My Dearest Candida (or should I say Jane?), Oh, how intrigued I am, being required to address this letter to you as

Miss Jane Wilton at Stratton Hall! Naturally, I am expiring of curiosity, for it is infuriating of you to tell me no more than that you are obliged to pose as a Governess to the Duke of Stratton's ward. I laughed at this until the tears ran down my cheeks, for I well remember what a naughty child you were—quite unmanageable until the extraordinary Miss Bone arrived to be your Governess!

But have no fear, your secret is safe. Your dreadful Uncle Montague is convinced you are residing here with me (and how I wish you were, dear Candida, for Guildford is extraordinary dull at present). Sir Montague has sent a letter for you which I duly enclose.

I was pleased to receive your all too brief letter about your life at Stratton Hall. Lady Brockway sounds too formidable and Lady Angelica quite bizarre! I am confused, however, by your reference to Lady Angelica's cousin, Sir Hugh Legatt, who, you say, hails from Guildford. I assure you, we are well acquainted with all the families of importance in this neighborhood, but I cannot recall meeting anyone of this name.

We are all in the best of health, and enjoying this glorious summer weather. I look forward to hearing from you soon and learning all!

I remain, your most affectionate cousin Clara.

Candida brushed away a tear as she reread her cousin's reassuring, friendly words. Clara had been fortunate enough to marry young, and very happily. She was devoted to her handsome husband and two thriving young sons. How Candida envied their contented life at their large rambling manor house in Guildford. There would be boating parties on the lake, with the boys screaming with laughter. Expeditions to Box Hill . . . dancing by starlight around the fountain on the terrace.

Lucky Clara, thought Candida with a wistful sigh. But how fortunate I am to have such an affectionate cousin. To be sure, without her loyal support, I should never have been able to masquerade as a governess here at Stratton Hall.

Resolutely, Candida turned to the missive from her Uncle Montague. Written in his spare gaunt hand, the letter was characteristically brief and to the point. He had returned home to Hampshire from his shooting party in the north, and found a letter awaiting him from the Duke of Stratton. The Duke declared his wish to be married immediately after Christmas, and to this end Candida was to present herself at Stratton Hall on December 27th.

Candida shook with fury. *Present myself* indeed! she raged. How dare he!

She read on, and to her surprise gathered that even Sir Montague had been taken aback by the indifferent manner in which the Duke was approaching his marriage.

Although I appreciate that the Duke is a man who bears many demanding responsibilities, nevertheless, I am surprised that he has not even requested a likeness of you, Candida. I have, therefore, taken it upon myself to send him a miniature of yourself which you will recall was painted to mark your eighteenth birthday.

Candida shot to her feet, her face ashen. "Oh no!" she whispered, horrified. "This will ruin everything! Oh, Uncle Montague, how could you!"

Startled, Lady Lucy laid down her brush. "Are you unwell, Miss Wilton? You look most strange!"

Candida laid a hand on the girl's shoulder, and with a great effort of will, controlled her voice. "I am perfectly well, Lucy! I stood up a little too suddenly, that is all. Oh, but your painting is coming along well! You have caught the blue of the sky to perfection."

Somehow, Candida managed to conduct a normal conversation with Lady Lucy about the art of watercolor painting, but her mind was in turmoil. So little time, she thought frantically. It is vital now that I find Lord Berkeley and persuade him that the Duke is the Robed Raider. For it is now only a matter of time before I, myself, am exposed as an imposter! At all costs, I must quit Stratton Hall before Uncle Montague's letter, and my portrait, are delivered to the Duke.

Chapter Nine

Conveniently for Candida, Lady Lucy's modiste was due to call at Stratton Hall that morning. Lady Lucy herself was furious at the prospect of being required to stand still for hours while the dressmaker fitted her new autumn ensembles. But for Candida the event was most fortuitous. It gave her an unexpected few hours free from her schoolroom duties. Hours which she knew she must put to good use.

With Lady Lucy (complaining bitterly) safely installed in her apartments with the long suffering dressmaker, Candida ran down the main staircase and turned the handle of the side door behind the bronze statuette of Diana. It was locked.

Candida was so angry, she felt almost physically ready to attack the door and break it down with her bare hands. But common sense prevailed. She went quickly up to the housekeeper's room, and politely asked Mrs. Brewer if she would unlock the door.

"I think I may have dropped my handkerchief in there the other day," explained Candida. "So silly of me to fuss, but it was the only one I possess with fine lace around the edge, and I don't want to lose it."

Mrs. Brewer understood perfectly, and with her keys jangling at her ample waist, led the way down to the side-room. Once inside, Candida maintained, for Mrs. Brewer's benefit, a plausible charade of searching for her lace-edged handkerchief. But all the time, her eyes were drawn to the back of the door.

It was bare. The Robed Raider's disguise had gone.

Candida felt despair clawing at her heart. As she thanked Mrs. Brewer and made her way out to the stables, Candida realized that without the robe, it would be extremely difficult to persuade Lord Berkeley that the Robed Raider resided within the walls of Stratton Hall.

My one piece of evidence, thought Candida bitterly, and I allowed it to slip through my fingers! Obviously, the Duke was wearing it last night when he abducted Hannah Sewell. Stratton Hall is so vast, the robe could now be hidden in any one of a hundred rooms, a thousand secret places.

The kindly groom saddled up a placid jennet, and Candida rode down into the village in search of Lord Berkeley. Observing her in the village square, Mrs. Sewell came hurrying toward her.

"Oh, Miss Wilton, I'm so glad to have caught you. I wanted you to have these. Just to thank you, you know, for being so kind last night."

She thrust into Candida's arms a beautiful nosegay of cottage garden flowers, dark, velvety snapdragons, red dahlias, wild pink roses, and gently blue borage.

"How pretty!" exclaimed Candida in delight. Then she inquired hesitantly, "Is there any news?"

Mrs. Sewell shook her head. "None. But I feel calmer in myself now that my husband's home. And Lord Berkeley's been down this morning, talking to everyone in the village. We all feel more reassured now."

"Has Lord Berkeley returned to the Hall?" asked Candida. "I did not pass him on the road."

"I believe I heard him express the intention of riding out over the cornfields to see that the stubble had been properly burnt," replied Mrs. Sewell.

After thanking the head gardener's wife most sincerely for the flowers, Candida turned left, up a steep flint and chalk path that would eventually bring her out near the first of the

Stratton estate cornfields. As she rode, her observant eye noted how the countryside had changed since she first arrived in Sussex.

The blazing, brilliant sunshine of August had gone now, replaced by the more mellow September light. In the hedgerows, the blackberries were ripening and the rosehips were turning a bright glossy red. The evenings, too, were beginning to draw in, arousing a longing for crackling apple-log fires and cinnamon scented mulled wine.

Candida scanned the horizon, the burnt off cornfields, and the lush green grazing lands—but there was no sign of the tall figure of Lord Berkeley. She rode on, over a chalky ridge and realized that she was now in an area of the Downs that she had not previously explored. It was rough land, clearly not used for cultivation or sheep. There were no workers, no farmers here. The only occupants visible to Candida were a family of rabbits, bobbing in and out of warrens on the hillside.

She sat still for a moment, smiling at their activity. And then a sudden movement caught her eye. Below her, on a narrow chalk path which skirted the high ridge, was a rider. His mount was a gleaming black hunter, and the rider was wearing a long, dark brown robe.

Candida sat stunned, amazed at the Robed Raider's audacity. It was one thing for the Duke to don his disguise at night—but to gallop thus in broad daylight! He must be drunk, Candida decided, urging her jennet forward. Clearly, his brain is completely addled. Having gulled everyone for so long, he probably believes that he could now actually stroll through Stratton village in his robe and *still* remain undetected!

And yet, Candida realized, he is not as stupid as to ride glaringly against the skyline. Cunningly, the Duke is keeping to the low path. But where is to he going? And for what purpose?

Candida had no hesitation in following him. It did not occur to her that she might be placing herself in danger. That if he turned and saw her—he might become violent, might even abduct her as he had snatched the other three unfortunate girls.

None of this entered Candida's mind for her only thought was that the Robed Raider might lead her to Hannah. At the very least, by observing him this closely, she was certain to discover more important information about him, which she would be able to pass on to Lord Berkeley.

As far as I am aware, thought Candida excitedly, beginning to enjoy the thrill of the chase, I am the only person who has seen the villain in daylight. My, but he is going at a lick! I hope my poor little jennet can keep pace with him.

Fortunately, Candida was an expert horsewoman. The jennet trusted her, and entering into the spirit of the adventure, gave of her best. The man on the black hunter finally left the chalk path, and cut across into a wild valley which Candida had never noticed before. At first sight, it appeared to be an overgrown mass of thorn, yew, and beech trees.

Candida reined in her horse, watching the Robed Raider dismount. He left the black hunter, and plunged into the tangled depths of the wood.

Perplexed, Candida trotted the jennet a little further on, then dismounted and approached the edge of the wood. What faced her was a fairly solid line of thorn trees, with two of them forming an overgrown but distinct gap, through which the Robed Raider had gone.

Taking a deep breath, Candida stepped between the thorn trees, into the wood. And then, as she surveyed the yew, the beech and thorn around her, she realized where she was.

Why it is not a wood at all, she thought. It is a maze! The Stratton estate maze. I recall Lord Berkeley and the Duke arguing over what should be done with it. And these thorns, beeches, and yews are not trees at all. They are overgrown hedges, which at one time formed the clipped walls of the maze.

In fact, to a discerning eye, the moss-strewn paths of the

maze were just visible. But which direction, pondered Candida, had the Robed Raider followed? There was no clue. Nothing to give Candida any guidance whatsoever.

As there is nothing else for it, she decided, I shall simply be obliged to trust luck. For one thing is certain: there is no turning back now. I know the Robed Raider is somewhere in this maze. And I am determined to find him!

Taking a deep breath, she plunged down the center path, then turned left, right, and left again. At every turn she was obliged to fight her way through slapping beech twigs, rending thorns, and patches of lethal stinging nettles. Before long, her hands were badly scratched and her dress and stockings torn beyond repair.

My, mused Candida, her natural sense of humor asserting itself, how fortunate it is that my days as governess are numbered. For at the rate I am ruining my dresses, I shall soon have nothing left to wear!

After five long minutes of rough exploration, Candida sensed that she was approaching the maze's center. The hedges here were so overgrown and dense that they blocked nearly all the light from the sky.

Candida shivered in the gloom that seemed unnaturally still. Not even a bird's song or a squirrel's rustle disturbed the uncanny silence.

So when the sound came, it was as loud as a pistol shot. As the sharp *crack!* echoed through the air, Candida whirled around, nerve-alert, too strung up even to scream.

She stood bemused, unable to believe her eyes. The sound had come, quite simply, from a person's foot treading on a beech twig. But it was not the Robed Raider who stood before Candida on the mossy path. It was the Lady Angelica Kerr.

She was, as always, dressed quite exquisitely in a wide hooped pale primrose satin dress. The powdered hair, brushed six inches high off her unlined forehead, was decorated with little yellow bows, each centered with a tiny pearl. In her jewelled hand she carried a large brimmed beribboned sun bonnet.

Lady Angelica seemed perfectly composed. "Why, whatever are you doing here in the maze, Miss Wilton?"

Relief flooded through Candida. For one terrifying moment she had believed that the Robed Raider himself was upon her!

"Did you see him?" Candida demanded urgently. "Did you see the Robed Raider?"

Lady Angelica's blue eyes widened. "The Robed . . . you mean he is here, in this maze?" Her voice rose to shriek. "Oh, but this is dreadful! I was out walking, and suddenly found I had blundered into what I believed to be a wood, but of course I now realize it is the Stratton maze. And the Robed Raider, you say, is in here with us? My, but what are we to do!"

She leaned weakly against a beech sapling and whispered, "You really saw him, Miss Wilton?"

"Not his face, unfortunately," replied Candida. "But yes, I most definitely witnessed him enter the maze."

"I cannot bear it!" wailed Lady Angelica. "I insist that we leave this horrible place immediately. Otherwise, the most appalling fate might befall us!" She grasped Candida's arm. "Come, I believe I can find the way out. But we must hurry!"

She drew Candida down a side path and began to run left, down a track lined with toadstools.

"No," said Candida confidently, "this is not the correct way out, Lady Angelica. We must turn right here."

"But how can you tell?" asked the girl in the primrose yellow. "It is all so overgrown, and frightfully confusing."

"I was terrified of getting lost in the maze," Candida told her, "so at each turn I made, I laid down a flower. See, there is a dahlia there, indicating that we must turn right. And further on, we shall find borage, wild roses, and snapdragons showing us the way."

Mrs. Sewell's nosegay, which Candida had tucked into the girdle of her dress, had proved invaluable in the maze.

Lady Angelica gasped in admiration. "My, how astoundingly clever you are, Miss Wilton! Lady Lucy is fortunate indeed to have you as her governess."

"There is no time to lose," said Candida, hurrying Lady Angelica down the path. "The Robed Raider left his hunter near the entrance to the maze. In due time, he is certain to come back and remount. If we position ourselves in a secluded situation nearby, we may be able to see his face."

"Yes, we shall identify him!" exclaimed Lady Angelica. "Oh, how brave you are, Miss Wilton, and what an adventure we are having!"

It is no adventure for Hannah Sewell, and the other two unfortunate girls snatched by the Robed Raider, thought Candida, her eyes fixed firmly on the ground as she followed the trail she had left with her flowers.

At last, the clear blue sky was visible once more over the Downs. The two girls had reached the edge of the maze.

"He left his hunter down in the hollow, near the stream . . ." Candida's voice trailed away. She blinked hard, wondering if the sunlight had temporarily blinded her, but no, the glossy black hunter was nowhere in sight.

"Oh, how infuriating!" cried Lady Angelica. "He must have doubled back, left the maze, and made his escape."

Candida nodded, twisting absently at a tendril of golden hair. "He must be very familiar with the layout of the maze," she mused.

Lady Angelica shrugged. "There's only one man in all Sussex who knows his way around the maze, and that's Greville."

"Lord Berkeley?" queried Candida, her face suddenly pale.

Lady Angelica stared at her. "Oh surely you don't believe . . . why, it is not possible. The notion is preposterous!"

Candida turned away, but Lady Angelica spun her around to face her. "You know something, don't you? Tell me! You must tell me what you know!"

"I . . . I found a dark brown robe in a seldom-used room at Stratton Hall," stammered Candida. "I told Lord Berkeley about it. But he brushed me aside, and refused to listen." She shook her head. "No, I will not believe it is he! I will not!"

Lady Angelica looked thoughtful, and began ticking off the points on her long fingers as she spoke. "Let us consider the facts. One; he is familiar with the maze. Two; the robe was found at Stratton Hall, and he behaved evasively when you mentioned it to him. Three—"

"But *why* should he want to abduct young girls in this dreadful manner?" demanded Candida, on the verge of tears.

"Mmm, tell me what color hair had Hannah Sewell?" asked Lady Angelica.

Candida spread her hands. "I have no notion, but her mother had very pretty auburn tresses."

"Ah!" exclaimed Lady Angelica in triumph. "It is likely, then, that Hannah inherited her mother's shade. Are you aware, Miss Wilton, that the other two victims of the Robed Raider each had red hair?"

"No, I did not know that," said Candida slowly. "But what significance does it have with regard to our suspicions about Lord Berkeley?"

"Why does he wear that hooded robe?" demanded Lady Angelica. "I'll tell you: to hide the scar on his left cheek. And why does he only abduct girls with red hair? Because it was a Parisian copper-head who caused that scar!"

Candida wanted to listen to no more of this. Each new piece of intelligence sounded so damning, so plausible when uttered by Lady Angelica. But she was now in full cry, and would not be checked.

"As far as I understand the incident," she said rapidly, "there was a quarrel, in Paris, between Bart and Greville over this red-haired girl. Greville accused Bart of treating her dishonorably. They came to blows over it, and in the course of the fight, Bart smashed at Greville with a silver candle-stick, scarring his cheek. Greville then gallantly escorted the girl to her lodgings. But the irony of it was, that when he returned home, he found that the ungrateful minx had stolen a pouchful of gold from his cloak!" Lady Angelica's thin face creased with laughter.

Candida had often wondered how Lord Berkeley had acquired that scar. Now she knew, and she dearly wished she did not! "Are you seriously suggesting that Lord Berkeley now has some incredible vendetta against girls with red hair? Oh, I can't believe that," said Candida impatiently, with a dismissive wave of her hand.

Lady Angelica's eyebrows rose. "My dear Miss Wilton! As a mere governess, you have travelled little and have but limited experience of the world. You must take my word for it that men's passions are strange, unpredictable things. When a man has been crossed by a woman, he neither forgives nor forgets!"

Candida fell silent. For a moment, she had forgotten her governess pose, and had spoken to Lady Angelica as herself, Candida Wellesley. I must not make that mistake again, resolved Candida. Although I have but a short time left in this demure role, I must ensure that I carry it through to the end. There is no point in exposing myself now, when my task is so nearly completed.

"Something has just occurred to me, Lady Angelica," said Candida quietly. "When the church bell sounded the alarm last night, Lord Berkeley appeared in the drive behind me, and we rode into the village together. So he could not possibly have been the person who snatched Hannah Sewell!"

Lady Angelica's cold blue eyes narrowed. "Did you witness him leaving either the house or the stables?"

"Well, no," admitted Candida. "I was in such a state of agitation over the ringing of the bell, my only thought was to reach the village quickly . . ."

"So it was possible for Greville to have snatched up Hannah, locked her in one of the disused cottages on the edge of the village, and taken the short cut through the coppice leading to the Stratton Hall drive." Lady Angelica brushed away a beech leaf entwined in the ribbons of her dress. "It would have taken a steady nerve to act thus. But Greville has always been capable of keeping a cool head in a crisis."

"That it should be he!" Candida whispered in disbelief. "I had thought, you see, when I found the robe, that the villain must be the Duke himself."

Lady Angelica threw back her powdered head and

laughed delightedly. "Bart! Why, surely you realize that such an ale-head as he would never possess the wit to pose as the Robed Raider! Why, in the middle of a midnight raid he would most likely have fallen off his hunter and rolled drunkenly into a ditch."

On reflection, Candida saw the truth of her words. How foolish of me to have suspected the Duke, she thought. For even if he had managed to effect an abduction of one of the girls, he would never have been able to resist boasting about his exploits in the morning.

Heavy with despair, she gazed at Lady Angelica. "What are we to do?"

"Nothing," replied Lady Angelica firmly. "Not until we have definite proof. For if we reveal now what we suspect, we may frighten Greville—if indeed he is the Robed Raider—into covering his tracks." She twirled her pretty sunbonnet in her hand as she considered the problem.

"The hunter," said Candida suddenly. "The Robed Raider's horse . . ."

"Black Knight from the Stratton Stables," cried Lady Angelica excitedly. "If we discover that Greville was riding that horse today, then we shall know for sure that he is the villain. You must find out, Miss Wilton. You must determine if Black Knight was Greville's mount today!"

Dinner that day was not served until the late hour of six o'clock. This was because of Lady Lucy who, having reduced her dressmaker to tears, had suddenly realized that she was ravenously hungry. Instead of ringing her bell and requesting that some light refreshment be brought to her, Lady Lucy had decided it would be more exciting to make her own foray into the kitchen.

It was half-past one, a time when Mrs. Brewer traditionally took a short nap. Lady Lucy had crept into the housekeeper's room, removed the larder door key from the bunch lying beside the sleeping woman, and run down to the kitchen. It was deserted for that short time, as most of the staff were enjoying a brief rest in the Servants' Hall. The red-haired girl had raided the larder, seized a large slice of delicious apricot tart, relocked the door and run away to her favorite hiding place down in the shrubbery.

Unfortunately, she also took with her the larder key. Cook, who of course, possessed a duplicate key, had been given special leave to visit her sick mother in Lewes. The panic and consternation in the kitchen when it was discovered that all the food was locked away, and the Duke's dinner was in jeopardy, was frightful. The undercook was in hysterics. Mrs. Brewer, annoyed with herself for not hiding her keys while she slept, screamed, raged, and pointed an accusing finger at the frightened scullery maids.

Finally, it was Tom Sewell, the head gardener, who came upon Lady Lucy happily dreaming away the afternoon down in the shrubbery. The larder key lay forgotten on the bench beside her.

By six o'clock, the weather had turned chilly, and a fire had been lit in the Morning Room. But despite the cheerful flames flickering in the hearth, the atmosphere as the company assembled for dinner was decidedly wintry.

The Duke was out of temper because he was monstrously hungry, and his dinner was two hours late. Lady Lucy, in disgrace, was by turns sulky and defiant. Lord Berkeley appeared withdrawn and remote, while Candida herself was still trembling with shock after her discoveries with Lady Angelica in the maze that afternoon.

The soup course was consumed in almost total silence, the only sound being that of the Duke, greedily slurping up the hot liquid with a disgusting vigor that set Candida's teeth on edge. However, by the time the Duke had demolished a plate of trout with almonds, his hunger had abated slightly, and he indicated that he was now ready for conversation.

He pointed his knife accusingly at Lord Berkeley and declared, "I have a bone to pick with you, Greville! I was all set to wake myself up today with a brisk gallop across the Downs, and then the head groom informed me that you had taken out my best hunter. What d'you mean by it?"

Lord Berkeley's voice was low and controlled. "You know as well as I, Bart, that Black Knight lately has been in a poor state. You've been riding him too hard, been neglecting to give him adequate cover when he's left outside in a chilling mist. I took him out today simply to ensure that he is fully restored to health."

Predictably, the Duke banged down his glass and began to shout. Lord Berkeley poured himself more wine and shouted back. Candida sat with downcast eyes, unable to touch another morsel of her fish.

So it was true! By his own admission, Lord Berkeley was riding Black Knight today. There could be no doubt then, that he was indeed the evil Robed Raider. She could deceive herself no longer, for every shred of evidence now pointed strongly in his direction.

Never in her life had Candida felt more wretched. She loved Lord Berkeley, and knew she should not, but she could not help herself.

Oh, what is wrong with me, she asked herself miserably. It has been proved to me now that Lord Berkeley is a man on whom I should turn my back without delay. Not only is he secretly betrothed to another woman—but he is also a ruthless rogue who takes pleasure in kidnapping young red-haired maidens purely out of a spirit of revenge for a girl who once bested him in Paris.

And still, despite it all, my heart quickens whenever I am in his presence. When our eyes meet, my pulse races, and at the sound of his voice my blood turns to liquid fire. I confess that despite all the dreadful things I now know about him, he is still the one man I would follow to the ends of the earth!

Her agonized reverie was interrupted by the entry into the Morning Room of a footman bearing a silver salver. He walked slowly around to the Duke's carved chair and stood respectfully immobile until his master finished hurling abuse at Lord Berkeley and refreshed himself by downing a glass of wine in one noisy gulp.

"Beg pardon, Your Grace," murmured the footman.

"The afternoon mail had just been sent up from the village."

The Duke snatched the letter from the salver, and waved the footman away. He ripped open the seal, and then exclaimed with a derisive snort,

"Why, it is a communication from Sir Montague Gore, the esteemed uncle of my dear fiancée!"

Candida paled. She gripped the table, her knuckles white, her eyes fixed in horror on the Duke. The amazing revelations following her exploration of the maze had quite driven from her mind the threat of her impending exposure by Uncle Montague. But now the moment had arrived, and there was nothing Candida could do but sit and wait for the blow to fall. Even flight was impossible, for the doorway was blocked by scurrying servants hurrying to bring in the succulent ham braised in honey.

The Duke grinned. "Sir Montague," he informed the table at large, "confesses himself surprised that I have not requested a portrait of my beloved, my sweet young bride." He hooted with laughter. "Does the old fool not realize that the only portrait that would interest me would be one of her jewels, her gold, her invaluable stock certificates? What do I care about the appearance of this Candida Wellesley? Once we are wed, and I have control of her fortune, I shall be happily besporting myself with all the most beautiful women in London."

Lady Lucy tossed back her red hair, and remarked boldly, "But Miss Wellesley might be ravishingly pretty, Uncle Bart. You might fall wildly in love with her."

"And pigs might fly," he retorted, pouring himself another generous measure of wine. "However, said Sir Montague has taken the trouble to send me a miniature of the lady, I suppose I may as well examine it, and discover the worst."

He drew out a small package tied in dark blue velvet. It contained, Candida was sure, the miniature which had been painted to mark her eighteenth birthday. She could well imagine the Duke's outraged reaction when he set eyes on the portrait and realized that the girl depicted was in truth sitting facing him across his own dining table. He will be livid at having been made a fool of, thought Candida, frantically. Sir Montague will be immediately informed. Oh, the repercussions will be terrible!

For one hopeful moment it crossed Candida's mind that perhaps the Duke would be so furious he would refuse to marry her. But that hope died as quickly as it had come. He will do anything to get his grimy hands on my fortune, Candida thought. And once we are wed, I have no doubt that he will retaliate by humiliating me in every way possible as punishment for my impertinence in daring to pose as a governess under his roof.

As the Duke began to tear away the velvet, Lord Berkeley arose and walked around the table to stand near his brother.

"You're a selfish oaf, Bart," he growled. "My glass has been empty for the past five minutes, but of course it would be too much trouble for you to pass down the decanter."

The Duke glanced up and replied with a surprised scowl, "You should have ordered the footman! Hey, watch out, you clumsy looby—now see what you've done!"

Lord Berkeley had reached across the Duke for the heavy crystal decanter, but on swinging it toward him, he had knocked the blue velvet package from the Duke's hands. It had fallen straight into the hot fire and as they watched, transfixed, it was in seconds no more than a heap of glowing ashes.

Candida breathed an almost audible sigh of relief. The Duke, however, leaped to his feet and seized Lord Berkeley by the shoulders. "Confound it, Greville! I've tolerated about as much as I can stand of your infernal interference in my life! You live in my house, drinking my wine, riding my best horses, and telling me how to run my estate. I won't stand for it, I tell you!"

Lord Berkeley shook him off and riposted thickly, "It's a good thing one of us takes an interest in the estate and the welfare of the tenants. Do you realize that I've spent the entire day gathering information about this Robed Raider who's terrorizing all the women in the village? And who was supposed to be leading the investigation? You! And where were you? Supping ale in a roadside tavern!"

The Duke roared, "How dare you criticize me for being in my cups! Why, you've certainly had a skinful tonight, and no mistake!"

The Duke was right, Candida realized in surprise. Lord Berkeley's speech was slurred, and there was a crazed gleam in his eye as he swung the glittering crystal decanter to and fro. Lady Lucy, sitting at the end of the table, was wide-eyed at the spectacle of her two inebriated uncles on the verge of coming to blows with one another.

Candida swept down the room, pulled the indignant Lady Lucy to her feet and hurried her from the room. As she closed the Morning Room doors behind her, the last thing she heard was the Duke's sneering remark,

"So he's abducted a few serving girls. What do they matter? There's always more where they came from . . ."

"My," breathed Lady Lucy as she accompanied Candida to the drawing room, "I have never seen Uncle Greville corned before. He truly had his dander up, did he not? What a ruck! I thought he was going to slice off the top of Uncle Bart's head with that decanter!"

Candida went immediately to the copper urn, and poured out the tea. After a few sips, she began to feel slightly more calm. But her agitation returned when she realized that in the heat of the moment when he addressed his brother, Lord Berkeley had referred to the Robed Raider—a man whose existence the entire household had been at pains to keep from the young Lady Lucy.

"Lady Lucy," Candida began in her most reassuring tone, "I hope you were not perturbed by the mention of a man they call the Robed Raider. You see—"

"Oh, do not fret, Miss Wilton. I know all about him," replied the red-haired girl airily. "Mr. Sewell told me when he found me down in the shrubbery this afternoon. I inquired after the health of his daughter, you see, and then he told me how she'd disappeared." She smiled. "I like Mr. Sewell. He talks to me as if I were grown up."

Candida set down her cup, reflecting that Lady Lucy was surely one of the most unpredictable girls she had ever encountered.

"I am not in the least afraid of the Robed Raider," Lady Lucy chattered on. "If he had the temerity to snatch me, I should pull that silly hood right down over his eyes, kick him hard on the shins, and run away, screaming at the top of my voice!"

"How do you know his robe is hooded?" inquired Candida curiously.

Lady Lucy shrugged. "Because I have seen it!"

"That day you fell downstairs?" began Candida tentatively, wondering if Lady Lucy had observed the robe hanging on the back of the small sideroom door.

"Oh no, not then." The girl frowned. "I was so confused that day, I remember little of what happened."

Candida drew the girl onto the sofa, and said with a calmness she did not feel, "Lady Lucy, this could be very important. Where did you see that robe?"

"Why, down by the seashore," said Lady Lucy innocently. "Do you recall that day when we walked by the sea, and then you could not find me when the mist came in?"

"Yes, I remember vividly," replied Candida somewhat tartly, recalling how anxious she had been.

Lady Lucy grinned. "Well, I found a cave hidden in the cliff wall. The entrance was very well concealed by a fall of rocks. I ran in there when I heard you calling. In the corner was this coarse brown woollen thing, all rolled up in a ball. I spread it out on the floor and sat on it, intending to wait until you found me. But the mist became worse, and I was frightened. I thought the tide might come in, right into the cave and drown me. So I ran out, and up the cliff steps."

Candida stared at her. "And that brown garment you sat on was a hooded robe?"

"Mmm." Lady Lucy nodded. "It was all horrid and scratchy. I'd have mentioned it before, Miss Wilton, had I known about the Robed Raider. May I have some more tea please? And may we play backgammon now?"

Chapter Ten

Not surprisingly, Lady Lucy won easily at backgammon and retired to bed in a state of triumphant high spirits. Candida sat alone in the drawing room envying Lady Lucy her youthful innocence. The two men had not joined the ladies after dinner, but had repaired immediately to the library, whence still issued the sound of raised voices.

Candida's one urge was to leave the house, saddle the trusty jennet, and ride down to the coast. She wanted to see for herself if Lady Lucy was right in her assumption that the coarse woollen garment she had sat on in the cave was in fact the Robed Raider's disguise. If the robe is still there, thought Candida, turning down the drawing room lamps, then there may well be other clues which will lead me, not just to the villain himself, but perhaps to the three abducted girls.

Candida sighed. *The villain himself,* she mocked herself. When are you going to face facts, Candida? When will you have the courage to stop referring to the Robed Raider in vague terms as *this villain* or *the blackguard,* and name him instead as Lord Berkeley? All the evidence points to Lord Berkeley. By refusing to acknowledge the truth, you are storing up untold suffering for yourself when justice finally prevails and he is unmasked.

She went slowly up to bed. If only I could go now, and investigate the cave, what a burden would be lifted from my mind, she thought. But it is impossible. Apart from the danger involved in a lonely, night-time ride across the Downs, there is Lady Lucy to be considered. I dare not leave her here, in this house, with Lord Berkeley in the strange, violent mood he has displayed tonight. If it is true that he is seeking a bizarre revenge by abducting girls with red hair, then Lady Lucy is in constant peril.

However, tomorrow Lady Lucy had been excused from her lessons. It had been arranged that she would accompany Lady Frances into the bustling town of Lewes, there to select the ribbons, laces, and other trimmings for her new autumn dresses.

Tomorrow, then, thought Candida as she drifted into sleep, I shall seize my opportunity and ride out to the cave. If luck is with me, I shall solve this mystery of the Robed Raider once and for all.

But luck, it appeared, had temporarily deserted Candida. She awoke the following morning with a headache so blinding that the merest chink of light entering her bedchamber caused her eyes to hurt most painfully. Ever since childhood Candida had suffered from occasional attacks of this nature, and she knew from long, bitter experience that there was nothing to be done but to lie still, with cold compresses on her forehead and wait for the hammering in her head to abate.

She was aware that these headaches usually followed a period of extreme exhaustion and stress. As she lay in the curtained bed, a kaleidoscope of confused images whirled around her tortured head.

She saw herself emerging from the darkness of the maze, and recalled her horrified disbelief when the black hunter, the Robed Raider's mount, was nowhere in sight. Then she was seated in the Morning Room, waiting with dread for the Duke to unwrap the portrait miniature which would expose her as an imposter. She relived the searing drama of Lord Berkeley swinging the crystal decanter, and knocking the blue velvet package into the fire . . . the Duke's fury, and the heated argument which had flared up between the two brothers . . .

Restlessly, Candida tossed and turned between the sheets, wondering if she would ever in her life find peace and tranquility again. The man I love is a dreadful monster, she thought feverishly, and I am surrounded by violence and deceit. Oh, how I long to cast off my governess's mask and be myself again. Life has been so confusing of late, that at times I have difficulty remembering just who Candida Wellesley is—if in fact, she exists at all?

Mercifully, sleep at last claimed Candida. She awoke around five, utterly refreshed and relieved to find that her headache had completely disappeared. As often happened after an attack of this sort, Candida was left with a longing to eat something sweet, and she was grateful to an understanding Mrs. Brewer who sent up some hot chocolate, and a plate of delicious bread and honey.

"Mrs. Brewer says there is no need to disturb yourself, Miss." The maid who brought in the tray smiled. "Lord Berkeley has been out all day, and sent a message that he would not be home for dinner. The Duke is dining with Sir Gerald Hawkshead, and Lady Lucy, of course, is with Lady Frances in Lewes."

Grateful for this intelligence, Candida hurriedly completed her repast. Then she dressed, pulled on her riding boots, and ran downstairs. She had but one thought in her mind, to ride with all possible speed across the Downs to the cliffs, to start her search for the Robed Raider's cloak.

But as she left the house, she drew up short, a cry of frustration on her lips. For advancing up the drive was a carriage bearing the Brockway arms. Doubtless, it was Lady Frances returning from Lewes with Lady Lucy.

And I cannot leave the child in the house unprotected, Candida realized, furious that once again her plans were thwarted. She stood aside as a footman sped down the front steps to open the carriage door. But no one emerged. Instead, Candida heard Lady Frances's voice calling imperiously.

"Oh, is that you, Miss Wilton? Kindly come here this instant and explain yourself!"

Bewildered Candida advanced toward the carriage. Lady Frances sat alone on the velvet seat, handing an assorted collection of packages to the Stratton Hall footman.

"As it happens, I was obliged to pass by so I thought it as well to deliver Lady Lucy's purchases. But I do not take kindly to being treated as an errand girl, Miss Wilton!" snapped Lady Frances crossly.

"I do not understand, Lady Frances," murmured Candida. "Where is Lady Lucy?"

The auburn-haired girl glared at the governess. "Where is Lady Lucy? How dare you ask me such a question! She is with you, is she not?"

"I have been confined to bed all day with a severe headache," replied Candida quietly. "I have not set eyes on Lady Lucy since last night."

Lady Frances frowned. "Miss Wilton. It is shameful of you to prevaricate so. Let me remind you of the facts. I went through into the haberdasher's workroom in Lewes to view her samples of mechlin lace. They were of quite inferior quality and I told her so in no uncertain terms. Then when I returned to the front shop, I found a note had been left for me by Lady Lucy, informing me that you had passed by and requested her to accompany you home at once. I was most vexed! Not that I particularly relish the company of that dreadful child, but the note itself was couched in the most impertinently curt tones! I—Miss Wilton! Where are you going? Come back here! How dare you run off when I am addressing you . . . !"

Breathless and deadly pale, Candida sped into the stables. "Please saddle that jennet for me. And quickly!" she instructed the groom.

He did as she bid, and within minutes Candida was galloping down the drive, toward the chalk and flint path which would take her up over the Downs. My God, he's outwitted me, she thought fearfully. The Robed Raider has seized Lady Lucy! I have no notion how he managed to persuade her to leave that message for Lady Frances, mentioning my name. But there is no doubt that he has abducted her. Oh, I just hope and pray that I am in time!

In the gathering dusk a sad smile crossed Candida's face as she recalled Lady Lucy's brave words about how she would react if the Robed Raider dared to lay a hand on her. *I should pull his silly hood right down over his eyes and kick him hard on the shins* she had declared.

But of course, it did not occur to her then that the villain would not necessarily appear before her wearing his disguise, thought Candida furiously. How easy it must have been for Lord Berkeley! He simply walked into the haberdasher's and convinced the bored Lady Lucy that it would be an amusing prank for her to leave a message saying she had left with her governess.

"We shall play truant for the day, you and I," he would have smiled. And Lady Lucy, delighted at such mischief, would have accompanied him without a murmur.

Up on the top-most ridge of the Downs, the wind blew strongly and the ribbons of Candida's hat slapped against her face. Impatiently, she pulled it off and threw it aside. The pins fell from her hair, and the golden tresses streamed out behind her, caught by the wind.

Far below, the lamps were being lit in the farms and village. But up here on the Downs, the only sound was that of the jennet's galloping hooves, and the distant whistle of the shepherd as he gathered his flock for safety against the gathering darkness.

Soon, a salty tang in the air told Candida that she must be near the sea. She turned away from the main cliff steps and trotted the jennet along the winding track that led to the other, rougher steps up which she had climbed that fateful day in pursuit of Lady Lucy.

At the top of the steps, she dismounted, and cast around for a secure place at which to tether the jennet. Then her eye fell on a battered wooden gate standing at the entrance to the path which led to a small, secluded fisherman's cottage. As she slipped the reins over the gatepost, Candida remembered that when she and Lady Lucy were lost in the mist that day, she had wanted to take shelter in the cottage. But—

Suddenly, everything went black, and Candida found herself frantically struggling for breath, for light, for air.

It was a sack, she realized, panic stricken. A sack had been thrown over her head. Strong arms were clamped around her body, and she was being kicked and pushed forward along the path.

Fear lent her courage and strength. As her captor shoved her forward, Candida dug in her booted heels and stood firm. At the same time, she bent her head forward and shook it violently, to release herself from the suffocating confines of the scratchy sack. It fell to the path, but not before Candida's tall captor had delivered a stinging blow to the side of her head.

Candida reeled from this punishment, but through the pain was still quick witted enough to seize her chance. In order to hit her, the man had been forced to release one of Candida's arms. Swiftly, she wrenched her body around. Fist clenched, she delivered a sharp blow to the Robed Raider's nose.

She had known, the moment the sack was thrown over her head, that she was in the clutches of the Robed Raider. As she turned to face him, the sight of his tall figure in the brown hooded garment frightened but did not surprise her.

But what *did* leave her gasping in amazement was the scream of pain the Robed Raider uttered as Candida's clenched fist made telling contact with his nose. For the furious shriek of agony that rent the autumn air was not the cry of an aggrieved man. It was the outraged screech of a wounded woman. "You meddling bitch! You've made my nose bleed! Well, you'll pay for that, Miss Governess. You see if you don't!"

Candida stood immobile, too stunned to move a muscle. For the piercing tones of her captor were unmistakably those of Lady Angelica Kerr!

Unfortunately for Candida, Lady Angelica was the first

to recover her wits. She slapped Candida viciously across the face, sending the girl reeling back against the front door of the cottage. Then Lady Angelica snatched up Candida's arms into a vicious grip behind her back, and marched her inside.

Candida found herself in a small bare parlor, lit by three flickering candles. An old blanket had been nailed up over the window and the air smelt damp and unhealthy. Recovering her fighting spirit, Candida turned, ready to claw the flesh from Lady Angelica's deceitful white throat.

"Don't move," instructed Lady Angelica quietly, in a voice loaded with menace. "I assure you, I know how to use this, and I would not hesitate!"

She was holding a pistol, levelled at Candida's heart. The hood of the robe was thrown back, revealing a bloodstained nose, and sleek brown hair tied back at the nape of her neck.

Lady Angelica laughed as she read Candida's thoughts. "The hair is a stroke of genius, is it not? Why, all Sussex knows that the vain Lady Angelica would never set foot from her house before her hair had been dressed to a fashionable height and powdered to an elegant shade of gray!"

Weakly, Candida leaned back against the damp wall. "Oh, how clever you have been," she whispered. "Your pretty, beribboned dresses . . . your powdered hair, festooned with glittering bows and fancies. You are celebrated as the most feminine creature in Sussex. No one would suspect *you* of riding a fierce black hunter, and abducting innocent young girls!"

"No," rapped Lady Angelica, "it is you who are the clever one, Miss Wilton. I must confess, when I saw you follow me into the maze the other day, my poor heart missed several beats. It was my own fault, of course, for being overconfident, and riding as the Robed Raider in broad daylight. There is a small arbor at the center of the maze which I find a convenient place to effect my change of clothing."

"But your hair that day was dressed and powdered," exclaimed Candida.

"A wig," smiled Lady Angelica, clearly quite overcome with admiration at her own inventiveness. "But I only just had time to throw on my yellow dress and the wig and confront you on the path. You were dangerously near to my arbor!" Her eyes narrowed reflectively as she regarded Candida. "I had always underestimated you before, Miss Wilton—I had assumed you to be a typical, insignificant governess. When I came upon you in the maze, I was planning to lead you down the wrong path, and snatch you away, to join my other pretty victims. But when you informed me that you had left a trail of flowers to guide yourself out of the maze, well, then I realized what a cool headed creature you are. I saw that you might be dangerous, I *knew* I should have to deal with you—once and for all!"

Candida shivered as she stared at the pistol in Lady Angelica's hand. If Lady Angelica was unbalanced enough to rush around the countryside abducting young girls, then it followed that she could be sufficiently deranged to pull the pistol trigger.

Bravely, Candida pushed aside her feeling of rising panic. I must keep my wits about me, she told herself firmly. I must encourage Lady Angelica to talk. Perhaps if I played upon her vanity . . .

"I am astounded at your courage in riding that enormous black hunter," Candida said admiringly. "Why, I could name a dozen strong men who would think twice about mounting such a spirited animal."

Lady Angelica took the bait. "Tush!" she declared with an impatient toss of her head. "I am heartily sick of men asserting that we women are feeble creatures who may not sit astride a horse, who cannot control a strong willed hunter, who may not ride to hounds. Well I, Miss Wilton, have proved the men wrong. I have done all these things. Yes, I have even ridden with the Duke of Stratton's own hounds!"

Candida had no need to hear more on this particular point. She remembered the letter from her cousin Clara: *I am confused by your reference to Lady Angelica's cousin, Sir*

Hugh Legatt . . . I assure you, we are well acquainted with all the families of importance in this neighborhood, but I cannot recall meeting anyone of this name.

"How amusing it was, listening to the men falling over themselves in praise of the horsemanship of Sir Hugh," laughed Lady Angelica. "The strong, *silent* Sir Hugh! For of course, I had to ensure that I uttered not a word on the hunt. Oh, what good sport it was!"

"Tell me—" smiled Candida—"that day at the maze. What *did* happen to your hunter? I saw you leave him near the entrance. Yet, when we emerged from the maze you had managed to spirit him away."

Lady Angelica looked pleased at this flattery. "When I arrived at the entrance of the maze, I didn't tether the horse. He has been carefully trained to graze for a short while on the sweet grass nearby, and then to make his way around to another, very small and very secret entrance which is on the other side."

Candida nodded. "How very clever. It was your insurance, then, in case anyone saw you entering the maze and became suspicious. You entered from one side, and left from the other."

"Just so, my perspicacious Miss Wilton," said Lady Angelica coolly.

Candida stood with her eyes closed, cursing her own stupidity. I should have realized, she berated herself, when I first encountered Lady Angelica in the maze and told her that I had seen the Robed Raider. She shrieked, and seemed almost about to swoon. Yet this was an out of character reaction for a lady who was quite accustomed to travelling about the countryside alone in her carriage at night—who I once heard scornfully refusing the Duke's offer of his footman as escort home.

And then again, I should have had my wits about me that day when Lady Lucy ran off into the mist. When I reached the top of the cliff steps, she was standing within one hundred yards of this cottage, accompanied by Lady Angelica! Oh, how stupid of me! And how fortunate that I happened upon them at that moment. Else for sure, Lady Angelica would have spirited the girl into this cottage and in the swirling mist I might never have found them.

And to think, Candida realized, that only minutes before Lady Lucy had actually been seated in a cave, on Lady Angelica's Raider's robe! She said aloud,

"That day in the mist... were you on the verge of abducting Lady Lucy then?"

A rueful smile touched Lady Angelica's lips. "It did cross my mind, yes. But then, of course, you came rushing out of the mist, oozing governessy concern. I seem to recall that you even put forth the intelligent suggestion that we all take shelter at the nearby fisherman's cottage!"

No wonder Lady Angelica was so reluctant to enter the cottage, thought Candida. For this was Lady Angelica's hideaway as the Robed Raider!

A triumphant note entered Lady Angelica's voice as she went on: "I was highly amused, however, at my device of encouraging Lady Lucy today to leave Lady Frances a message saying she had returned home with you! I imagined you might have some difficult questions to answer when it was discovered that the chid was nowhere to be found."

"But she is to be found," Candida retorted quietly. "I have found her. She is here in this cottage, is she not?"

Lady Angelica shrugged. "You'll see, soon enough. It was stupid of me not to realize that you suspected me of being the Robed Raider. I knew you were a clever governess, but I didn't appreciate quite *how* clever. However—" she flashed a malicious smile at the golden haired girl—"now you are here, I may as well make good use of you."

Candida shivered at the menacing tone. She then proceeded to ask the last, most intriguing question. "Why?" she inquired. "Why have you been masquerading as a robed man and abducting these young girls?"

"The answer is quite simple," replied Lady Angelica. "The whole aim and object of my little enterprise is to raise funds for myself. Regrettably, my father's gambling debts have left my mother and me in considerably reduced circumstances. I don't believe anyone in Sussex society realizes how desperately poor I am. Oh, I keep up a magnificent front, naturally. I am always dressed in the height of fashion and I affect all manner of elegant airs and graces. But, underneath my modish clothes, my petticoats are thin and torn, and my shoes are stuffed with paper."

"But how will these abducted girls provide you with funds," queried a mystified Candida.

"I sell them," said Lady Angelica with an air of surprise, as if the answer was perfectly obvious. "I am in contact with a French pirate. A monstrous rogue, but there you are, one cannot always choose one's business associates. He, in turn, is in touch with an incredibly wealthy Arabian Sultan, who has a passion for girls with red hair."

Candida's blue eyes widened in horror. "You have sold these English girls into slavery?"

"Don't be absurd," snapped Lady Angelica. "They will not be slaves, they will be concubines of the Sultan. It is an honored, cherished position. They will lead lives of luxury, waited on by handmaidens, their only object in life being to please the Sultan."

"But Lady Lucy is only twelve years old!" cried an aghast Candida.

"Oh, you governesses are such prim, narrow-minded creatures!" laughed Lady Angelica. "I assure you, in Arabia, such youth is highly prized by the Sultan."

"How . . . how many girls have you sent to him?" whispered Candida.

"Regrettably, none have actually left these shores yet," sighed Lady Angelica, in her agitation waving the pistol in what Candida considered to be a thoroughly dangerous manner. "The first two girls were both supposed to be on the high seas weeks ago, but unfortunately my French pirate's ship was grounded on some rocks. However, he will be dropping anchor in English waters tomorrow night. So you and Lady Lucy can look forward to an enthralling sea voyage, Miss Wilton!"

Candida's chin rose. "So, I am also to be sold to the

Sultan? But I do not have red hair, Lady Angelica." Candida was beginning to feel less terrified of the pistol in Lady Angelica's hand. Clearly, then, it was only intended to frighten her. By killing her, Lady Angelica would gain nothing—whereas by keeping her alive, she could sell her to the French pirate for shiny gold pieces.

"Ah, yes, your hair," agreed Lady Angelica. "We shall be obliged to dye it red, in an infusion of box leaves."

"But will the Sultan not be furious when he discovers he has been deceived?" murmured Candida.

"Yes, I expect he will have you thrust into a weighted sack and drowned," said Lady Angelica carelessly. "I am given to understand that this is how disobedient concubines are usually disposed of."

"But you," persisted Candida, playing for time and thinking furiously, "will not the Sultan seek reprisals against you?"

"Against me, a noble English lady?" declared Lady Angelica indignantly. "I should think not! He will have my French pirate garrotted of course, but that will be no great loss."

"Except that you will have lost your, er, trading partner," suggested Candida.

Lady Angelica looked not at all perturbed. "Oh, in truth I am a little fatigued with this venture. There is a limit to how long one can roam across Sussex stealing red-haired girls. With the sale of you five pretty maidens, I shall have amassed a sufficient fortune to take me to Paris."

Candida nodded. "Where no doubt, you will speedily attach yourself to a wealthy French Count?"

"Certainly not," rapped Lady Angelica. "I shall settle for no less than a *Duc*. To the French nobility, there is a tremendous cachet, you know, in marrying into the English aristocracy."

She waved the pistol at Candida. "But we have conversed long enough, Miss Wilton. Come, let us adjourn to the kitchen, boil some water, and dye your hair. I do believe you will make the most ravishingly pretty copper-haired damsel."

She opened the parlor door, and indicated that Candida was to precede her through to the small kitchen. Obediently, Candida walked forward. They entered a tiny, dark passageway, at the end of which was the open door of the kitchen.

With an outward air of reluctance, Candida stepped into the kitchen. Then she suddenly blazed into action.

Shooting out a hand she slammed the kitchen door behind her. Candida felt a surge of elation as she heard the wooden door make contact with the metal of Lady Angelica's pistol, and the clatter of the firearm to the stone floor.

Wasting not a moment, Candida wrenched open the door and dived for the surprised Lady Angelica's throat. The older girl struggled but the force of Candida's attack overpowered her. With a gasp of satisfaction, Candida pushed the taller girl backward into the parlor, banged shut the door, and locked it.

Then began what Candida knew was a race against time. She was sure that Lady Lucy and the other abducted girls were hidden here in the cottage. But where?

The cottage was small, and provided few hiding places. Instinct drew Candida to the dank stone steps leading to the cellar. Candle in hand, she descended the narrow stairs, praying that the cellar door would not be locked.

To her relief, she saw that the door was secured by large top and bottom bolts. She rammed them back, and pushed open the heavy, creaking door.

The four girls were lying on the damp floor. They were bound hand and foot, with scarves around their mouths and their young eyes wide with terror.

"Do not be afraid," Candida said hastily, to reassure them, setting the candle down carefully on the floor. "It is I, Jane Wilton."

Relief flickered across Lady Lucy's pale face, and she began to wriggle and moan. Candida ran across, and snatched the scarf from the girl's poor, bruised mouth.

"Oh, Miss Wilton!" whispered Lady Lucy. "Lady Angelica! She persuaded me to come with her—"

"I know," murmured Candida soothingly. "Don't speak now. You must save your strength."

Frantically, she wrestled with the tough rope binding Lady Lucy's hands. At last, the tight knots eased. Candida flung the rope to the far side of the cellar and gently rubbed the circulation back into the young girl's wrists.

"Now you must do exactly as I say, Lady Lucy," she whispered urgently. "First, set Hannah and the other girls free. Then, together, make your way upstairs."

"But Lady Angelica!" cried Lady Lucy. "I know her now to be a ruthless, evil creature, Miss Wilton! She will have no mercy—"

"She will be powerless against the three of you," Candida reassured her. "And in any event, it is my belief that now she is discovered, she will be more intent in saving her own skin than taking revenge on you. I am going to seek help. When you see the rescue flares of the riders coming over the Downs, I want you to start screaming and shouting to attract their attention and show them you are here." She took the girl by the shoulders, and said, "Will you do all that, Lady Lucy? Will you do exactly as I say?"

"Yes, Miss Wilton." The girl reached out and hugged her. "Oh, I am so grateful that you came and rescued us!"

There was no time to say more. Candida fled up the stairs, wrenched open the front door of the cottage and ran out into the night. As she reached the end of the path, she heard a crash, and the splintering of glass.

It was as she had anticipated. Candida had flung Lady Angelica with such force into the parlor that she would have lain for some time, stunned and winded. Then, recovering her breath and her wits, she would have attempted to open the door—and realized that it was locked.

Thus her only means of escape was through the window. Candida stood at the gate for a moment, watching. The resourceful Lady Angelica had obviously torn down the blanket which had curtained the window, and wrapped it around her hands as she smashed through the glass. Gingerly, the robed Lady Angelica maneuvered herself out to freedom through the jagged panes.

But still Candida did not move. At all costs, she thought, Lady Angelica must be prevented from re-entering the cottage and terrorizing those four young girls. It is vital that she catches sight of me, so that I may act as a decoy.

Lady Angelica jumped clear of the window, and glared around her. The candlelight from the parlor revealed the tense, vengeful face of an animal cheated of its prey. Deliberately, Candida swung open the creaking garden gate.

The jennet, of course, had gone. Candida had no doubt that when Lady Angelica first threw the sack over her head, she had untied the horse and set her to roam free across the Downs. There was nothing to be done, Candida realized, but to run—and fast!

Lady Angelica had heard the noise of the gate, and was swift in pursuit. Instead of heading inland, toward the upward sweep of the Downs, Candida kept to the cliff track, guided by the large white stones placed at intervals to mark the lethal edge of the cliff.

Candida soon realized that, fleet of foot though she was, Lady Angelica had the advantage. For Lady Angelica was running in the loose garment of the Robed Raider, which she had hitched up for freedom around her knees. But Candida was encumbered by the wide, hooped skirts of her governess's dress.

She stumbled on along the grassy track, feverishly aware of the sheer, long drop only inches to her right. If one of the guiding white stones had been moved . . . if she was unlucky enough to trip, and lose her footing, she would be pitched headlong over the cliff, onto the jagged sea-lashed rocks.

And Lady Angelica was gaining on her. Gasping for breath, Candida told herself that desperate measures were called for. In another minute, Lady Angelica would be upon her. The brown-haired girl was taller, and stronger than Candida. If it came to a face-to-face struggle, there was no doubt who would emerge the victor. And who would be the one tossed over the cliff edge to certain death in the rocky watery depths a hundred feet below.

A dark, blurred shape loomed ahead. With a sob of relief, Candida recognized it as a large thorn bush. She flung herself behind it, gathered up her strength, and wrenched up her skirt to her waist.

Lady Angelica came rushing up the path, her hair dishevelled, her face intent in the soft moonlight. When she drew level with the thorn bush, Candida stepped out onto the track. As Lady Angelica drew up short with a gasp of surprise, Candida reached up and rammed over her head the rigid hoop which she had withdrawn from beneath her dress. Then with a violent shove, she pushed the girl who was now effectively caged from head to elbows, back into the spiky midst of the thorn bush.

Lady Angelica's scream of rage and frustration was loud enough, Candida was sure, to be heard at the other end of Sussex. But Candida paid no heed. She turned her back on the shrieking girl, and ran on, up and up the path, her eyes set on a large, roughly triangular shape on the topmost height of the cliff.

Candida had told Lady Lucy that she was going for help. But to the casual observer, there was nothing on this high, deserted clifftop which would possibly be of assistance.

Yet, still Candida sped on, until at last she reached the topmost height and the strange tall shape that loomed high in the moonlight. She threw herself down on the springy grass, tearing at the turf for a small box she had been told would be hidden there, wrapped in an oilskin.

A shriek of fury made her start, and turn. Lady Angelica had managed to extricate herself from both the hoop and the thorns. She was advancing now, spitting with rage, up the path, toward Candida.

Candida delayed no longer, but set to work. There was a scratching sound, followed by a small flare. Then the flare became a flame, crackling first, then roaring into a brilliant orange as the bushwood caught fire.

With a sob of relief, Candida sat back on her heels and watched the bright flames blazing upward, brilliant against the night sky. For the first time in five years, the magnificent Stratton Down Beacon was afire, signalling for miles across the Downlands its scorching warning-call of danger and distress.

Chapter Eleven

See, Lord Berkeley had directed, pointing inland on a golden August day when Candida had first arrived in Sussex, *there is another beacon on top of that hill, and a permanent watchman also. If ever he observes this clifftop Stratton Down beacon afire, then he sets light to his own hilltop beacon. And that, in turn, is clearly visible from Stratton Hall.*

A chain of fire! an impressed Candida had exclaimed, never dreaming that only weeks later, she would be the one to set the nighttime countryside shimmeringly alight.

She held her breath, looking toward the dark hills, her eyes straining for the first lick of flame from the answering, inland beacon. What if the watchman had fallen asleep?

Then I am lost, Candida realized fearfully, pushing back her golden hair with smoke grimed hands. For unless the hilltop beacon is lit, there is no chance of anyone at Stratton Hall learning of the drama being enacted here on the clifftop.

She cast an anxious glance back down the path. Lady Angelica stood immobile, as if frozen to the spot. She, too, was gazing, almost mesmerized, toward the high hills.

One minute . . . two minutes . . . and still the hill remained in darkness. Candida wiped her perspiring fingers on her dress. Lady Angelica turned her head, and a smile of triumph played around her lips. She began to move upward toward the fair-haired girl standing illuminated by the leaping flames on the cliff.

Desperately, Candida moistened her dry lips. She was doomed. She knew it. The clifftop path ended here. There was nowhere left to run. Nowhere to go but down into the foaming sea.

And then, miraculously, a glow appeared on the horizon. Swiftly, the sky lightened as the hilltop beacon blazed an answer of recognition and the reassuring promise of rescue.

Lady Angelica hastily took to her heels and disappeared back down the cliff track. Candida sank to her knees, tears streaming down her cheeks. For a chilling second, it occurred to her that Lord Berkeley might not be at home. (The Duke would no doubt be too drunk to stir himself to ride out to the coast.)

Resolutely, Candida pushed the thought aside. Of course Lord Berkeley would be there. Of course he would come. He would not fail her.

She stayed by the beacon, too weak to move. The four girls, she knew, would be safe enough at the cottage. Help would soon be at hand, and Lady Angelica would molest them no more. At this moment she was probably hurling herself onto her black hunter and riding hell for leather toward the county border with Kent.

Soon there came more lights, moving fast over the hill and down toward the coast. It would be Lord Berkeley, riding fast, leading the rescue team. She saw them gallop toward the cottage, and knew that Lady Lucy and the girls had done their work well in attracting attention as Candida had instructed.

Yet still, Candida remained by the beacon, its flames just beginning to die down now, and its heat very intense.

Ten minutes passed before Candida saw him: a lone figure, galloping at a furious pace along the cliff path toward her. She stood up, and ran to meet him.

Lord Berkeley flung himself off his horse and opened his arms to her. Without thinking (for to Candida it was the most natural action in the world) she gave herself into his embrace. His arms enfolded her, and at once his lips found hers.

They kissed with a blazing passion that fully matched the fire of the beacon behind them. Candida's blood raced as at last she surrendered to her desires, responding rapturously to the urgency of the dark-haired man's embrace. He kissed her long, and hard, and lovingly . . . Feeling his hands in her hair, his demanding mouth on hers, she wanted this moment never to end. She wanted only to stay here in his arms forever.

He too, appeared reluctant to release her as he kissed her again and again, with a masterful ardor that told her—as if she did not already know it—that she was his. Now and forever, she belonged to him, and him only.

"My God, Candida," he murmured at last, his voice deep and low, "how I have wanted you!"

"And I you," she whispered. "Oh, these past weeks . . ."

Her voice trailed away as the shock of realization left her stunned and breathless. She gazed into his gray eyes and exclaimed softly, "You called me Candida! You addressed me by my correct name . . . ?"

Smiling, he took her hands in his. "There is so much we have to talk about! Do you remember that fateful night when my brother had the impertinence to invade your bedchamber?"

Candida shuddered. How could she ever forget that night? "You came," she murmured. "You came and rescued me."

"I was up in one of the attics, sifting through all manner of old papers and documents which had lain there for decades," he said. "But among all the scrolls of parchment and old household account books, I found something else. It was a small portrait of a beautiful golden-haired young woman. And I could not believe my eyes, for the portrait was of the new young governess at Stratton Hall."

"Of me?" cried Candida in surprise. "But how could that be? The last portrait I sat for was in honor of my eighteenth birthday, and was sent only days ago by my Uncle Montague to the Duke."

"Quite so," agreed Lord Berkeley, tenderly stroking

Candida's long hair. "When I turned the portrait over, the name written on the back was that of the Lady Majorie Wellesley."

"My mother!" exclaimed Candida. "She and your mother, the late Duchess, were childhood friends. They devised a pact whereby my mother's firstborn girl should marry your mother's eldest son."

Lord Berkeley nodded. "I know. As I sat that night in the attic, all became clear to me. I realized why you had come to Stratton Hall and posed as a governess. Oh, Candida, how my heart went out to you for your courage! With every fibre of my being I appreciated what despair you must have felt when you first set eyes on my brother and realized what manner of man you were betrothed to!"

He went on: "But there was no time then for further reflection. I heard my brother's voice and your scream echoing from your bedchamber. I raced down, and threw him out. It took every ounce of self-control I possessed not to mill the life out of him there and then for daring to lay a finger on the woman I loved!"

Candida gasped, and laid her head on his shoulder as he murmured, "Yes, I knew I loved you, and when I looked at you there on the bed, with your beautiful hair streaming over your shoulders, I was overcome with passion for you."

"And I too," breathed Candida. "I remember how your eyes darkened as you gazed on me. I confess, I wanted only to feel your arms around me—I did not care about the consequences!"

"Had circumstances been different, I admit, I would have made love to you then, and there, and right through the night," he said, in a tone that sent a thrill of desire through Candida's trembling frame. "But by then, I knew who you were. I knew I must turn my back on you, never again to look upon you with love."

"But why?" cried Candida, mystified. "Surely you could not believe that I would go through with this marriage to your brother? I shall never wed him, *never!*"

Lord Berkeley gazed out to sea, his eyes troubled. "Candida, had I still believed you to be Jane Wilton, a pretty young governess, I should have proposed to you on the spot and swept you down immediately to be wed in the village church. But you are not Jane Wilton—you are a beautiful and extremely wealthy young woman. Whereas, I am a second son with nothing financial to offer you but my small annual allowance. I am a proud man, Candida. I will never let it be said that I married in order to live off the fortune of my wife."

Candida drew herself up, her eyes blazing. "And what, pray, do you imagine Society will say when they learn that you are engaged to a wealthy heiress by the name of Lady Frances Brockway! Or, do you intend to do the decent thing and return her fabulous dowry to her father? I'm sure Lady Frances will be enchanted at the prospect of starting her married life with you in a grace and favor cottage on her father's estate!"

Lord Berkeley took a step back, a hand raised mockingly to shield his face. "My, what a firebrand you are, Candida! I can see that marriage to you is certainly not going to be dull!"

"But how can you marry me," stormed Candida, infuriated that he should laugh at her, "when you are already betrothed to Lady Frances?"

"Candida, I assure you, I am not and never have been engaged to Lady Frances. For heaven's sake! Credit me with possessing some taste, some discrimination!"

"But Lady Lucy heard you express your love for her, one day at Brockway Hall," stammered Candida indignantly. "You gave her a ring, the stones of which spelled *dearest!*"

Lord Berkeley roared with laughter. "Ah, yes," he replied thoughtfully. "I remember now. We agreed to keep our liaison secret until after my brother was wed."

Candida turned away, blinded by furious tears. He came up behind her, and firmly encircled her with his arms. Angry now, she struggled to free herself, but he was too strong for her. Holding her close, he murmured,

"Forgive me. I do not wish to distress you. Candida, the truth is that Lady Frances and I were merely rehearsing our lines for the annual harvest supper play!"

As his blessed words sank in, Candida went limp with relief. "I . . . I remember now. The play was written by Lady Angelica, was it not? Oh, what an irony!"

Gently, he turned her to face him and kissed away the tears on her cheeks. "Oh, how foolish I have been," whispered Candida. "I had completely forgotten about the harvest supper play." Then she said urgently, "Lady Angelica! Those poor girls down in the cottage—"

Lord Berkeley laid a finger over her lips. "Be still, my love. My trusty bailiff will by now have escorted the girls back to Stratton Hall, where Mrs. Brewer will be ministering to them. By now, no doubt Lady Lucy is tucked up in bed enjoying a huge hot supper, and quite revelling in being the heroine of the hour."

Candida smiled. He was right, of course. "And Lady Angelica?"

"The Night Watch have been alerted. But I suspect that she will evade them. Lady Angelica knows this countryside like the back of her hand. Every nook and cranny, every cave and badger's set is familiar to her. In fact, it was precisely this point which first alerted me to the fact that she might be the Robed Raider."

"You suspected her?" asked Candida with surprise.

"Not at first," Lord Berkeley said gravely. "In the beginning, the Robed Raider had me completely foxed. But then Lady Angelica became over-confident, and careless. As you know after Hannah Sewell disappeared I questioned every man, woman and child in Stratton village. No one, of course, mentioned Lady Angelica directly in connection with the Robed Raider. But it was interesting how many of the villagers remarked, quite casually, that they had observed her up on the Downs, riding a black hunter."

"But she was not dressed as the Robed Raider?" queried Candida.

"Oh no. She was probably merely exercising the animal. Then one little girl in the village told me that she had seen Lady Angelica out very early in the morning, riding the black hunter astride."

"And this was when you first began to suspect her," said Candida, pushing back with the toe of her riding boot some glowing embers which had rolled away from the center of the fire.

Lord Berkeley fingered a stray lock of black hair. "The notion seemed preposterous. Lady Angelica! So finely dressed, so full of feminine fancies. But then I remembered that there is another side to the lady. I have known her from childhood and I am aware that she is a spirited and also steely hearted girl. And of course, I knew that the Robed Raider was someone who possessed an intimate knowledge of our Sussex countryside. Yet, I could not at this stage accuse Lady Angelica point blank, as I had no proof—and for the life of me I could not surmise why she should be abducting these girls."

"I can give you the answer to that," replied Candida. And she told him about Lady Angelica's reduced financial circumstances, and about the French pirate and the lascivious Sultan.

"Stap me!" muttered Lord Berkeley. "I always knew Lady Angelica was a cold-blooded lady, but I never dreamed she was as merciless as this."

Candida sat down on the springy grass, and drew close to the fire. Lord Berkeley removed his cloak, and placed it around her shoulder. They sat in silence for a while, gazing out on a moonlit sea, and a sky full of stars.

Then he said, "There is a mischievous smile playing around your lips, Candida. What are you thinking of?"

Her blue eyes danced with laughter as she turned to him. "I thought the Robed Raider was you! When I found that woollen robe at Stratton Hall and you were so abrupt with me—"

Ruefully, Lord Berkeley rubbed his chin. "I fear I *was*

somewhat curt. Please forgive me. But the robe, too, was intended for the harvest supper play. It is a tradition in the family, you see, that the play remains a total secret until the moment it is performed. We all make fearful fools of ourselves, and the tenants enjoy it enormously!" Then he tilted Candida's chin up to face him, and said with mock severity, "And what, pray, did your fertile little mind imagine that I was going to do with a parcel of abducted red-haired girls?"

She told him then about her encounter with Lady Angelica in the maze. "Lady Angelica said," Candida went on in a very small voice, "that after an incident with a red-haired girl in Paris, you were seeking revenge by persecuting any girl you could lay hands on with that color hair."

Lord Berkeley sat astounded for a moment. Then he shook with laughter. "Trust Angelica to come up with such an outrageously fanciful notion, no wonder we always chose her to write our harvest supper plays. She has the most spectacular imagination."

Candida's eyes were fixed on the fire. "Did you . . . did you really have an encounter with a red-haired girl in Paris?" she inquired in a casual tone which did not deceive him for one minute.

"Yes. I fought my brother for her, and received this scar on my cheek for my pains. Then I escorted her home, and later found she had stolen my money." Observing the drawn expression on Candida's face, he drew her close. "This was many many years ago, my love. When I was but a green youth. Since then—I will not deceive you—there have been other women, but I have never in my life loved anyone as I love you, Candida."

She believed him.

As she lifted her face for his kiss, she knew she would not have wanted it to be any other way. Of course a man of his age—nigh on thirty years—would have enjoyed romances with other women. But it was she, Candida Wellesley, whom he truly loved. It was she with whom he desired to spend the rest of his life.

A thought suddenly occurred to her. "Last night," she

murmured, "when you swung that crystal decanter and knocked my portrait into the fire before the Duke could set eyes on it . . . were you really drunk?"

He smiled. "I hope you were convinced by that little exhibition of my theatrical talents! Heavens, if you could have observed your face as Bart read out that letter from your Uncle Montague, and you realized that he held in his hands a portrait of you!"

"I didn't know whether to jump out of the window, hide under the table or stab myself with the carving knife," admitted Candida. "Thank heavens, you were quick witted enough to take action."

She warmed her hands before the fire and remarked, "How strange to think that for all this time you have known my true identity. You have watched me going about my governess duties—playing a demure and respectful role—and not once did I suspect that you knew the truth."

"I could not understand why you stayed at Stratton Hall so long," he said. He hesitated, and then went on. "My brother—forgive me—I do not wish to sound disloyal to my own kin. Bart has many good points. He has taken very seriously his guardianship of Lady Lucy. He never bears a grudge. He—"

Candida laid a hand on his arm. "It is very noble of you thus to defend your brother. There is no need for either of us to cxpress the truth in words. I have lived under the same roof as the Duke! I have formed an opinion of his character, and I know I could never marry such a man."

"Then why did you not leave Stratton Hall within days of setting foot in the main hall?" he asked.

"There were many reasons." Candida smiled. "Most important, I was headlong in love with you. Come what may, I wanted to be near you—even though at that time I had no hope that my feelings were reciprocated. And then, I gradually became very fond of Lady Lucy. I felt she had suffered a wretched childhood, and I wanted, as best I could, to show her affection and genuine friendship."

"You have certainly succeeded," said Lord Berkeley

quietly. "I assure you, Lucy is now your most devoted admirer! Admittedly, she will never be a demure little miss, that is not in her nature. But somehow, you have managed in your lessons with her to divert all that wild, unruly energy into more fruitful channels."

Candida blushed at the compliment. She hurried on; "Well, then apart from Lady Lucy, I admit I was intrigued and heavily involved with the Robed Raider mystery. I knew I could not quit Stratton Hall until the villain was exposed."

It was getting late. Candida was deeply reluctant to move from the clifftop, and the low, friendly flames of the dying Beacon fire.

After some time, however, Lord Berkeley gently pulled Candida to her feet. "We must go back," he said. "There is much to be resolved."

Candida gazed up at him. "What will we do?"

He kissed her smooth brow and said, "How strange life is! I had determined that I must turn my back on you forever. And yet, tonight, when I saw you silhouetted against that blazing Beacon, I was powerless to fight against the love I felt for you. It is as if there are times in life when one's reason ceases to function. All that matters is what one *feels* . . . what one instinctively knows to be right."

"I felt the same way," whispered Candida. "To run toward you as I did, and throw myself into your arms! Why, in the elegant salons of Society such behavior would be scandalous. Yet here, up on the clifftop, with only the moon and stars as witnesses, I felt free to follow the impulse of my heart."

He looked into her eyes and said gravely, "Will you wait, Candida? Will you wait for me until I have made my fortune, and am in a position to support you as you are accustomed?"

"Oh, Greville, what foolish talk is this!" cried Candida. "I love you with all my heart. You say you love me. It is irrelevant which one of us has happened to inherit a fortune. I have wealth enough for both of us—"

"I am only too well aware of that," he replied coldly.

"We must have this quite clear between us, Candida. Under no circumstances whatsoever will I permit myself to live on your money!"

"But—"

He raised a commanding hand. "I am a second son. As I have no inherited fortune, then I must earn my wealth. So I ask you again, Candida. Will you wait for me?"

She gazed deep into his gray eyes. "Yes," she whispered. "I shall wait for you forever, Greville."

So they kissed for the last time on the clifftop. But through the joy of her passion, Candida's eyes were damp with tears.

They rode together on his horse back across the Downs to Stratton Hall. The great house was ablaze with lights. A throng of villagers stood in the drive, and in the lamplight Candida recognized the weatherbeaten face of Tom Sewell, the Stratton Hall head gardener. Candida could well imagine his heartfelt relief at being reunited with his daughter Hannah.

Lord Berkeley took Candida around to the garden door. "We will talk more tomorrow," he said.

Candida nodded, understanding that for the moment, he had a duty toward the tenants. They would be anxious to know what had happened—why the Downland beacons had suddenly burst into flame. And Tom Sewell, naturally relieved that his daughter was returned to him, had a right to be informed of the incredible identity of the Robed Raider.

Fortunately, Mrs. Brewer was occupied with Lady Lucy, and Candida was able to run up the back stairs into the privacy of her bedchamber. With the door safely locked behind her, she sank down on the bed and buried her head in her hands.

So much had come to pass in the last few hours. It was difficult to believe that it had all really happened. Most important, she clung to the joyous intelligence that Lord Berkeley loved her!

For some time, Candida sat and relived their extraordinary hour together, out on the clifftop. She knew that for the rest of her life, she would never forget the ecstasy of the moment when Lord Berkeley had first taken her into his arms and kissed her.

But as she sat there on the bed, a chill stole over Candida. "What is to happen to us now," she whispered. "We love each other. Yet, he steadfastly refuses to marry me until he has made his fortune. But that could take years!"

It is not, thought Candida in anguish, that I am not prepared to wait. I know I could never love another man as I do Lord Berkeley.

"But there is no need to wait," mused Candida impatiently. "Through an accident of birth, I happen to possess great wealth. Why can we not be married now and share our financial good fortune?"

Yet from the grim expression on Lord Berkeley's handsome face as they discussed the matter, she knew he would never agree. He is the type of man who will insist on being master in his own home, Candida realized. He is too proud to allow the gossips of Sussex to accuse him of marrying petticoat-wealth.

Candida drew her knees up to her chin and concentrated all her thoughts on the problem. And when at last she fell into bed, she had arrived at the only possible solution.

I shall rise at first light, she resolved, and ride straight back to Hampshire. There I shall tell Uncle Montague the full story. That the Duke of Stratton is a drunken dissolute, and that I have fallen irrevocably in love with his brother. I shall make it clear to my uncle that I am quite determined to marry Greville.

Once he sees my mind is made up, he will be more inclined to assist me with the most crucial part of my plan. Somehow, some of my great wealth must be secretly transferred to Greville. Lord Berkeley must have a financial advisor in London who handles his stocks, and investments. Uncle Montague knows all these people. Surely it would not be beyond the wit of man for it to be "arranged" that some of

Lord Berkeley's stocks should suddenly increase in value. There is no need for him ever to know that it was part of my fortune which thus swelled his wealth.

Candida sank back against the pillows, relieved that the decision, at last, had been made. By tomorrow evening she would be back in Hampshire, and her fateful interview with Uncle Montague would be completed.

Yet, before she drifted into sleep, Candida's thoughts, quite unaccountably, turned to that summer's day at Brockway Hall, when Lady Frances had involved them all in asking questions of the *Oracle* which Lord Berkeley had given her for her birthday . . .

That which I desire, Lord Berkeley had asked, *will it come to pass by day or by night?*

I did not know then that he loved me, mused Candida, stretching languorously between the sheets. I had no notion that he was referring to the avowal of our love!

The reply the *Oracle* gave, however, was strangely prophetic. What Lord Berkeley desired, said the *Oracle,* would come to pass *by night, by fierce heat and blazing light.*

Up by the burning beacon we declared our love for one another, thought Candida. But the smile on her lovely face suddenly froze as she recalled what the *Oracle* had decreed for her.

Shall I marry? had been the question posed on Candida's behalf by Lady Frances.

And chillingly, the *Oracle* had declared, *Yes, to him whom destiny has chosen for you.*

"This is the most extraordinary tale I have ever heard in my life." Sir Montague Gore's astringent tones sliced through the air of the austere library at Gore Lodge.

Candida stood before him in her dark blue governess's dress, tired and hungry after the long day's ride from Sussex, across the county of Surrey and home to Hampshire. But so anxious was she to bring matters to a conclusion with her uncle, that she had come straight in from her hired carriage and sought an immediate interview with Sir Montague in the library.

Sir Montague adjusted his eyeglass and peered down at his niece. "Now let me see if I understand the facts correctly: you are giving me to understand firstly, that you travelled alone to Stratton Hall and presented yourself in the guise of Miss Jane Wilton, governess?"

Candida waved her hands. "I was not alone all the way, Uncle. My maid, Bessie chaperoned me as far as Hazelmere."

"Hazelmere," repeated Sir Montague, in a voice which suggested that they might be referring to the New World. He went on in a neutral tone, "This was, as I remember, after you persuaded me to write to the Duke, recommending the services of this Miss Wilton person."

"I . . . I am sorry I deceived you, Uncle," stammered Candida. "But you see—"

He held up an authoritative hand. "Once installed at Stratton Hall, you then proceeded to develop an infatuation for one Lord Berkeley, the Duke's brother."

"It is not an infatuation!" flared Candida in a storm of passion. "I love him. With all my heart and soul I love him!"

A flicker of distaste crossed Sir Montague's gaunt features. As a confirmed bachelor, he counted himself fortunate that his comfortable existence had remained undisturbed by any hysterical affair of the heart.

"In addition, you have evidently been rushing around the Sussex countryside in pursuit of a berobed man—who ultimately is revealed to be not a man at all, but one of the female sex?"

Candida turned away. Her uncle's caustic tone made everything which had come to pass at Stratton Hall sound utterly unbelievable. She shivered. It was a cool September night, and although an apple-log fire burned in the library hearth, Sir Montague was standing with his back to the mantel, effectively blocking all the heat.

She took a deep breath and tried again. "Uncle, I realize

that what I have done has come as a great shock to you; but you must understand that I could not agree to marry the Duke without first seeing for myself what manner of man he was. And believe me, having lived beneath his roof for the past month, I know him to be a coarse, unfeeling drunkard! I could never wed him!"

"Foolish girl! You were prejudiced against him before you even set foot in Stratton Hall," snapped Sir Montague. "Admit it!"

"I confess, I was not impressed by the cold tones of his original correspondence with you, when he indicated that I was to *present myself* at Stratton Hall for a wedding immediately after Christmas," agreed Candida. "But even you yourself, Uncle, were surprised that the Duke showed so little interest in me, that he did not request my portrait."

Sir Montague frowned. "I did, in fact, send him your likeness."

A gleam of laughter danced in Candida's eyes as she recalled the arrival of the portrait, and Lord Berkeley's quick witted impersonation of a man in his cups. "I regret to say that the portrait was knocked into the fire before the Duke had the opportunity to see it," she murmured.

"How very fortunate for you," commented Sir Montague dryly.

"Uncle," said Candida in her most persuasive tone, "if you could but meet the Duke, and converse with him for half an hour, I am convinced you would understand why I refuse to marry him. It is bad enough that he spends his days and nights in an alcoholic stupor. But when he is reasonably sober, his only topic of conversation is horseflesh. And he has no sense of responsibility toward his estate, and his tenants. He—"

"Candida," interrupted Sir Montague, his bony fingers drumming on the mantel, "what is the family motto of the Wellesley family?"

"Why, *Duty Unto Death,*" said Candida.

Sir Montague nodded. "Quite so. And how did your father and your brother meet their deaths?"

Candida's eyes misted. She whispered, "You know perfectly well how they died, Uncle."

"Indeed I do. But I want you to tell me," said Sir Montague severely.

Candida bit her lip. What irony, she thought, that I have spent the last month in charge of a schoolroom, and I stand before my uncle, now dressed in my drab governess gown. Yet *he* is catechizing *me* as if I were a naughty twelve-year-old girl with ink stained fingers!

"I am waiting," remarked Sir Montague distantly, settling his wig more firmly on his domed head.

Candida dug her nails into the palm of her hand and forced herself to remember that dreadful night. "Our house caught fire. My father and brother insisted on plunging into the blaze to rescue the servants and perished in the attempt!"

Sir Montague gazed coldly over her head. "And your dear mother. What were the circumstances of her death?"

Candida's control broke. "You are a cruel, hateful man! You must know that for the rest of my life I shall bear on my shoulders the guilt that it was my birth that killed my mother!" She flung herself into a deep leather chair and buried her head in her hands.

"Duty Unto Death" intoned Sir Montague. "Your parents, and your brother all lived and died upholding your proud family motto." He walked across and laid a cold hand on her shoulder. "You must go to your room, now, and rest. I want you, also, to think of your family, and the proud Wellesley tradition they died to uphold. Remember your mother, your father, your brother. Brave souls, all. I know you will not fail them, Candida."

She opened her mouth to argue, to explain, but he would hear no more. He escorted her upstairs and left her alone in her bedchamber.

Candida gazed around the room with a sigh of relief. After four weeks sleeping in the characterless governess's room at Stratton Hall, it was a delight to be back among familiar surroundings once more.

When the fire at her own home had compelled her to

move here to Gore Lodge, Candida had chosen this room on the top floor as her own. She had selected it for its tall, arched windows which allowed the sunlight to stream in, and afforded a splendid view beyond Sir Montague's manicured estate, to the windblown Hampshire hills beyond.

She sank down on the silk-covered bed, and rubbed her tired eyes. It had been such a long day. She had arisen at daybreak and gone immediately to Lady Lucy's apartments. The girl was sleeping peacefully, undisturbed by nightmare memories of her ordeal at the hands of the Robed Raider.

Candida left a note by her bed, explaining briefly that she had been suddenly called away. *But I promise I will come back very soon* Candida had written, not wishing Lady Lucy to imagine that her governess had uncaringly abandoned her.

She left another note for Lord Berkeley. *I have gone to talk to my Uncle Montague. I am confident that once he is aware of all the facts, he will accept that my engagement to the Duke must be broken. I remain your most loving and devoted Candida.*

It had been easy then, at Stratton Hall, to write such confident words. Basking in her joy and elation that her love for Lord Berkeley was returned in full measure, Candida had felt headily assured that she could, if required, fly easily to the moon.

But once confronted with Uncle Montague's forbidding face, all Candida's optimism had evaporated. She had been so immersed in all the dramatic happenings at Stratton Hall that she had quite forgotten the unyielding nature of her Uncle's temperament.

"How foolish I was to imagine that he would respond in an understanding manner when I talked to him of my love for Lord Berkeley," she whispered. "My bachelor uncle knows nothing of love. To him, duty is all. Oh, I am aware that my dear mother declared on her deathbed that it was her dearest wish that I should wed the Duke of Stratton. But I am convinced that had she known the manner of man he would grow into, she would never have compelled me to marry him!"

Candida stood up, resolutely ignoring the exhaustion sweeping over her. "I must speak to my uncle again. Immediately. Somehow, I must make him understand the depth of my love for Greville!"

She ran to the door, and turned the handle. An expression of disbelief crossed her face. The door was locked!

Furiously, Candida rattled the handle. "Uncle! Unlock this door this instant! How dare you keep me prisoner!"

There was no reply. Almost beside herself with rage, Candida ran to the fireplace and picked up the heavy brass poker. She drew it up over her head and battered the heavy oak door with all her might. "Let me out!" she screamed. "Uncle! Do you hear me? Release me at once, you unfeeling monster!"

Relentlessly she wielded the poker, ramming at the door again and again. At last, she heard heavy footsteps along the outside corridor.

"Stop that noise!" ordered Sir Montague. "Do you want all the servants to hear?"

"It is your own fault if they do!" retorted Candida. "How dare you lock me in!"

"As your legal guardian, I have every right to place you under my care and protection," replied Sir Montague coldly.

"Care!" Candida threw down the poker in disgust.

"You are a young, undisciplined girl with no experience in the ways of the world," Sir Montague informed her. "Left to yourself you would heedlessly ruin your life by seeking to marry a second son with barely a penny to his name."

Candida's scornful laugh rang out. "Do you imagine that the Duke of Stratton is rich beyond measure? He has gambled and drunk his fortune away. He admits that he is marrying me solely for my fortune!"

"I am not at all surprised," replied the infuriating Sir Montague. "Your hysterical complaints are irrelevant. The important thing is that he is a Duke. And as Duchess of Stratton you will not only be revering your mother's last wish, but you will also bring credit to the entire Wellesley family."

"To yourself, you mean," raged Candida. "It is you who relish the glory of being related to the Duchess of Stratton!"

She took a deep breath; "I have no desire to be a Duchess! I am going to marry Lord Berkeley. He is the man I love."

"On the contrary," said Sir Montague coolly. "You will wed the Duke of Stratton, as arranged."

"The date of the wedding is fixed at four months hence," retorted Candida. "Do you seriously imagine you can keep me prisoner here for all that time?"

Sir Montague's reply was crushing. "Indeed not. I intend that the wedding shall be brought forward. We shall travel together to Sussex tomorrow, and you shall be joined in holy matrimony with the Duke within twenty-four hours of our arrival at Stratton Hall!"

Chapter Twelve

Stunned, Candida reeled back onto the bed. This she had never expected! She knew her Uncle Montague to be a determined man, but she had never anticipated that he would go so far as to bring forward the date of her wedding.

Wearily, Candida slipped into bed. Well, I am determined, too! she thought fiercely. It is all very fine that Uncle Montague declares that he will have me wed with all possible speed to that obnoxious Duke. But he will have to drag me bodily to Sussex. For I shall fight him every inch of the way!

Her last thought before she succumbed to sleep was of Lord Berkeley. He will save me, she thought. He will not allow them to marry me to the Duke. Lord Berkeley, the man I love, will stand before them all and declare his love for me . . .

At dawn the following morning the key in the lock turned. The door was softly opened. Quietly, Sir Montague Gore stepped into his niece's bedchamber.

Purposefully, he advanced toward the curtained bed, followed by his anxious housekeeper. With a swift movement he swung back the bedcurtains and instructed the housekeeper, "Awaken Miss Wellesley."

The woman leaned forward and shook the sleeping girl. As Candida opened her drowsy eyes, and reluctantly relinquished the companionship of her dreams, Sir Montague pushed the housekeeper aside. In his hand he held a goblet, half full of a cloudy liquid.

He put the goblet to Candida's mouth, and said softly, "Drink."

Still half asleep, Candida had drunk down half the liquid before she realized what was happening. Suddenly wide awake, she attempted to dash the goblet from her uncle's hand. But although he was sparsely built, he possessed a wiry strength which easily proved the master of her. He forced the remaining measure of the sleeping draught down her throat and tossed the goblet aside.

Candida lay helpless in the bed, fighting against the waves of darkness. "You—you—*fiend*—" she murmured weakly. "But Greville—he—he will—defeat you!"

Her eyes closed. "Capital," muttered Sir Montague. "She will trouble me no more until we arrive at Stratton Hall. And by then her fate will be sealed." He turned to the housekeeper and snapped, "Dress Miss Wellesley—in a pale silk gown, if you please. And when you have finished, take that appallingly dull governess's dress away and burn it!"

When Candida awoke she found herself lying on the velvet sofa in the Blue Drawing Room of Stratton Hall. The Duke and Sir Montague were standing by one of the long windows. The curtains were drawn against the gathering night, and the lamps were lit.

I have slept a drugged sleep all day, thought Candida in despair. And my uncle has conveyed me to Sussex.

She glanced around, wondering why Lord Berkeley was not present. Observing the movement of her head, Sir Montague addressed her.

"Ah, you are awake at last, my dear! I hope you feel refreshed after your long journey? No doubt you are in need of refreshment. You will find a tempting cold supper on the table just behind you!"

Candida was indeed extremely hungry. Realizing that she would require all her strength for the battle to come, she sat up and tucked into the cold meats and fruits which lay under a white cloth on the sidetable.

The Duke himself poured her a glass of wine, which he brought across to Candida.

"So!" he declared, "you had the temerity to come into my house and pose as a governess, Miss Wellesley!"

She met his gaze boldly. "I regret nothing!"

He roared with laughter. "If there's one thing I like it's a filly with spirit! My, we shall make a good team, you and I, Miss Wellesley. Methinks I shall enjoy breaking you in!"

"What you enjoy is immaterial to me, my lord Duke," retorted Candida. "For I am not going to marry you."

"Oh yes you are!" grinned the Duke. "At six o'clock tomorrow morning down in the village church. Everything is arranged. My only regret is that my dear brother will not be present. But Greville is away in Lewes today, giving statement to the authorities about Lady Angelica's little escapade. He is not expected back until late tomorrow morning."

Candida paled. It could not be true! Fate could not have dealt her such a bitter blow! She had been so sure that Lord Berkeley would be here, to declare his love for her. He alone could overcome the determination of Uncle Montague and the Duke.

But Lord Berkeley was in Lewes, and unaware of her plight. And by the time he returned to Stratton Hall, the deed would be done. She would be bound in matrimony to the hateful Duke!

Candida sipped her wine, lost for words. Sir Montague, however, was as articulate as ever.

"I do believe you are forgetting your manners, Candida my dear. You have, after all, done the Duke a great wrong! To enter his household masquerading as a governess, and then to indulge in a foolish flirtation with his brother."

Candida leaped to her feet, her eyes blazing. "I love him!" she declared fiercely. "How dare you demean our love by referring to it as a foolish flirtation? He is a noble, good, upright man. Lord Berkeley is everything, in fact, his brother is not!"

The Duke's hand moved fast through the air and struck her hard on the cheek. "Impertinent bitch! My, when we're wed I'll teach you who's master. Within one week, I'll have you kneeling at my feet, kissing my boots. I'll make you—"

Sir Montague cleared his throat. "Candida! Apologize this instant to your betrothed."

"Never! And he is not my betrothed!" Candida spat, shielding her face as the Duke pulled her toward him and raised his hand once more.

Sir Montague hastily stepped between them. "My lord, calm yourself. It would not do, tomorrow, for the Rector to receive a bride whose face was covered in bruises."

The Duke was shaking with rage. But reluctantly, he released the defiant girl. "Spurn me, would you," he hissed, "in favor of my beloved brother! Well, listen well to this, my girl. You'll never set eyes on Greville again, d'you hear? I shall turn him out and forbid him ever to cross the threshold of Stratton Hall again. And once we're wed, if I hear you so much as breathe his name, I'll take a horsewhip to you and thrash you to within an inch of your life. Do I make myself quite clear?"

Candida shrank back from the cold menace in his pale blue eyes. She had no doubt that he meant every chilling word.

Sir Montague addressed the Duke. "I fear that my niece possesses a wilful nature, my lord. But I am convinced that the responsibilities of marriage will soon have a welcomingly calming effect. For the meantime, I feel it best that she should be kept under restraint. Is there a secure room in the house where she may reside until the hour of the nuptials?"

The Duke nodded. "The cellar. She can scream blue murder in there but the servants won't hear. And there are no windows from which to either escape or attract attention. What's more," he grinned, "I possess the only key."

Sir Montague's gaze was level. "That sounds most satisfactory, Your Grace. However, as Lady Candida's legal guardian I must obtain from you a serious understanding that she will in no manner be disturbed during the night . . ."

"Have no fear," the Duke laughed. "She shall remain a virgin until I take her into our marriage bed."

With no more delay, Candida was thrust unceremoniously into the cellar and given one candle to relieve the darkness. As the Duke pulled shut the huge oak door, Candida was in time to catch the expression of unease on her uncle's gaunt face.

"Yes, Uncle," she declared, with scornful dignity. "Well might you look ashamed. To treat thus your own kin on the eve of her wedding. It augurs well, does it not, for my future happiness as the Duchess of Stratton!"

Sir Montague frowned. "You have brought this upon yourself you cat-witted girl! During your night in the cellar you would do well to reflect upon your noble family motto. *Duty Unto Death,* Candida!"

The door was banged shut and the Duke noisily turned the key.

"Duty Unto Death?" Candida screamed, beating the door with her fists. "I would choose death, then, rather than marry that drunken pig. Do you hear me, Uncle? I would rather die!"

Unheeding, their footsteps faded away up the old stone stairs. Candida collapsed, sobbing, against a hogshead of claret.

"Oh Mama," she whispered, "why did you wish this fate upon me? If you were only here now, to save me from this wretched marriage."

But her mother lay peacefully in her grave. And Candida was dismally aware that apart from her Uncle and the Duke, there was no one in the world who knew of her dreadful plight.

But someone else did know. When Candida had been dragged, kicking and struggling, from the drawing room down to the cellar, a girl with tousled red hair had crept fearfully out from behind the sofa.

Lady Lucy had dived behind the sofa only seconds before her Uncle Bart and Sir Montague had entered the drawing room with the unconscious Candida. Owing to an unfortunate incident earlier in the day Lady Lucy was not anxious to be in the company of her uncle. (She had leaped out of a hedge and startled a new horse which the Duke was breaking in. The nervous horse had bolted and tipped the Duke headlong into the ornamental lake.)

Safe behind the sofa, Lady Lucy had listened with fascination, amazement and growing terror to the conversation between the three adults. There was so much for her young head to absorb!

First, it transpired that Miss Wilton was not a governess at all, but a wealthy heiress named Miss Candida Wellesley. And she was in love with Uncle Greville. But the wicked Sir Montague was forcing her to marry Uncle Bart!

Bemused, Lady Lucy opened the French doors and stepped out onto the terrace. Away in Stratton village, the church clock chimed eight. By the time it strikes eight once more, thought Lady Lucy, Miss Wilton—Miss *Wellesley* will be the new Duchess of Stratton.

The girl shook her head, knowing not what to make of it all. She wandered around to the kitchen garden and saw before her a light gleaming in one of the potting sheds. Inside, Mr. Sewell, the head gardener, was setting out the wallflowers which would be planted to bloom next spring.

Lady Lucy felt a surge of relief. She had never in her life been able to keep any piece of intelligence to herself. And now, she knew she would simply expire if she did not tell someone what she had overheard in the Blue Drawing Room!

Lady Lucy liked Tom Sewell. He talked to her in a nice quiet voice, and didn't regard her as a nuisance as did so many grownups. And, she reasoned, he was only a humble gardener. There would be no harm in telling him about the dramatic events in the Blue Drawing Room this evening . . .

As the church bell struck eleven, the Stratton village night watchman observed a candle still burning within the Sewells' flint cottage. The watchman smiled. That would be the conscientious Mrs. Sewell, busying about in her kitchen, setting everything ready for her husband's early breakfast. The watchman walked on, thinking of the comely girl he was betrothed to marry next year and the breakfasts they would share together.

Back at the flintstone cottage, Mrs. Sewell was indeed in her pin-neat kitchen. But her thoughts, as she sat at the scrubbed table, dwelled not on such mundane matters as men's breakfasts.

At last, she stood up, and walked resolutely upstairs to the room she had shared for over thirty years with her husband Tom. She set down the candle on the floor, and shook him awake.

"Tom! I have made up my mind. You must go to the Hall and tell them the truth."

The head gardener sat up with a start. "Are you deranged, woman!"

"No," his wife said quietly. "I am seeing sense for the first time in my married life."

"But—but it will be all around the village with the speed of a forest fire," he protested, waving his hands and knocking off his nightcap in his agitation. "Do you want everyone to *know?* We'll never be able to hold up our heads again!"

"Tom, I'm forty-seven years old," said Mrs. Sewell. "And we are none of us immortal. I'm not prepared to go to my grave, whenever that may be, with this on my conscience."

Her husband sighed deeply. "But we promised, Mary! We gave our solemn word of honor that we would never breathe a word of what we did!"

"I know that!" Mrs. Sewell twisted her wedding ring. "But times change, Tom. Circumstances alter things. I've sat downstairs this night, and I've thought long and hard about what Lady Lucy told you."

"The ramblings of a young girl," said Tom Sewell scornfully. "She was probably inventing it all, just for mischief."

Mrs. Sewell shook her head. "She's a devious young minx, to be sure. But even she couldn't devise a tale as tragic as this. And I haven't forgotten Miss Wil—Miss Wellesley's great kindness to me, to our family. When our Hannah was snatched away that night, I was nearly out of my mind with grief. But Miss Wellesley comforted me. She even came back here and stayed the night with me, and wouldn't leave in the morning until she was sure I had control of myself once more."

"Yes, but—"

"And then there's Lord Berkeley to think of," Mrs. Sewell swept on. "You've said yourself a million times what a good, just man he is. You know for a fact, Tom, that he's worth ten of that Duke!"

At this, Tom Sewell turned away, and would not meet her eyes. He trembled. "Mary, I can't do it. I can't go up there to the Hall at this time of night, and rouse them all from their beds, and say my piece. I'm a simple gardener, not a talking man. And how do I know they'd believe me?"

Mary Sewell stared at him stonily. "Tom Sewell, answer me this. Have I been a good, loyal, and devoted wife to you?"

He nodded. "Yes," he whispered. "No man could have wished for a better wife. I've been fortunate, Mary, I know that."

"I've stood by you, Tom," Mrs. Sewell said remorselessly. "I've never breathed a word to a soul about—you know about what. But I'm telling you this. If you won't go now up to the Hall, then I will! I'll tell them all I know. And then I shall take my Hannah and I shall leave this cottage, and you will never set eyes on either of us again. I mean it, Tom!"

Tom Sewell groaned, and covered his face with his hands. After over thirty years of marriage, he knew his wife well enough to understand that when she used this particular tone, there was no arguing with her. And deep down, he knew she was right. He recalled that an old shepherd had once told him of an ancient proverb: *Take what you want in life. And pay for it.*

"Fetch me my clothes, Mary, and a lamp," he said numbly. "I'm about to pay my tithe."

Incarcerated in the cellar, Candida heard nothing of the commotion in Stratton Hall that night. She was unaware of

Sir Montague, attempting vainly to retain his dignity as he descended in nightshirt and cap to the main hall, summoned there (by all unlikely individuals) by a humble gardener! She was deaf to the disgruntled cries of the stableboys, roused from their slumber by no less a personage than the Head Steward, who galloped off into the night bearing an urgent message hastily scrawled by a stunned Sir Montague. And she knew nothing of the second rider who stormed across the moonlit Downs, cursing Fate, and gardeners, and all womankind.

Candida was, in fact, sleeping fitfully when she was awoken by the scrape of a key in the lock. She leaped to her feet, blazing with fury.

The Duke, she thought. He has reneged on his promise to Uncle Montague. He has come here, on the eve of our wedding, to ravish me. To take his revenge because I fell in love with his brother!

Candida shivered. She knew the Duke would show her no mercy. She would be beaten, humiliated, forced to submit to his every depraved desire. And after his educative years in Paris, Candida had no doubt that his demands on her would be bestial beyond belief.

Shaking with terror, she ran and stood behind the door. I shall not give in without a fight, she resolved fiercely. Make no mistake, you shall pay the price for my enforced submission, my lord Duke. For I shall leave my mark on you!

As the door swung open, Candida sprang. With the instinct of an animal at bay who has nothing else to lose, she lunged toward him, hands outstretched ready to tear out his throat.

But he was taller than she—stronger—and ten times more powerful.

He disarmed her by the simple expedient of crushing her to him, into his embrace.

"Be still, Candida!" he commanded quietly. "You are safe now."

"Oh Greville! It is you!" gasped Candida in relief, gazing

up at the face of the man she loved. "I—I thought you were the Duke—"

He smiled down at her. "You were not mistaken, my dearest. I *am* the Duke of Stratton."

Candida's eyes widened. "Your brother! He is dead? He has met with an accident? Oh, Greville, you didn't—"

The dark-haired man shook his head, and glanced around at the gloomy cellar. "My God, Candida! What a dismal setting for our reunion! Come with me now to the drawing room and I will explain everything to you."

In the Blue Drawing Room, Candida found a bemused Sir Montague sitting by the hearth. Although it was the middle of the night, Stratton Hall blazed with light and movement, as servants scurried to and fro bringing fresh logs for the fire, wine and sweet biscuits.

Sir Montague was, by now, formally dressed in a dark brown velvet frock-coat. Even so, the dramatic events of the night had left their mark, for his wig was decidedly askew.

"Never in my life," he informed Candida, "have I known such a night as this. To be so rudely awoken with a demand that I must descend and converse with a common gardener! And then to listen to his astounding tale—"

"Oh please, will someone begin at the beginning and tell me what has been happening here tonight!" cried Candida. "I am fair ready to expire with suspense!"

The man she loved guided her to the sofa, and sat down beside her. "It all began," he told her, "over thirty years ago, when my mother was brought to bed of her first child. I am given to understand that my mother suffered greatly, and when her son was born, she lay close to death. Moreover, the child was a small, sickly creature. Before he was wrapped in the traditional swaddling clothes, my father, the old Duke, looked at the boy and realized that his son and heir would probably not last the night."

"But he was wrong," said Candida. "The child lived to become a lusty young man—your brother."

"No, he did not live," Greville replied gravely. "He

breathed his last in the small hours. He was taken away, and buried in a secret place underneath one of the young oak trees on the estate."

"Then . . . then who was the boy who grew up to become the Duke of Stratton—" queried an astounded Candida.

"He was an illegitimate child, fathered by Tom Sewell," said the dark-haired man. "I gather that during the early days of his marriage to Mrs. Sewell, they quarreled, and Tom Sewell sought solace for the night with one of the milkmaids. It so happened that both she and my mother, the Duchess, were brought to bed at the same time. For the unfortunate young milkmaid, the strain of giving birth was too great, and she died that night, along with my mother's son."

"So Tom Sewell was persuaded to let his lovechild be laid in the Stratton Hall cradle," said Candida.

"It was my father who initiated the deception," said Greville. "He was desperate for an heir—and my mother appeared on the point of death. He was not to know then that she would recover, and bear me. And I have no doubt that from the Sewells' point of view, giving the baby to the Duke was a very practical solution. Mrs. Sewell was prepared to stand by her husband, but she had made it clear that there was no question of her rearing another woman's child."

Candida shook her golden head as she digested this information. "Of course," she whispered, "I remember now. That night when I stayed in her cottage she referred most scathingly to the Duke. *'He's a bad 'un'* she said, *'Blood will out, you mark my words.'* But she was tired, and upset, and I paid scant regard to her words."

Sir Montague spoke: "It goes without saying, of course, that the late Duchess knew nothing about the exchange of boy children. She believed she had borne a healthy, robust son who would continue the proud tradition of the Stratton line."

Candida gazed with shining eyes at the man seated beside her on the sofa. "So you are the true Duke of Stratton!"

He raised her hand and kissed it. "And you shall shortly be my Duchess. I have already formally requested your uncle's permission for us to marry."

"And I shall not, after all, be defying my mother's last wish," sighed Candida happily. "Oh, what a weight that is off my mind!" Then a frown creased her pretty brow. "There is just one thing which puzzles me. How did you know that Tom Sewell was telling the truth. For myself, I know him to be an honest man. But with such a serious allegation as this, surely you required proof that the person then entitled Duke was in fact Tom Sewell's son."

"Quite correct, Candida," intoned Sir Montague. "Naturally, at first I was loath to accept what the gardener told me. But his sincerity was obvious. And apart from that, he informed me that all children fathered by a Sewell always had a strawberry shaped birthmark on their right forearm."

"Why, yes," exclaimed Candida. "I recall seeing just that on Hannah Sewell's arm when she was held captive at the fisherman's cottage.

Sir Montague went on: "The Duke, as we then believed him to be, had been listening to Sewell's tale with mounting indignation. But when I declared that to settle the matter once and for all he must show me his arm, he became positively abusive."

"Bart has that strawberry mark on his arm," said the Duke. "Naturally, having grown up with him, I have seen it often."

"He stormed from the house," recalled Sir Montague, "using language fit to put a sailor to the blush. Meanwhile, of course, I had instructed the Steward to ride to Lewes to request Lord Berkeley to return immediately."

Outside, the sky was beginning to brighten. Sir Montague rubbed his eyes, and said briskly, "Well, the Rector will be waiting to perform a marriage ceremony. Since all the arrangements have been made, it seems convenient, and sensible to avail ourselves—" He paused, considerably affronted by the Duke's outburst of laughter.

"I am surprised, Your Grace, that you regard your nuptials to my niece as a matter for amusement," Sir Montague said testily.

"I fear you misunderstand, Sir Montague," replied the Duke. "My laughter was more an expression of disbelief, than of frivolity. Have you forgotten that Candida has spent this night shut in a cellar, believing herself doomed to marry a man she loathed? I assure you, I will not permit my bride, my future Duchess," he smiled tenderly at Candida, "to go to her wedding with that dire memory so strongly in her mind."

Sir Montague had the grace to look ashamed.

The Duke went on: "Naturally, I am eager to marry Candida with the least possible delay. But she must come to her wedding with a tranquil heart, and a mind unsullied by the recollections of this dreadful night. In addition, one must be mindful that a Stratton wedding will be a great occasion—not just for Candida and me—but for the tenants, also."

"Why yes," murmured the future Duchess, "we must declare the day a holiday for them."

"Indeed so," the Duke approved. "There will be feasting, and music, and dancing through the night . . ."

"And I shall be a flower girl at the wedding!" declared a piping voice from the door. Lady Lucy rushed into the drawing room, almost tripping over her lace-edged nightshift. She flung herself at the Duke and cried, "I overheard two of the maids talking about Uncle Bart, and you being the true Duke, and your wedding to Miss Wellesley. Oh, it is all so exciting!"

The Duke repressed a smile, and declared with mock severity, "Really, Lucy, I hope when you go away to school that you will be severely punished for your regrettable habit of eavesdropping at every possible opportunity."

"Oh!" wailed the red-haired girl. "You would not be so cruel as to send me away! I want to stay here, with you and Miss Wellesley!"

"But I imagined it was your dearest wish to go to a boarding academy," teased Candida.

"I have changed my mind," declared Lady Lucy fervently. "Please promise I may stay here with you."

Candida hugged her. "Of course you may! We should be quite lost without you."

"Back to bed with you now, Lucy." The Duke smiled.

Sir Montague arose and said wearily, "Allow me to escort you upstairs, Lady Lucy. I confess, I am quite overcome with fatigue."

When Sir Montague and Lady Lucy had left the room, Candida arose and went to the window. "So much has happened," she murmured. "So much is explained. It is plain now why you and Bart were so unalike as brothers. You differed in every respect. In appearance, character, and temperament. But what will happen to him now?"

The Duke stood beside her, his arm around her slender shoulder. "I suspect that he has gone in search of Lady Angelica. They are in many ways very alike, you know."

"Yes," Candida agreed. "He admitted that he only desired to marry me because of my inheritance. It was obvious that he greatly admired Lady Angelica." She turned to face the Duke. "Oh, Greville, to think that he has squandered so much of your family fortune!"

"Let us not dwell on the past," he said firmly. "I have in mind many plans which will make the Stratton estates vastly more profitable. It was impossible to implement these schemes before because Bart would not allow me a free hand. But now I am in sole charge, and with you at my side, anything is possible."

Candida felt a surge of happiness at his words. So much has happened since I first set foot in this house, she mused. "I can hardly believe that we are truly to be wed," she whispered. "It all seemed a wonderful dream!"

"When we are married, Candida, I shall of course expect you to curb your impulsive ways," said the Duke severely. "I was furious with you for taking it into your head to rush back to Hampshire so suddenly. Especially as the first I knew of your escapade was when the messenger from Sir Montague came to rouse me at my lodgings in Lewes."

Candida stared at him in horror. "Curb my impulsive ways? Oh, you sound like Uncle Montague himself!" Then her eyes danced as she realized he was mocking her. She went on: "But I advised you of my plan to return to Gore Lodge. I left a note with your valet."

"I did not receive it," explained the Duke, "for the simple reason that I did not return to Stratton Hall last night. After Hannah Sewell and the abducted dairymaid had been reunited with their parents, I thought it my duty to escort the third girl, Verity Laine, back to her boarding academy in Lewes. And as I knew I should be needed in Lewes the following morning to give my evidence at the Assizes, I stayed overnight there."

"What a shock it must have been when you received my uncle's message asking you to return immediately to Stratton Hall," commented Candida. She paused for a moment, and then said anxiously, "Greville . . . you said that you had fallen in love with me when you still believed me to be a governess. I do hope you will not expect me to be a demure, self-effacing little wife. For that is not in my nature at all!"

The dark-haired man roared with laughter. "I am well aware of that, my headstrong young beauty! I knew you to be a woman of spirit and rare character that night when I found you wandering in the moonlight, with your governess's cap tossed aside and your glorious hair streaming free over your shoulders. That is the Candida I love!"

He bent and kissed her then, with an ardor that set her a-tremble with desire. After a long time, Candida opened her eyes, and gazed out at a dawn sky streaked with crimson and gold.

Safe within his arms, Candida sighed with joy as she greeted the new day—and the new life she would share with the man she loved so passionately.

ABOUT THE AUTHOR
Caroline Courtney

Caroline Courtney was born in India, the youngest daughter of a British Army Colonel stationed there in the troubled years after the First World War. Her first husband, a Royal Air Force pilot, was tragically killed in the closing stages of the Second World War. She later remarried and now lives with her second husband, a retired barrister, in a beautiful 17th century house in Cornwall. They have three children, two sons and a daughter, all of whom are now married, and four grandchildren.

On the rare occasions that Caroline Courtney takes time off from her writing, she enjoys gardening and listening to music, particularly opera. She is also an avid reader of romantic poetry and has an ever-growing collection of poems she has composed herself.

Caroline Courtney is destined to be one of this country's leading romantic novelists. She has written an enormous number of novels over the years—purely for pleasure—and has never before been interested in seeing them reach publication. However, at her family's insistence she has now relented, and Warner Books is proud to be issuing a selection in this uniform edition.